THE SAINT

FIFTH REPUBLIC SERIES
BOOK THREE

PENELOPE SKY

HARTWICK PUBLISHING

Hartwick Publishing

The Saint

Copyright © 2025 by Penelope Sky

All rights reserved.

CONTENTS

1

FLEUR

I sat on the couch in front of the TV, the news showing the charred body that hung from Notre-Dame. Sunrise had hit the city and I'd been up nearly all night, but I felt no fatigue, not when the adrenaline was still pumping away. Until Bastien walked in that door, I would be on alert.

I was in his t-shirt and his boxers because I had nothing else to wear. I wasn't in the mood to blow-dry my hair, but after being locked in a wet coffin, I needed to be bone-dry. A blanket was draped over my shoulders and snug around my body because I was still cold, despite the hot shower and the steam that fogged the glass in the bathroom.

Gerard had left food and water for me, and I'd drunk all the water but ignored the food because I had no appetite.

I guess dying was an appetite suppressant.

The last thing I wanted to be was alone right now, forced to think about everything that had happened over and over. Anytime I visualized that coffin, tears welled in my eyes. I still felt the sting of the splinters that had impaled my fingertips. I still felt the cold rainwater against my skin. It had been so dark in that coffin that I'd only known where the water was by touch.

And I remembered how it felt to drown...quite vividly.

I'd held my breath as long as I could and pounded on the coffin lid even though it was hopeless. I'd wanted to die while fighting rather than die while submitting. But then my lungs took over and forced me to gasp—and that was when all the water flooded in.

It was painful...so fucking painful.

And to spend the last few seconds of your life knowing you were going to die was the worst part. To wait for it to end, to want to rush it just to make it stop, to be in complete darkness while it happened.

I didn't feel my tears until they reached my lips. My eyes were glued to the TV, seeing the same clip they showed over and over, the body ablaze, because someone had caught it on camera from their apartment window.

That was the man who had ordered my death.

Good riddance.

I heard footsteps approach, and I turned to the door, knowing Bastien was finally home now that the deed was done. I already felt the relief before he walked in, felt the peace that only he could give.

The door opened, but it wasn't just him. Adrien was with him.

Bastien was still coated in filth and mud because he hadn't changed since pulling me out of that coffin. It was even on his face and neck, dried in place. He glanced at the TV to see the news before he looked at me again.

My eyes were on Adrien.

All that relief, all that peace…just evaporated.

Adrien stilled at the sight of me, hesitating at the ferocity that must have been in my gaze.

I released the blanket and got to my feet, wearing clothes that were far too big for me, and I walked up to him, seeing him tremble slightly at my approach. His eyes remained locked on mine but were packed with fear. So many things I wanted to say, so many things I wanted to do. I nearly asked for Bastien's gun so I could shoot Adrien in the arm. But he wasn't worth the emotional investment. "I wish I'd never met you." I wished I could take back those years, take back my vows, take back my heart.

He flinched like I'd punched him, like those simple words were sharper than a dagger. "They were going to come for you, no matter what I did, Fleur. I saved you. I called Bastien and saved you—"

"Bastien saved me."

"Because I called him—"

3

"All of that could have been avoided if you'd just told them that Bastien and I are together. That's all you had to fucking say, and they would have let me go." My eyes burned with furious tears. "I died, Adrien. Fucking drowned in mud."

He clenched his eyes closed to shut out the pain of my words. "I know—"

"You don't know. You don't know what it's like to fucking die."

He opened his eyes again, soaking wet with tears that were sincere. "I was so scared, Fleur. You have no idea."

"No, you have no idea how scared I was. Trapped in the dark with a fucking camera in my face. The cold water inching closer to my mouth, and every move you make just sucks up the oxygen and makes the water pour in more."

He closed his eyes again, like he couldn't bear it. "It all happened so fast. I knew Oscar and Bastien did business together, so I assumed he would honor the code. I never imagined my beef with him would come anywhere near you. If I'd known that, I would have caved to him immediately. I would never risk the person I love most—"

"You have no right to say that to me, Adrien."

Bastien stood there and let us have it out in the middle of his living room, his clothes caked in mud and smelling of dirt and rain.

Adrien winced at my words. "I'm so sorry—"

"I don't forgive you."

"I should have told him what you are to Bastien. That would have fixed everything. But in the moment—"

"I'm done with this conversation." I was exhausted, physically and emotionally, and my throat was so raw from coughing, it hurt to talk. The world continued to spin, and I needed it to go still, needed the world to go quiet. "I want to be with Bastien right now and for you to leave." It was hard to believe Adrien had ever been my husband when my brief relationship with Bastien felt more like a marriage than ours ever had.

Adrien looked defeated, clearly wanting to fight on but knowing his time was up. He started to turn away, also covered in dirt from shoveling the mud off my coffin. "I'm glad you're okay."

"I'm not okay." It was hard to believe I would ever be okay after that.

He stilled, his eyes on the floor, and then walked out.

When the door clicked shut, I closed my eyes and released a strained sigh. After a beat, I looked at Bastien.

His bright eyes were locked on mine, the only part of his body that wasn't covered in filth. Even his hair had mud in it, like he'd dug me out of that grave with his bare hands. "It's okay not to be okay, sweetheart. But you will be."

Bastien tossed his muddy clothes and mine in the trash then cleaned off in the shower.

I waited for him in bed, the curtains drawn closed to block out the sunlight. The doors to the living room were closed too, shutting out the light that came in from the terrace. I should sleep, but a part of me wondered if I'd ever be able to sleep again.

I knew the nightmares would come.

Bastien joined me a moment later, sliding into bed in just his boxers.

I was on him right away, circling his neck with my arm, hiking my leg up over his thighs, laying my forehead against his chin with my eyes on his throat. All I wanted was to be close to him, our bodies and souls touching, and once that happened, I felt better.

And worse.

His fingers lightly played with my hair as he lay with me. Didn't ask how I felt, didn't ask what I needed. Just comforted me with his strong silence.

My lips started to tremble as the emotion seeped through the cracks in the door of my heart, just the way the rainwater had dripped through the openings in the wooden coffin. My heart cracked, and the emotion poured in like a waterfall. I attempted to stifle my tears, but whenever I tried, it turned into sobs.

Only when I felt safe could I accept the violence. Only when I was in Bastien's arms could I confront my own death.

He didn't hush me or silence my cries with kisses. He just let me cry, let me shed the rainwater that had absorbed

6

into my pores. Let me explode with terror and pain and fear. Let me feel everything I needed to feel so it would pass.

My eyes remained on his throat, and I watched him swallow more than once.

I cried until I was spent, cried until the physical and emotional exhaustion built to a crescendo…and I fell asleep.

When I woke up, he was still there, but wide awake like he'd been alert for a while. I turned to look at the crack in the curtains to gauge the time of day by the light. It was dark, so the day had passed while we'd slept.

I immediately thought of what happened the day before, but knowing it was officially in the past made it a little more bearable. Processing something that had happened a few hours ago was just too hard to do.

"Hungry?" he asked.

"Not really."

"You should eat something."

"The only thing that sounds remotely good is pancakes…but it looks like it's dinnertime."

"That can be arranged." He grabbed his phone off his nightstand and texted Gerard, his private room service.

"You didn't have to do that."

"I want you to eat." He snaked his hand up my shirt and lightly grazed my side and stomach with his fingers, his touch warm like summer sunshine. "I know it's hard, but it'll help." He lay there and stared at me, his blue eyes gentler than they'd ever been. His stare usually had an intensity that never faded, only grew with the duration of his gaze. But now, it was softer than a silky rose petal.

We lay together in silence, just looking at each other, the night deepening out the window.

A while later, his phone vibrated with a message. He checked it before he returned it to the nightstand. "Breakfast is served."

I already knew before Gerard texted—because I could smell it. I could smell the melted butter on the fluffy pancakes, the crisp applewood-smoked bacon, the scrambled eggs covered in gooey cheese. "I guess I'm a little hungry."

Normally, he would smile at that, but his mouth remained hard in a near-grimace. "Attagirl." He left the bed and put on his gray sweatpants, his ass tight in the fabric, his junk slightly outlined in the front.

If this were yesterday, I'd be jumping him, but today, I felt nothing.

We sat at the dining table where the food was covered with silver domes. Gerard had brought coffee even though it was seven in the evening, prime dinnertime. Bastien removed his cover and showed the T-bone steak and scrambled eggs. Instead of having coffee or juice, he poured himself a scotch.

8

I had blueberry pancakes and scrambled eggs with cheese and a couple slices of bacon, my favorite meal. The steam from the food hit me in the face the second I removed the lid, and the smell incited my appetite.

I could tell Bastien wasn't as hungry as he usually was because he didn't inhale his food like a bear. He took bites here and there, focusing on his drink more than the meal. His eyes drifted out the window often, his mind somewhere else. He hadn't died by drowning, but he was clearly fucked up by what happened too. Maybe he felt responsible for what had gone down. Maybe he just felt like shit about it.

"Are you okay?"

His gaze flicked back to me, his eyes wounded in pain. "No."

I echoed his words back to him. "It's okay not to be okay."

His eyes drifted away again, rejecting my affection. "Don't worry about me, sweetheart."

"Hard not to."

He continued to stare out the window, half of his food still on his plate, which was a first. His broad shoulders were sunken under an invisible weight, and his eyes lacked their usual shine, even when the glow of the city reflected in them like Christmas lights.

"So…what happened?"

He took a heavy breath, his chest rising when I broached the topic. "Long story. The Aristocrats demanded that Adrien stop his business because it's an insult to the French people. I relayed that message to Adrien—more than once—but he chose to ignore it. Oscar and the Aristocrats have always respected the Fifth Republic and agreed with its politics because it protected the longevity and high status of the French empire. So, I expected this behavior from him the least."

"Why didn't you tell me this before? I could have talked to Adrien."

"Separation of church and state."

"What does that mean?"

"I know you want no association with my criminal activities," he said. "I did what I could to keep Adrien alive since I knew you wouldn't want him killed, but he wouldn't listen to me."

"That doesn't sound like him. To just disregard a threat like that."

He was quiet for a while. "I think he was too depressed to see reason. That business was all he had left."

Because I'd left him. I felt a twinge of guilt, but it was very brief. "I never want to see him again." I'd already said that straight to Adrien's face, but I said it again because I meant it. Adrien panicked, and if Bastien weren't in my life, that panic would have gotten me killed. "If he hadn't cheated on me, I would be dead right now."

Bastien didn't disagree with that and continued to look out the window as if he hadn't heard me. "You can talk about it…if you want." He still wouldn't look at me, like he carried the burden of shame for a crime he didn't commit.

I wouldn't put Bastien through that. What he had witnessed was already eating him alive. "It's okay."

"I know some good people if you want a professional."

"You have a therapist?"

"No," he said. "But I know all the good ones."

"I'm okay, but thanks." I'd died just yesterday. I needed to accept that fact before I could move past it.

He continued to look out the window, a view he must have seen a hundred times, his expression somber and writhing in subtle pain.

"Bastien?"

His eyes refused to obey.

"Why won't you look at me?" Did he see me differently? Did he carry the blame, when Adrien was cursed to bear that alone?

He inhaled a deep breath, his big chest rising slowly before he let it out easily. But he didn't say anything, choosing to bottle up his feelings in an airtight container. He shut me out completely, his jaw tight and the cords in his neck strained. "Because you were dead, Fleur. Because when I got there, you were fucking dead…"

2

FLEUR

I didn't leave his house for three days—and neither did he.

All I had were the clothes I'd arrived in, which had been thrown in the trash, so I wore his boxers and t-shirts, lying with him on the couch while he watched TV, sleeping all day in bed because it didn't matter how much I slept at night, I was always tired. I didn't get into the tub and knew I never would again.

Bastien was always there, his hands on me, his kisses on my neck and collarbone, his warmth a beacon of sunshine in my winter of misery, but he was different. Quiet and distant, visibly scarred. He'd never been a man of many words, but now, he didn't say anything at all.

I knew I needed to move my stuff from my apartment because I couldn't keep living like this, wearing clothes that were at least five sizes too big. I only had a couple more things to pack up, but that shouldn't take more than an hour or two. It seemed crazy to think about packing when I'd literally died a few days ago, but sitting around the house without my things wasn't a long-term solution.

We'd just finished lunch, sitting across from each other at the table. I noticed Bastien wasn't working out in the morning like he usually did. He seemed to have completely stopped his life, like I did. He wasn't on his phone either, like he'd abandoned all of his responsibilities to be with me night and day. But he still wasn't really there with me.

"I need to go to my apartment," I said. "I can't keep wearing your clothes, as comfy as they are."

His eyes were on me until the moment I said that. Then they darted away, focused on the view again. "I get it."

I had no other choice but to show up in Bastien's sweatpants and one of his sweatshirts. All I had were my shoes. I waited for him to say something more, offer to come with me or call his guys to move my stuff, but he did none of those things.

He just wasn't the same, and I didn't like that. "Can your guys still move my stuff, or…?"

His eyes came right back to me as quickly as they'd darted away, but now a stillness gripped his entire body, a tightness in his muscles and his tendons. His eyes hardened, his eyebrows furrowed, and despite how stern he looked, he seemed truly present. "You still want to live with me?"

"Of course I do." Nothing had changed between us. My feelings for him were still a bonfire of emotion. If anything,

I wanted to live with him even more and never wanted to set foot in that apartment again.

His stare remained locked on mine, and it was the first time he really looked at me, at least in the way he used to.

"Unless you don't want me to—"

"Of course I do." He swallowed like there was emotion in his throat he had to beat down. His eyes were packed with intensity and desperation and heat so hot I could feel it across the table. "I wasn't sure if that was something you still wanted."

"Why wouldn't I?" I blurted, having no idea why he'd made that assumption.

His stare continued, but the sharpness of it went dull and his presence started to recede once again. It was the only time I'd witnessed him withdraw rather than push forward, to make his presence small rather than command the entire room.

"This is why you've been so distant…"

His eyes dropped momentarily as he shifted his jaw, as if debating with himself whether he should speak further. "I've been waiting for you to leave me. Waiting for the shock to fade and a new fear to replace it."

His words hurt me like a paper cut on my heart.

"I should just shut my fucking mouth right now. But you were right to leave me. As long as you live in my world, you'll always be a part of it, which means you could be a victim of it...as we just learned." He looked away. "You were right to want a law-abiding citizen with a nine-to-five. You were right to fucking run from me." He swallowed and let out a sigh. "If I were a better man, I would do the right thing and walk away...but I fucking can't." His eyes watered momentarily. "I can't fucking do it."

"I'm not leaving, Bastien."

His eyes remained elsewhere, the moisture still coating them. He had better control of his emotions than others because he could fight the tears before they even had a chance to truly form. But his fingers tightened into a fist on the table, and he clenched them.

"It wasn't your fault. Adrien is the only one to blame."

His eyes didn't find mine again, glued to the table, the restraint visible in the tightness of his body.

"If I'd never met you, I'd be dead right now." Oscar would have taken me, and Adrien would have had no way to get me back. "You were the one who found Oscar. You were the one who got my location before it was too late. You were the one who dug me out of the ground and brought me back to life."

He closed his eyes for a second, flinching at the sting of my words.

"Even if you tried to leave me, I wouldn't let you."

His eyes came back to mine, still angry and broken but steeped in emotion.

"Because I never want to be apart from you." This had all happened so fast, an underwater riptide that had pulled us far out to sea. The moment our eyes met, we were taken by the current, and I drowned in his blue eyes. This wasn't the kind of relationship I'd wanted and not when I'd wanted it to happen—but that was done now. My heart had planted roots in his earth, and the sharpest ax couldn't cut me down. I wanted to be with him always, for the rest of my life, for better or worse.

He stared at me for a long time, seconds that turned into a full minute. The pain that throbbed in his eyes slowly faded, the tears that had coated his eyes dried out within a single blink. But the emotion still burned on the surface, poignant and motionless like a winter fog. "Let's get your stuff, sweetheart."

It was my first time back in that apartment, and I was glad it would be my last.

I would face a penalty for breaking my year-long lease, but I didn't give a damn. Like hell would I ever be able to sleep in that apartment again. I had good memories with Bastien, because we'd slept together for the first time in my bed, because we'd shared a pizza at my dining table one evening, fucked on the couch when he stopped by for a quick hookup. But that wasn't enough to make me want to stay, not when I could be with Bastien every day.

The boxes were still everywhere, some tipped over from when the men had broken in and pushed them aside. I only had a few essentials left, some of my clothes and shoes and other accessories I used every day.

I stepped into my bedroom and looked at the bed. I still remembered the sound of their footsteps, the way I thought it was Bastien, until I realized too late that it wasn't. The flashbacks were quick, the cold of the tile against my cheek, the darkness from the coffin.

Even when he stood behind me, he recognized my unease. "I'm here, sweetheart."

I looked at the rumpled sheets then the closet before I released a sigh. "I know. Just need to grab a couple more things…" I opened the door and got to work, knowing the quicker I finished the task, the quicker I could leave.

Bastien stepped into the other room and called his guys to come by.

I threw the rest of my stuff in a suitcase, the items I used on an everyday basis so they would be easier to retrieve once we returned to his house.

Bastien stacked up the boxes near the doorway so the guys would have an easier time getting them out of the apartment when they arrived. When he had nothing else to do, he took a seat at the kitchen table and lit up a cigar, not caring about his manners since we were leaving the apartment for good in the next hour.

Twenty minutes later, the guys arrived and started to carry the boxes away.

Instead of letting his guys do all the work, he grabbed a box and carried it down too, the cigar still between his lips.

I finished my suitcase then rolled it toward the front door, a couple more boxes stacked there, waiting to be carried out. I still had things at Adrien's house, items that had been too big or too valuable to move when I'd stormed out. My intention had been to go back and get them at some point, but that opportunity had never come.

Now, I would send Bastien to retrieve it for me so I wouldn't have to look at that son of a bitch.

The guys took the last of the boxes, and Bastien grabbed the suitcase.

"Anything else?" Bastien asked.

I shook my head. "Everything else came with the apartment."

"Alright." Instead of rolling the suitcase across the floor, he carried it by the handle. We took the stairs to the bottom floor and then stepped onto the street. My things seemed to have been packed in another car that had already driven off because there was nothing in Bastien's SUV except the suitcase he put in the back.

The car pulled away from the curb, and I looked at my apartment for the last time.

It was a decent place in a good spot, my shelter after I left my husband and stepped into a life of insecurity and isolation. Despite what had happened that night, I would always have love for it, because it was where I started over... even though I had been so fucking scared to do it. The rage and sting of betrayal had pushed me to leave Adrien, and the pride and stubbornness were what had kept me away. That apartment had never been home, but a stepping-stone to this moment, to the man beside me—home.

He had an enormous closet and only used a fraction of it. He was a simple man and a creature of habit, so his wardrobe was a couple pairs of jeans, some t-shirts, and long-sleeved shirts. All dark colors, with the exception of a few lighter grays. He owned one sweater and two jackets. That was it.

Instead of collecting expensive watches like Adrien, he seemed to collect guns. He didn't appear to collect cars either because he had a driver in a black SUV take him everywhere. The only luxury he really seemed to care about was his estate, which was probably worth a number I couldn't even write out correctly.

I spent the day hanging my clothes in the closet and organizing my stuff, wanting to get rid of the boxes that filled his rooms as quickly as possible. There was plenty of space, but they were still an eyesore that would drive Gerard crazy.

I put all my cosmetics in the drawers of his large bathroom. I had plenty of counter space for all my things, the mirrors going all the way to the ceiling and outlined in gold accents. I felt like a princess in a palace, rescued by a handsome prince who still seemed too good to be true.

Bastien spent that time at his desk, working on his laptop and firing off texts on his phone. He rarely made phone calls. I'd only seen him make a handful of calls since I'd known him. He had the ability to run his empire in utter silence.

It'd been five days since I died. It took that long to start to feel normal again. The fatigue had finally passed, and I wondered if I'd been so tired because my brain hadn't recovered from the lack of oxygen...for however long I'd been dead. It might have only been a minute or two, but that was long enough to do enough damage to affect me like this.

I didn't suffer from nightmares, but I suspected that was because Bastien was there beside me, my dream catcher, a beast that guarded my unconscious mind from unwanted visitors.

I felt so safe with him that if he hadn't asked me to live with him, I might have asked him instead. "Babe?"

He looked up from his laptop right away, his eyes locked on mine with the attention of a soldier when addressed by his commander. The nickname didn't make him grin like I'd thought it would. He'd stopped being distant with me, but he was still emotionally mauled by what had happened. I was the one who had died, but I pitied him for having to see it. To pull my body out of the cold water then do his best to bring me back.

"You don't have to stay with me." He hadn't left my side in almost a week. He didn't have a schedule like the rest of the world, but I knew there had been days when we didn't see each other because he was so busy with work. He'd never been absent from his obligations for this long. "I know you have work to do."

He studied me as he searched for the confirmation in my face.

"I'll be okay." I felt safe in his palace next to the Seine. Whenever the anxiety would come for me, I would look to the Eiffel Tower for direction like it was the North Star and I was a sailor lost at sea. "Life goes on."

He left the desk and came toward me, wearing only his sweatpants and nothing else, hard and chiseled and tatted, a fine piece of man that I got to see every single day. He cupped my face and dug his hand deep into my hair as he tilted my chin up to look at him. "Life goes on for everyone else, but not for me, not when my life is bound to yours."

The hardest and most dangerous man I'd ever met could be the gentlest and most romantic. "It's okay, Bastien." I held on to his forearms as his heat transferred into me like flames from the hearth.

"Luca has been covering for me."

"But Luca isn't you." I wanted him there with me always, but I would never weaponize my pain to manipulate him into staying. "Really, it's okay. You've given me enough of your time."

"I've been here because I wanted to be—not out of obligation." He tilted his head slightly as he looked at me. "Because I've needed this time as much as you have." He brushed my cheek with his thumb. "I've seen some bad things. Done worse things. But that was the single most horrifying moment of my life."

I tightened my fingers on his forearms. "I know."

He stared at my lips before he dipped his head and kissed me, slow and soft, giving me his full lips before a bit of tongue, kissing me with heat for the first time since Oscar had taken me. But then he pulled away, his blue eyes looking hard into mine. "I'll go back tomorrow—if you're sure."

"I'm sure."

"You're safe here. No one can get into this house without a wrecking ball."

"I'm not scared. Not anymore." I wasn't scared someone would take me or hurt me. I wasn't scared that Bastien would sneak around behind my back and break my heart. I wasn't scared of anything—not when he was mine.

A slight smile moved on to his lips, but it was faint, so faint it was almost lifeless. "Attagirl." He kissed me again, cradling my face to his as he pulled me in, kissing me nice and slow, giving me his lips and his breaths and a bit of his tongue.

The frost in my fingertips melted at his touch, and my heart started to beat again, pounding with the vitality that he breathed into me when he brought me back to life. My hands felt my favorite feature, his big and hard chest, feeling the surge of heat that burned from the muscles underneath his flesh.

His arm circled my waist and squeezed me to him tight, his neck bent down to meet my kiss. Our mouths moved together in a dance we'd practiced many times, but it still felt brand-new, the touches between us electric.

His hand moved to my ass underneath the baggy shirt I wore, and he squeezed both cheeks in a single hand as he gave a quiet moan into my mouth, like he desired me with a bottomless depth.

There wasn't a single time we were together when we hadn't ended up in bed together for sex except these last five days. I'd been in too much shock to desire him, and he'd seemed to feel the same way. But once he knew I was okay, doing better, at least, he came alive like he'd been suppressing his desire this entire time.

He lifted me and carried me into the bedroom, laying me on the bed that Gerard had made while we were at my apartment. Bastien pulled off my underwear and didn't care that I hadn't shaved in a couple of days, my mind distracted by the past that haunted me in the present. He dropped his bottoms then moved on top of me, helping me get the shirt over my head so my warm tits could feel the cold air.

He helped himself between my thighs, his arms anchored behind my knees as he towered over me.

His chest was above me like the sky, his hard stomach tight and clenched as he worked his core. I grabbed on to his big-ass bicep with one of my hands while I planted the other against his rock-hard chest, a chest so strong a bullet would bounce off it. "Jesus Christ, you're so fucking hot."

His smirk was barely visible because he was so much taller than me, but I saw it when I tilted my head back, moaning when his big dick entered me with the hardness of a steel bar. He entered smoothly through my slickness, able to squeeze into my tightness because I was ready for him at a moment's notice, watching him walk around the house in just his gray sweatpants low on his hips, seeing the flush of his muscles after he worked out, the tendons that were like spider webs across his skin. He was the single hottest motherfucker I'd ever seen.

He rocked into me nice and slow, his mouth just inches from mine, his warm breaths like a tropical breeze over my skin.

We had been in the midst of a serious conversation just minutes ago, but now I was so red-hot that I was about to hit a threshold I hadn't known was on the horizon until I was already at the edge of the cliff. "Bastien..." I felt the tendons in his neck, felt the heartbeat in his chest, felt the warmth from his internal furnace. I could come just by looking at the man.

His rocking turned into a pounding, his strokes even and hard, hitting me in the perfect spot on repeat. His skin started to tint and moisten with a sheen of sweat, smelling like a man, and that was a turn-on in itself.

I was already ready to go, but my body halted, extending the buildup for a second longer because it was just so good.

But his breathing turned harsh and irregular, fighting the fire in his dick because he wanted to come inside me. He held off for me, waiting for me to go first, and like the gentleman that he was, he didn't edge himself, too proud to show a sign of weakness.

I'd been fucking him long enough to know his tells and his moves, to know how he felt even when he tried so hard to hide it.

I let myself go, both of my hands gripping his wrists for something to hold on to, like I was at the top of the tracks on a roller coaster and I was about to go into a drop. When I fell over, my nails were like claws, and I came around his fat dick with a mixture of cries and screams, with tears that burned my eyes before they streaked to my ears. "Bastien…" No man brought me to the heavens the way he did, made me see the stars that the strongest telescope could never detect.

He didn't wait for me to finish before he let go, unable to hold on to the railing a second longer. He made the jump, his cock thickening a little more inside me before he released, giving his final pumps full of mounds of seed.

I loved watching him come inside me. Just made me want to fuck him again.

He seemed to have the same idea because his dick was still hard when he finished. He started his thrusts again, this time pounding into me hard enough to make the bed shift and the headboard tap lightly against the wall. He fucked me like he'd wanted to fuck me for weeks and months, like he'd spotted me across the bar and eye-fucked me all night before he finally got me back to his house. His desire bled from his pores, and he took me like it was his mission to claim me, to erase my past and own my future.

3

BASTIEN

Luca walked into the warehouse in his tactical vest, like he'd just moved product. He talked with the guys across the room before our eyes met, and he joined me at the table.

I sat there, a cigar in my mouth and a cold drink in my hand. It was my first night back on the job. It'd been a long twelve hours, and I still had several more to go. It was the first night that Fleur would be by herself, but I knew she could handle it.

She'd died and come back to life, so she could handle anything.

"How's she doing?"

"She's better," I said after I released the smoke from my mouth.

"And you?"

I gave a shrug. "I'll get there."

"Did you work it out, or did she take off?"

"She said she's not going anywhere." It was hard not to smile as I said that, proud of my woman for being tough and touched that I was worth fighting for. For most of our relationship, I had done all the chasing, but now she chased me. "She moved in."

"Yeah?" he asked. "Happy for you."

"Thanks, man. It's nice to see you supportive for once."

"You know I'm protective of you."

"I'm a grown-ass man and don't need you to protect me, asshole." I smirked when I said it, so he knew it was all good between us.

"It's been quiet. The Aristocrats haven't made their move."

"They will. Give it time."

"Won't Adrien be their target instead of you?"

"No, they'll want both of our heads. Adrien crossed them, but I hung Oscar for all the world to see." And I didn't regret it. He'd killed my woman, so I burned his ass alive. Didn't care that his wife was a widow, that his kids wouldn't have a father. He violated the code—simple as that.

"Maybe we should hit them first, then. Nip this in the bud."

"Everyone will think I'm a psychopath if I do that."

"You are a psychopath."

I smirked. "We need to be diplomatic. Set up a meeting. Give us an opportunity to talk it out before we go nuclear. Everyone needs to see that I'm not a vindictive monster who can't think straight."

"Well…you did burn Oscar as he hung on Notre-Dame."

"That was because he buried my girl alive—and everyone should know what those consequences are."

"Then I'll see if they're receptive to a negotiation," he said. "Does this negotiation include Adrien?"

I took a drink from my cool glass and finished the last of the scotch. "That fucker is on his own."

"They'll kill him for his involvement in this."

I gave a shrug. "Fine by me."

"What about Fleur?"

"He's the reason she almost died, so I don't think she cares too much."

He sank back into the chair then lit up his own cigar and released a couple clouds of smoke, enjoying a moment of silence between us, two friends smoking and drinking, what we did best.

"Thanks for covering for me."

"No one even knew you were gone."

"Well, don't do my job *too* well."

A little grin moved over his face, but then it was gone when he brought the cigar to his lips. "It's quiet tonight, and we should appreciate it because I know it's not going to stay that way. Not when we've got a fight on two fronts."

"We've survived this long," I said. "I wouldn't worry about it."

"But we've always known our enemy—and now we don't."

I let the cigar sit between my fingertips, the smoke slowly rising to the ceiling.

"Just something we've got to remember."

I was out all night and most of the day. I worked so long that I still came home after Fleur got off work. It was the first time I'd come home and found her already in my house —because it was her house too.

She was on the couch when I walked in, still in her pencil skirt and tucked-in blouse and heels, like she didn't know what to do in a house that didn't quite feel like her own. But when I walked through the door, her eyes lit up in a special way, and she looked so damn happy to see me.

She left the couch and walked up to me, five inches taller than normal in those pumps, and her eyes softened with affection and excitement, a look I'd always remember as long as I lived, and kissed me.

She hooked her arms around my neck, and her face was nearly level with mine when she wore those heels. Her tits pressed into my chest, and she kissed me like she'd been thinking about me every moment that we'd been apart.

This was what I'd wanted when I'd asked her to move in, to come home to her every day, to feel my cock harden when I walked in the door knowing she was there, either naked in the shower or in lingerie in the bed or in my t-shirt on the couch. Whatever version was sexy as hell, and I was here for it.

I squeezed her ass in her skirt and kissed her back.

"I missed you, babe." She spoke between our kisses, saying it in a breathy voice.

I moaned into her mouth because she made me feel so wanted. There were no walls, no insecurities, no reasons to hold me at arm's length. This was what I wanted the moment I saw her, for us just to fucking be together.

I scooped her into my arms and sat on the couch with her on top of me, wanting her tits in my face, her soft hair against my skin, her pussy on my dick. I yanked her skirt up over her hips then popped open my jeans. In a hurry, we both tugged at our clothing to access each other. She undid the buttons of her blouse so her cleavage was visible in her bra. She pulled my shirt over my head because she liked my chest, liked to touch it and kiss it and look at it.

She guided my length inside her then slowly sank, slowly pushed down over my big dick until her ass touched my balls. She breathed and winced at the size but did it anyway because she was a fucking champ.

She started to rock nice and slow, rising up to my tip and sitting back down on my base, taking her time like she wanted me to enjoy it after a long day.

My hands gripped her ass when it popped out of her skirt. I guided her the way I wanted, each thrust purposeful but easy, like we had all night to fuck. I kissed her chest and nipped at her collarbone, smelling her perfume and then her sweat because she did all the work to fuck me.

I got to enjoy it, watch her fuck me like she'd been thinking about it all day.

I unbuttoned her blouse the rest of the way and helped her out of it before I unclasped her bra, letting her perfect tits come free, little nipples on plump tits, firm and perky, nicest pair of tits I'd ever seen.

She started to move faster, riding my dick harder as she arched her back and came down on my length, moving like a seductress who was about to steal my soul. She ran her fingers over her chest, leaned back to make her tits tilt to the sky, smeared my length in her cream that was thicker than the milk in her morning coffee.

"I'm fucking obsessed with you." I worshipped her body with my stare, with my big hands, wanting to come inside that little pussy because it was all mine. I didn't thrust up to meet her movements, sat still and let her fuck me like I'd paid for it. She was so fucking good at it, so confident and sexy, like she knew what I wanted the moment I walked through the door.

"I wanted to show my appreciation." She reached her hand behind her and played with my balls as she continued to ride me, making me inhale a sharp breath at her touch. "For everything you've done for me…"

My fingers dug into her ass, and I felt my cock twitch inside her because I'd never been this fucking hard in my life. It was like a taunt, watching me try to hold it together while she was a fucking fantasy. "Sweetheart…"

"Come inside me."

I sucked in a breath through my teeth. "Jesus."

"It turns me on." She exaggerated her movements, taking my length all the way to the base before she rose up again, her palms planted on my chest, her tits fucking amazing. "I like to feel it."

I couldn't keep it together, not after she teased me and fucked me the way I liked. She was paradise, and my dick didn't want to leave. When I fucked whores, I never cared about their pleasure. But if I was with a woman I met at a bar or on the street, I stepped up and acted like a gentleman. Now that I was in the first real relationship of my life, it felt wrong to shoot my bullet before she shot hers. But she had me by the balls—literally—and I was too weak to fight it.

So I felt the heat swallow me whole, and I felt my gun fire off an entire clip of bullets. My eyes were on hers, seeing her cheeks flush in arousal as she watched me come inside her. My hands squeezed her cheeks before I tugged her at the speed I wanted, taking her harder until my final pumps were finished.

I was winded, though I hadn't moved, winded because she took the breath straight out of my lungs. I was fucking obsessed with this woman, and I was relieved that I didn't have to hide it anymore. That she seemed just as thoroughly obsessed with me.

No surprise that my dick was still hard when it was sheathed inside her, when the perkiest tits were against my chest, the greenest eyes locked on mine like I was the man she should have married in the first place.

She rocked herself slowly, like she could feel the come between our bodies, her neck bright red like that really did turn her on. She moved into me and kissed me, slow and sexy kisses, her hips still grinding against me. "Now it's my turn."

She seemed to be feeling better because she'd gone to work and then fucked my brains out when I came home, so I took her out to dinner. Just because we lived together now didn't mean I would stop doing those things.

Besides, I wanted to show her off.

I knew every man looked at her and wished he were the one nailing her.

But that privilege was all fucking mine.

She sipped her water before she looked at the menu, wearing an oversized sweater as a dress with thigh-high black boots. She was probably trying to be casual, but it was one of the sexiest things I'd ever seen her wear.

I'd have to fuck her again when we got home.

"What are you getting?" she asked.

"The chicken."

"Still cutting back on the red meat?"

I gave a shrug. "Doctor's orders."

"Good for you for getting checked out," she said. "And good for you for caring. I need you to live a long time."

My parents used to fight about my father's cholesterol levels all the time. My father would always dismiss my mother's concerns, probably because he knew he was more likely to die from a bullet than a heart attack. "It runs in the family, so…"

She gave a slight nod in understanding.

The waiter came over to take our order, and I stuck to my roasted chicken, while she got a salad and a soup. She'd been eating very little the last week, and she seemed to be continuing that streak.

"You didn't have to go back to work." I'd told her boss she would be unavailable for a while. If he didn't like it, it wasn't like he could voice it. Not when I could fire him—or worse.

Her mood dampened noticeably. "I had to get out of the house."

"You could have gone to yoga or shopping…better options."

"I don't do yoga."

She could bend in all sorts of ways, a hot pretzel underneath me, so I'd assumed she'd been doing yoga all her life. "Fooled me."

"And I don't need to go shopping."

"I've never heard a woman say that."

She chuckled slightly, my words lifting her spirits a little bit.

I wanted her happy, soaring with the clouds, her smile big and infectious. But I knew it would take time to get there. "You don't need to work at all, sweetheart. It's not like you have rent."

"I broke my lease, so I still have to pay it until a new tenant comes in—"

"I already took care of it." I'd paid her landlord for the next six months. That was more than enough time for him to find a replacement.

She stared at me blankly for a few seconds. "You didn't have to do that."

"You're my woman. You're my responsibility."

"I don't want to be a responsibility."

"It's a privilege to have you as a responsibility."

She shifted her eyes away, desperately trying to be angry, but I could tell she wasn't.

"You don't need to work."

Her eyes came back to me. "But I like working."

I smirked as the laugh inched into my throat. "No, you don't." She hated going to work in the morning. She never complained about the work itself, but she didn't have anything good to say about it either. Didn't blame her. The idea of sitting behind a computer all day sounded mindless and boring.

"I mean, I like working for my own money."

"What do you need money for?"

"Food, clothing, essentials—"

"I provide all of that."

She released a sigh, a little smile on her lips. "That's sweet, Bastien. Really, it is. But when I said I didn't want you for your money, I meant it."

"And I believe you."

"It's fine," she said. "I don't mind working."

"You didn't work with Adrien."

"Well, that was different."

"How?" I was used to barking orders and having people obey, and it was frustrating when I couldn't apply that to her. Most women would be happy to let a man take care of them, but she chose to be difficult about it, and it was starting to piss me off.

She hesitated before she answered. "We were married..."

I knew I would marry her someday, so I didn't see why she couldn't rely on me now. Her yearly income wasn't even equivalent to a penny of mine. "You said you were in this with me. You said you wouldn't leave even if I asked you to."

"And I meant that, Bastien."

"Then let me take care of you." It would be different if she were passionate about her job and it meant something to her, but working as an assistant to some suit was not fulfilling. "My woman should not be working—unless it means something to her. I know for a fact this job is just a means to an end—means you no longer need."

Her eyes moved out the window, and she sighed. "I don't want to fight."

"We aren't fighting."

"What about you? Do you like working?"

I smiled because the question was ridiculous. "You think I still need money?" She'd seen my house, seen the funds that my investment company earned, billions of dollars. And she thought I was a slave to the clock? "I'm in the game because I was born in it, and I'll die in it. Because the power and the adrenaline give me a fucking rush like nothing else—not even you."

She stared at me for a while before she grabbed her water and took another drink.

My stare was locked on her face like a laser from a sniper.

She was in an invisible corner with nowhere to go, but she still tried to find a way out.

"When I asked you to move in with me, I asked you to be the woman of the house. The woman who waits for me to come home. The woman on my arm for every dinner and social event. The woman who is *mine* in every sense of the fucking word." I didn't raise my voice, but I felt the raw frustration burn in my chest. "I want to take care of you—so let me do my fucking job."

"I said I don't want your money—"

"I understand," I snapped. "But I want to give it to you anyway, so just let me."

We'd been arguing for so long that the waiter arrived with our food. He placed the dishes in front of us, probably aware of the tension that was tighter than a taut rope because he didn't say a word before he walked off.

She looked down at her food but didn't seem interested in it. "Maybe we should have talked about this before I moved in."

"You should have assumed all of this before you moved in. What is the problem, Fleur?"

She was quiet for a while, her eyes still on her plate so she wouldn't have to look at me. "The last time I was financially dependent on a man, he cheated on me and I had to start over with nothing. No education or resources or—"

"You might as well just slap me in the fucking face."

She lifted her gaze to look at me. "My feelings have nothing to do with you, Bastien."

"You were left with nothing because you refused to take half of the estate, which you were fully entitled to. Let's not forget that."

"He was the one who built all that wealth."

"It doesn't fucking matter, Fleur. And your feelings do have to do with me, because right now, in this fucking moment, you're with me, not him, and you don't trust me. You don't trust that this relationship will be different from your last one."

"It's not that I don't trust you—"

"Then prove it."

She crossed her arms over her chest, rubbing the fabric of her sweater as she stared at the food we probably wouldn't eat. "Okay." She lifted her chin and looked at me, her eyes still timid. "I'll quit."

It was what I wanted, but not in the way I wanted it. I didn't want to have to fight for it.

"I don't want to fight. I'm so happy with you."

My anger still burned beneath the surface, a simmer after the boil.

"It's not that I don't trust you, because I trust you more than anyone I've ever known."

My anger started to ebb, to slowly dissipate because I could hear her sincerity.

"I didn't fall in love with you because you're rich or because you're powerful."

My eyes narrowed on her face.

But she didn't seem to have any idea what she'd just revealed to me, like her feelings were so second nature she didn't even register her words. "And the last thing I ever want you to think is I'm with you for the wrong reasons. Because if you lived in my old apartment and could only afford to take me to McDonald's, I'd be perfectly fine with that."

She really had no fucking idea what she'd just said. It was so far compartmentalized that she didn't see the truth even when it stared at her right in the face. I couldn't fight the grin that moved over my lips. The anger was long gone when I heard the words directly out of her mouth, words that Adrien had shared with me first without remembering it.

"What?" she asked, the confusion in her features fully sincere.

"Nothing."

Her eyes flicked back and forth between mine like she knew that wasn't the truth.

I changed the subject before she could ask me for a better answer. "All I want is for us to be together fully and completely—and you've finally given that to me."

4

BASTIEN

She didn't have to submit a two-week notice or formally quit, not when I was her boss, so she was just done. We didn't talk about it again, and I was glad it was over. It was one of the worst fights we'd had, but it couldn't have ended better.

I couldn't wipe the smile off my face for days.

I worked mostly nights, leaving after she went to bed. When I came home, it was usually late morning, and she was dressed and ready to go even though she had nowhere to be. I kissed her and grabbed her ass like I always did, happy that she was the face I saw after a long night on the streets.

"How was work?"

"Fine." I pulled the envelope out of my back pocket and opened the flap to reveal the debit and credit cards that were all in her name. I placed it on the table. "These are yours. Buy whatever you want. I have space in the parking garage under the building if you want a car."

Her eyebrows flicked up at the offer, but she didn't say anything.

I waited for resistance or argument, but it never came.

Finally, she said, "Thank you."

I moved into her again, my hand squeezing both of her ass cheeks as I kissed her hard on the mouth. "Attagirl." I gave her ass a hard spank before I walked away.

"Bastien?"

I turned back to her, dead tired and ready for bed, but she was always my priority.

"Could you do me a favor?"

My eyebrows furrowed before I walked back to her. "Anything."

She hesitated before she made her request. "I still have a lot of stuff at Adrien's. Stuff that I couldn't bring to the apartment because I was in such a rush to get the hell out of there. I don't think I can look at his face again and not punch him, so…could you get it for me?"

"Of course."

"There's the rest of my clothes—"

"You have *more* clothes?" She already took up eighty percent of the closet.

Her trepidation vanished as a sly smile moved over her lips. "And shoes…lots of shoes."

"Jesus Christ."

"You might want to rethink giving me your credit card." The smile was still there, and it was nice to watch her tease me again.

I didn't need to rethink it, not when that was the exact reason I gave it to her. "Good thing we have extra closets in this house."

"I was thinking the same thing."

"Or I'll have to remodel one of the rooms *into* a closet."

"Ooh, I like that idea."

I smirked then reached for my phone to text Adrien. *I'm coming by tonight to get the rest of Fleur's stuff*. I didn't wait for his response, too tired to care about whatever nonsense he might say. "I'm going to shower and head to bed."

"Alright. But how tired are you...?" Her hand absent-mindedly went to my arm, and she lightly grazed the skin, her fingers finding a tendon and following it down to the inside of my elbow.

There was nothing sexier than a sexy woman wanting you. Compliments and advances from girls all over this city were nothing compared to hers. "Never too tired for that."

I'd worked a lot that week because of the time I'd taken off, and even though she wasn't working anymore and had a lot of free time, she didn't seem to mind that I had other obligations besides her.

She'd started working out in my gym, using the treadmill and some of the free weights. She bought books at the bookstore down the street and read them in cafés, and Gerard told me she used the kitchen to bake cookies from scratch. So, she filled her day with activities that were a lot more interesting than work. And I knew she felt better because she wouldn't have gone anywhere by herself just a week ago.

I'd never pictured myself as a one-woman kind of man, let alone asking someone to live with me, but once I had her, my life felt perfect. Complete, even.

I stopped by one of our warehouses before I headed to Adrien's because that was the most convenient route for the night. When I walked in, the music blared and the bass thumped. The guards were relaxed like they weren't on duty.

There were girls everywhere, so Luca had probably paid for a private show with the burlesque girls from Moulin Rouge or Crazy Horse. Luca was a hard-ass like I was, but he loved the drink and women just a bit more. He had a girl on his lap when I walked inside, the girl wearing nothing but sparkly panties. The top hat that was supposed to be on her head had somehow ended up on his instead.

I made myself a drink, the guys oblivious because they were too busy having fun. I knew if I shut it down, everyone would be resentful, and I'd learned that being a leader was about give-and-take. There were times to be strict, and there were times to let loose. We'd just finished our product shipment, and the tariffs had been paid for the month, so there was nothing pressing at the moment.

"Look who it is." One of the girls spotted me and walked over. "It's been a while since I've seen you around." She was in a sparkly silver bodysuit and a top hat, bringing the wardrobe from the show straight to the warehouse.

It took a second for me to remember her name, but it came to me eventually. "How are you, Marie?"

"You know, busy," she said. "Between Moulin Rouge and university, I don't have a lot of time for much else."

"Quit university."

She rolled her eyes. "I need a job."

"You'll never make as much doing anything else as you do doing this."

"Yes, but I'll get old someday, and no one is gonna watch a middle-aged woman in a burlesque show."

"If she's hot, who cares."

"You'd fuck a middle-aged woman?" she asked incredulously.

"She'd probably give good head, so I'd be game."

She laughed at what I said, like I'd made a joke or my honesty was just amusing to her. "I miss you."

Marie and I had a fling shortly before I'd met Fleur. It'd lasted about a week. I fucked her in the alleyway of the building after one of her shows, and then she came to my house a couple times. But it fizzled out and I lost interest. "I'm seeing someone."

"For now," she said. "But when that's over, maybe we could meet up again."

Before I'd settled down, my personal life was a mixture of regulars and women I met on the town. And sometimes I would just pay a whore, depending on my mood. But now, that felt so long ago that it didn't even feel like me. "I'm gonna marry this girl."

She looked surprised then winced and swallowed, trying to catch herself from showing her disappointment. But the emotions were practically written in permanent marker on her face. "Oh…I did not expect that."

"I didn't either. But that's how it goes."

"Well…congratulations."

It was a hollow sentiment, so I didn't respond to it. Luca's girl finally left his lap, so I hurried over before he got sidetracked again. "I gotta talk to Luca." Without looking, I left her side and took the empty seat beside him. "Didn't realize there was a party tonight."

He had a shit-eating grin on his face. "Yep."

"Thanks for the heads-up."

"I knew you would have just shut it down."

"And you'd be right."

"Just because you're sticking your dick in one woman doesn't mean the rest of us have to do the same." He lit up a cigar and took a couple puffs to get it going. "So, how's she doing?"

"A lot better." With every passing day, a little more color returned to her face. "I'm going by Adrien's now to pick up the rest of her stuff."

"Finally, some fucking closure."

"She quit the firm."

"Why?"

"Because I asked her to."

"She seems like someone who would put up a fight about that."

"Oh, she did." I grinned.

"Why do you care if she works or not?"

"Because she's doing it for a paycheck, not because she's passionate about it. Why does she need money when I can buy her anything she fucking wants?" I took one of the cigars off the table and lit up. "Now she goes to the bookstore and reads in cafés. She works out, bakes shit."

"Why does she need to work out?"

"For her health, asshole. People die of heart attacks in their thirties. It's not that rare." It wasn't because I thought she

49

needed to lose weight or have a tighter ass. I was fucking obsessed with her body.

"Is that why you don't order steak anymore?" he teased.

"As a matter of fact…"

"Turning into an old man."

"Just trying to live to be an old man someday."

He smiled before he puffed on the cigar again. "I'm glad she's out and about instead of hiding behind a locked door."

"Me too," I said. "The conversation got a bit heated, but it ended on a high note."

"If she's a prideful woman who wants to work, let her. Kinda sexy, if you ask me."

"She didn't work with Adrien, so when he fucked around, she felt destitute. Doesn't want to feel that way again."

"She could have taken a lot more than half if she wanted to."

"I told her that."

"But she's got too much pride—one of the reasons I like her."

"I just didn't appreciate being compared to him."

His eyes shifted back and forth in confusion. "I don't think she did. She just wants to be more independent after what happened to her. Pretty reasonable. I think you're just pissed off because you weren't getting your way."

"She doesn't *want* to work. And I *want* to take care of her. I know I made the right decision because she's been happier than a little bird at the first sight of spring. Doing what she wants when she wants."

He pulled the smoke into his mouth then released it as a cloud out of his nostrils.

"I will take care of her—and I won't stick my dick where it doesn't belong." That was all women wanted. Didn't need to be in several relationships to figure that out.

"Does she have any idea how fucking psycho you are for her?"

I continued to conceal the depths of my emotions from her, to run a marathon instead of a sprint, to play the game by her rules. "I'm sure she does. I think she's psycho for me too, but she's doing her damnedest to hide it...unsuccessfully."

"Unsuccessfully?"

I felt myself smile at the memory. "At the end of our argument, she basically said she was in love with me, without realizing that she'd actually said it. Like it's been true for so fucking long that it just slipped out. Adrien told me she said the same thing, but he was drunk out of his mind, so I wasn't completely certain I could believe him. But looks like he was telling the truth."

"Why won't she say it to your face?"

"I think she's scared."

"Scared? If she still wants to be with you after being buried alive and literally dying, she doesn't seem like she scares easy."

"I think she's afraid to admit to herself that her heart is at risk again. That I have the power to break her worse than Adrien did. Which is ridiculous because I would never hurt her."

"To be fair, I'm sure Adrien said the same thing."

"I'm a man and he's a boy. It's different, and she knows it's different."

He gave a nod in agreement.

"You know how much pussy gets handed to me?" Nearly every night, I ran into a woman who made a pass at me, whether it was at a bar or a meeting spot or someone's estate. There wasn't enough time in the day to fuck all those women, even if I wanted to. "And you know how easy it is to turn it down? So fucking easy, man. Because that's my fucking wife. How Adrien didn't know that is fucking beyond me."

"I think he just assumed he wouldn't get caught."

"I would never get caught," I snapped. "She would never know, and you would never rat on me if you knew. It's about not wanting to do it in the first place. I just wish she understood that."

"I don't think she would have moved in with you if she didn't understand that, Bastien. If she didn't trust you like she does, she would have left the second you pulled her out of that coffin. She wouldn't grab her shit and move in with you. She wouldn't trust you to take care of her. Maybe the road is a little bumpy at times, but she's never lost her grip on the wheel."

I was impatient for more, but Luca made me see reason, that just because she wanted to wade into the water instead of jumping in headfirst with me didn't mean she was any less committed.

"You already know how she feels, and that's all that matters," he said. "It doesn't matter when she's ready to say it."

I arrived at Adrien's house, the rest of the guys waiting by the SUV smoking cigars and waiting for orders.

The butler showed me inside. Adrien was standing in the sitting room like he'd been pacing to pass the time. The second he realized I was there, he gave a sigh. "How's she doing?"

"She's fine."

"Fine? What does that mean?"

"She had a rough couple of days, but she's been doing well ever since. Goes shopping, runs on the treadmill, bakes cookies. She doesn't take baths like she used to, but I'm sure warming up to that idea will take more than a couple weeks."

The relief swept over his gaze. "Good...that's good. Has she gone back to work?"

"She quit."

"Why?"

I shouldn't subjugate myself to this conversation, but I wanted him to understand he'd been replaced, that he'd thrown her away and I'd put her back together. That when he'd tossed out the trash, there had been a diamond in the rubble—and now that diamond was mine. "Because she doesn't need money when she has me."

He didn't appear stung by that response, his only concern for her well-being. "I've been worried but knew a call or text wouldn't be welcome."

"Bother her, and I'll kill you."

His eyes immediately flew back to mine, his stare shifting as if trying to understand if I meant that threat.

Yes, I fucking did. "She made her wishes clear."

"I just want to know she's okay—"

"That's my job now, asshole. You've been fired and replaced." I snapped my fingers. "*Like that.*"

He looked away, like the truth of my words dug under his skin.

"Where's her stuff?"

"I tried to pack everything, but...it was too hard." His hands went to his hips, and he looked at the stairs. "I didn't expect it to end like this."

"If you didn't want it to end, all you had to do was not fuck other people."

He turned to me. "You're a real prick."

"You expect me to feel sorry for you? Expect Fleur to feel sorry for you? No one gives a damn, Adrien. Were you thinking about Fleur when you were balls deep inside someone else? Were you thinking about her when you came in a bitch's mouth and told her to swallow? Were you thinking about her—"

"*Stop.*"

"Then take me upstairs so I can get her shit and go home."

Adrien said nothing else before he finally headed upstairs to the primary bedroom he used to share with Fleur. The bed was covered in piles of clothes, and the shoes were placed on top. There were other things, a jewelry box, a box full of pictures and keepsakes, a couple pieces of décor.

I called the guys downstairs. "Bring at least twelve boxes— and all the tape." I hung up then looked at Adrien across the bed, unable to believe I was standing in the room where Fleur used to sleep every night before she met me. "The only grace I'll give you is the fact that I think this was all meant to happen. Fleur was meant to be mine—so this was destined to go to shit."

I had the guys put the boxes in one of the spare bedrooms so she could go through them at her convenience. Adrien let us go without a fight. Didn't mention the Aristocrats or his plans for the business. He still had a target on his back, but this time, I wouldn't help him.

It was early morning when I walked in the door. She wasn't on the couch or in bed, and when I stepped into the bathroom, I found her in the shower, her soiled workout clothes on the floor where she'd left them.

I stared at her through the fogged-up glass, seeing her sexy curves soaking wet. She grabbed my bar of soap and rubbed it over her chest, over her plump tits, and then across her throat, her movements slow like she was in no rush and had nowhere to be.

I dropped my clothes in a pile on the floor and joined her.

When she felt the draft from the cold, she quickly turned toward me with wide eyes, like she assumed the worst instead of the best. But when she realized it was me, that bright affection entered her gaze, sunshine through the clouds in her eyes.

Wordlessly, I greeted her, hooking my arms around her soapy body and bringing her into me for a long kiss. I gripped her tight ass in one hand, while I squeezed her around the torso with the other. The kiss continued, growing from soft and slow to hot and fiery, full of tongue and little moans masked by the sound of the falling water. Shower sex was not my favorite, not when there were so many obstacles and the height difference between most women and me was so great, but I wanted this woman whenever she stepped into the room. Her kiss was scorching, her touch like a spark to a pyre that burned my soul.

I scooped her into my arms and lifted her into position, letting her guide my length to her entrance, and I lowered her down to sheathe it fully.

She moaned as she hooked her arms around my neck, being supported by my hands on her ass and my arms under her thighs.

I lifted her up and down, thrusting my hips on her way down, taking her in the shower like she weighed nothing. Since my arms were the size of her head, she really did weigh nothing.

Her skin was red, flushed by the heat growing inside her. Her eyes had a heavy glaze over them like she was lost in the heat between us, lost in the passion that set our world ablaze. I knew she was impressed by my strength because she was more turned on than usual, watching me lift her over and over without having to slow, my bulging arms the size of tree trunks. I listened to her body and studied her touches and kisses, so I knew her favorite position was missionary. She was always so fucking wet, and she came so damn fast. But it seemed like she enjoyed this even more. "You like this, sweetheart?"

Her answer was immediate. Didn't have to pull it out of her. "Yes…"

I started to fuck her faster. "You love it when I fuck you like this?"

Her breaths ran rampant, uneven and uneasy. "Yes."

I kept up the fast pace because of the adrenaline and the throbbing arousal in my dick. I lifted three times her weight in a session in the gym, so my muscles didn't fatigue as quickly as they would with a higher weight.

She was about to come. Her eyes glazed over like she saw stars, and her lips parted to begin the incoherent stream of sighs and cries and moans. She was so pretty when she came, her eyes growing wet with tears that were desperate to be free. Then there was the crescendo, the moans intermixed with my name, and the sudden tightness of her pussy.

I could tell how wet she was, even in the shower. It was so distinctive around my dick, so slick. I brought her down on my length the exact way I wanted and gave her my final pumps, filling that pussy with another load.

I held her close and felt her ankles lock together at the top of my ass. It took just a few seconds for my breathing to return to normal. I stepped farther under the showerhead so the water could hit us both to wash away the sweat.

Then she kissed me, kissed me hard, like she was far from done with me. "You're so fucking hot. I can't believe you're mine."

5

FLEUR

Bastien worked every single night for two weeks, and while I was disappointed he was gone so much, I didn't complain. He'd bailed on all his responsibilities when I'd needed him most, so I couldn't be greedy with his time.

I went through all the things that Bastien had retrieved from Adrien's and put the clothes and shoes away in the closet in one of the additional bedrooms. It was more than a spare room, but a smaller primary that was worthy of an important guest. The walk-in closet was perfect for all my extra things. Adrien had also included my wedding dress in the contents. It was zipped up in a bag, so I assumed Bastien hadn't noticed.

Even if that had been a special day, it felt weird to keep it, so I tossed it in the donations bag.

I could only organize my belongings for so many hours without getting overwhelmed, so I would take a book down to one of my cafés and read it while enjoying a midday

59

coffee. I did cardio for an hour every day now because I was afraid I would gain a bunch of weight since I spent most of my time sitting on my ass. And Bastien was so fucking hot that I had to at least try to stay fit.

I'd thought I would be lost and bored without having a job to occupy my day, but it was the opposite. I didn't miss staring at a computer screen and looking at spreadsheets and booking appointments for my boss. I didn't miss the meetings and the mandatory luncheons and the bullshit.

I didn't miss worrying about rent and what temperature I could afford to keep the heater and how much I could afford in groceries for the week. I didn't miss hearing people argue down the hallway from my apartment because the walls were practically made of paper. I didn't miss having to do my laundry in my kitchen. Now, I didn't have to do laundry at all.

No laundry. No cooking. No dishes. Nothing.

When I'd been with Adrien, I'd still had to do everything else. I was a housewife, and I earned my keep by doing everything so he didn't have to do anything. With Bastien, I felt like a queen in a castle whose only responsibility was to fuck the king when he came home.

I sat at the table at BO&MIE, a café that had café crème and raspberry croissants, my favorite. I was upstairs near the window, reading my book while I sipped my coffee. I normally went in the morning when it was quiet, but I'd come around lunchtime today and it was louder than usual with all the people, so I had my earphones in while I read.

The chair across from me was pulled out, and someone put down their tray of food, baked rigatoni and a croque monsieur sandwich.

I assumed it was some jerk who had come to make a pass, but my eyes lifted and locked on the prettiest blue eyes I'd ever seen.

He smiled at my surprise as he sat across from me, his tray holding enough food for two people, maybe even three. "Mind if I join you, sweetheart?"

I paused the music in my earphones and closed my book. "How did you know I was here?"

"I track your phone."

"Oh…" I didn't know that.

He grabbed his fork and started to eat his pasta. He seemed to pick up on my disapproval because he said, "It's a two-way street. You can see where I am whenever you want."

"I can?"

He took my phone from the surface of the table and tapped his name in my contacts. The map popped up, showing both of our dots in the same spot. "If you're ever worried about me." He returned the phone to the table. "Want any of this?"

It did look good, fresh pasta drenched in sauce with the cheese baked on top. "Sure."

He scooped half of it onto the little place that held his croissant and slid it toward me. "I ordered cheesecake too, but the prick forgot to give it to me." He gave me his fork and left to retrieve another one.

His sandwich looked good too, so I cut that in half and crammed it onto my plate.

When he came back, he handed me the fork then smirked when he realized I'd taken some of his sandwich too. "Attagirl."

He was the only man in the world who encouraged me to eat. If I started to gain some weight when I was with Adrien, he would make little comments to indicate he noticed, like asking me to make salads and soups for dinner, things that didn't have carbs. He thought he was being clever, but he was just an idiot.

That experience had made me strict with my diet. I ate whatever I wanted, but I always kept it under a calorie limit. I usually had a coffee and croissant for breakfast then skipped lunch and had a big dinner with Bastien before he went to work.

"Why are you awake?" I asked.

"I'm off tonight, so I just took a nap."

"You are?" I asked a little too enthusiastically.

He smirked. "I'm all yours, sweetheart."

"Ooh…what should we do?"

"I don't care as long as you're naked."

I smiled and nearly rolled my eyes, but instead, I speared a piece of pasta with my fork and popped that into my mouth.

"You must like this place. You're here nearly three times a week."

That meant he watched me on his phone often. "I love their raspberry croissants."

He smirked and continued to eat.

"What?"

"Those are my mom's favorite too."

"Well, she has good taste."

"Guess so." He continued to eat, inhaling his food like usual, arms on the table as he towered over his meal. "We have a wedding this Saturday. Totally slipped my mind until Luca reminded me."

"We, as in you and me?"

"Did you think I was going to take Gerard?"

The chuckle escaped uncontrollably. "I'd love to see that."

"He's not my type."

"He does all your cooking and cleaning and laundry, so he better be your type."

His smile could win awards. "You've got me there." He grabbed his sandwich and took a big bite, a manly bite. He chewed as he stared at me across the table then glanced at the book I'd been reading. "*The Chateau*. Any good?"

"I like it. It's about these two sisters who get trafficked working in a labor camp, and while the older sister is there, she falls in love with one of the guards...who ends up being more than a guard—and that's as far as I've gotten."

He gave a slow nod. "That does sound good. You like romance?"

"I read everything. I just finished *Mistborn* by Brandon Sanderson."

"I didn't know you liked to read so much." He continued to eat, but his eyes were glued to my face like he was truly enraptured by my words. He wasn't half listening, but actually invested in what I had to say.

"I used to want to be a literature professor."

"What changed?"

"Well, I got married, and that dream kinda just died..."

"You still have time—if that's what you want to do."

"I thought you didn't want me to work?"

"I said I don't want you to work *for* money," he said. "Working for passion is very different."

I'd have to return to university and take classes and write dissertations and spend the next six years of my life studying and writing papers, and that sounded like so much work now that I was almost thirty. "I'd rather read whatever I want in a café and wait for my man to wake up than lecture a bunch of undergrads."

His eyes lit up as if he liked that answer. "You seem to be adjusting well."

"I'm not gonna lie, I don't miss the office."

That smile stretched across his lips like that answer truly made him happy. All he wanted to do was take care of me. It gave him more than happiness, but purpose and pride. "I assumed."

"I doubt my boss misses me either. I was the worst assistant ever."

"You were not."

"As if he'd ever complain about me to you. You wanna know how I know I sucked?"

He cocked his head slightly.

"He never asked me to do anything. Like, ever. I could have sat in that office and played solitaire all day, and it wouldn't have mattered. I had to find things to do for him."

"That doesn't mean you sucked. It just means he was scared shitless of pissing me off."

"What did you say to him when you hired me?"

"That my woman would be working for him, and I'd shoot him in the back of the head if he gave you a hard time."

My eyes nearly popped open.

He chuckled. "Sweetheart, come on. You think I'd say that?"

"Uh, yes."

He smiled before he took another bite of his sandwich. When he swallowed, he spoke again. "I just told him you were my girl and needed work. That was it. I'm not sure if he even wanted an assistant. Maybe he thought I planted you to spy on him, so he walked on eggshells the whole time."

"Well, that would mean he's hiding something."

"We're all hiding something, sweetheart."

"Even you?" I asked, turning those words around on him.

He looked me dead in the eye, the smile nowhere in sight. "Yes."

I hadn't expected him to say that, so my own smile drained out of my face.

He seemed to have lost his appetite because he didn't touch any more of his food. He drank from his water then sat there, arms across his chest, as if he expected me to interrogate him about these secrets.

But I didn't want to ask. Didn't want to violate his privacy.

He continued to stare at me. "I'll tell you if you want to know."

My eyes flicked down to my plate, only a few bites left. "You don't have to tell me anything, Bastien. You're entitled to your privacy."

He cocked his head in the other direction, his eyes narrowing as he stared at my face. Several beats passed, and he didn't say anything. "I'll have to tell you eventually, but now isn't the best time." Probably because we were surrounded by people and families and tourists.

"Why do you have to?"

"It's just something you should know. Something I'm not proud of, but I'm not sorry about either."

I felt my heart tumble into the abyss, and I didn't want to think about whatever it was a moment longer. "Whose wedding are we going to?"

He clearly hadn't expected the change in subject because he stared at me for nearly a minute before he answered the question. "One of my producers. His daughter is getting married at the Four Seasons."

"Now that I have all my stuff back, I have something to wear."

"Doesn't mean you can't buy something new too."

"You seem to have forgotten how many clothes you moved over for me."

He gave a slight smile before he grabbed his fork and took a few more bites of his meal, his appetite back at the change in subject. "I'm sure the guys who moved everything could never forget."

"Luca will be there?"

"Probably."

"Probably?"

"He's kinda flaky."

"Will you know anyone else there?"

"I'll know a ton of people there."

"A drug dealer wedding…that's a first." It was hard to picture criminals doing normal things like everyone else.

"I've been to a lot of drug dealer weddings and birthday parties and bat mitzvahs." He finished his tray of pasta then wiped his mouth with his napkin. "Not all criminals are bad. Some of them are just trying to provide for their family like everyone else. They sell drugs, but they run it like a family-owned pizza parlor."

"Is that the kind of wedding we are going to?"

He nodded.

"And the others…?"

"The others need to be policed by me. Otherwise, a lot of bad things would happen to good people."

I remembered the first night we'd met and how he handled the burglars. He'd spoken to the police like he knew them well. "I thought you were a cop when we first met."

"I remember." There was a hint of amusement in his eyes.

"If I didn't know you, I would have a hard time believing all of this."

He soaked up my words like a dry sponge that was suddenly damp. "There's a lot of stuff that happens in Paris that most people don't know about. The French Emperors have been a secret society that has existed on and off for centuries, founded by Napoleon Bonaparte before he became the first French Emperor. It was an important part of his strategy, to take hold of the country from the inside out. Over the centuries, the organization has changed, faded into the background, and then come into prominence when the Republic needed it. It's grown to what it is now, protecting the Republic in the shadows. We have partners all over the world, and those people are the best sources of information for global terrorism and other threats to the Republic and our allies. I report what I hear to our generals."

All I knew was the man before me, the man with a heart full of justice and kindness. It was easy to forget his position in light of that. "I had no idea."

"I'm a descendant of Napoleon—on my mother's side."

"Wow."

"We still have a couple things that once belonged to him. The Aristocrats allowed me to keep them because it's mine by blood."

"Allowed?" Bastien didn't seem like a man who needed permission.

"Their intentions started pure, but they've become extremists through the generations. They are more like a cult these days, declaring war on anyone who doesn't revere the French Republic. I thought Oscar was more practical than his peers, but I learned the hard way that he wasn't."

I shouldn't care enough to ask this question, but a part of

me would always care. "Do—do you think they'll try to kill Adrien?"

Bastien didn't bullshit me. He never did. "Absolutely."

"Would they spare him if he gave them what he wanted?"

"This isn't your problem, sweetheart. I warned him many times. He got himself into this mess, and even when he had a way out, he still didn't take it. Your concern is misplaced." He spoke calmly, like my interest in my ex's well-being didn't upset him.

"What about you?" I asked. "Will...will they try to kill you because you killed Oscar?"

He stared at me across the table, the light coming through the window and striking his face with the most beautiful glow. His eyes were like pools of clear blue water. "That's my problem, not yours."

"It is my problem, Bastien."

"I'll handle it, like I always do," he said calmly. "Don't waste another minute worrying about it."

"Do you have a plan? Are you going to kill them first?"

He smirked. "That sounds like the opposite of *not* worrying."

I appreciated the fact that he tried to shield me from sources of nightmares and shadows of anxiety, but he was the single most important person in my life, and the idea of losing him scared the shit out of me. "I fucking love you, so how am I not supposed to worry?" I raised my voice more than I should, but my frustration got the best of me.

His smile was brighter than the sun on a summer day. He relaxed in the chair, arms across his chest, staring me down with blue eyes that were both soft and amused at the same time.

His mood had completely changed, and I didn't know why. "What?"

"How many times are you going to tell me you love me before you realize what you're saying?" He cocked his head, that smile still wide on his mouth.

A tornado of anxiety burst in my chest and turned every organ and bone upside down. Fear hit me like a ton of bricks because I was scared. I'd gone to sleep one night, and then I woke up to a whole new life, a life I hadn't wanted. But the roots I'd planted were too deep to run. My addiction to this man was so strong that a detox would kill me. It had all happened so fast, and it wasn't until that very moment that I'd stopped to take a breath and accept this reality. It had always felt temporary, a moment in time that I should treasure before it was gone, but now, I knew this was it.

This was forever.

"I—I forgot I have a doctor's appointment." I grabbed my book and stuffed it into my bag, feeling his hard stare on my face. "I'll see you later." I left my chair and slid between our table and our neighbor's before I passed behind him.

He didn't order me to sit down. Didn't force me to face the conversation like a man.

He just let me go.

I went across town to Mason Louvard to get one of their famous crookies, a chocolate chip cookie baked into a croissant, my go-to when I wanted to eat my feelings. But there weren't enough crookies in the world to make this unease go away.

I sat at a table alone, my coffee sitting in front of me even though I'd had enough caffeine for the day. It was the only time I missed my old apartment, so I could have somewhere to go alone. But now, I lived with Bastien, so he'd be there waiting for me when I walked inside, prepared to finish the conversation once I was ready to have it.

Would I ever be ready to have it?

How had this happened?

How had it happened so fast?

The divorce papers had just gone through, and now I was living a whole new life with someone else. I was back in a position I didn't want to be in, not when I hadn't had enough time to heal and let go of the past.

But I must be ready...if I was the first one to say it.

It'd been hours, and Bastien hadn't tried to call or text. He gave me space, even though it must have been hard for him. It must have hurt him to watch me run away...again. Just when I thought about him, he texted me. *I have stuff to do, so the house is yours. I'll be home in the morning.* He didn't want me out in the city, sitting alone in cafés while I tried to juggle my feelings.

I texted him back right away. *Please don't go. I'll head home now.*

His three dots didn't appear. I had no idea if he was mad or not. It was hard to tell through a text. Now that I had debit cards and credit cards with no limits, I paid for a cab when I normally would have walked. Having unlimited funds made life easier, saved me time, made everything more convenient.

When I returned home, the gate immediately opened for me as if the guards had been expecting me to show up. I took the elevator to the top floor, my heart dancing in my throat, and then I approached the double doors that led to the primary bedroom—the suite I shared with him.

I was scared, scared of something that had already happened, something that had already come true. I stared at the door handle made out of gold before I turned it and stepped inside.

Bastien was in one of the armchairs in the living room, shirtless and barefoot, his knees wide apart as he sat in his gray sweatpants. His elbow was propped on the armrest, his fingers against his temple, and he stared at me with an empty look.

He showed no anger. No resentment. Nothing at all.

I moved to the end of the couch, the spot closest to the armchair, feeling his stare follow me then burn into my cheek.

The fireplace was cold because it was a warm day, the sun coming through the open curtains. It was almost five now, so the sun would be going down soon. I focused on the fireplace because it was so hard to look at him.

"Sweetheart."

I blinked once or twice before I found the strength to meet his stare head on. When my eyes locked on his piercing blue eyes, I felt a rush of adrenaline.

"You're the one who said it—not me."

"I know…"

"Several times."

"Yeah…"

"I've taken it slow like I said I would. My foot was on the brake, but you stepped on the gas."

"I get it, Bastien."

"Then why am I being punished right now?" His tone turned clipped, the anger coming out.

"Punished?"

"You tell me you love me, and then you leave," he said. "That's called whiplash."

I stared at the fire.

"Look at me."

I sucked in a deep breath and met his look.

Now, he looked furious, his eyes hard and angry. "What is the problem, Fleur?"

"There is no problem."

"Then why did you run?"

"I didn't run. I just needed a moment."

"To what?" he snapped. "You can tell your ex-husband you love me, but you don't have the balls to say it to my face?"

I sucked in another breath. "He told you that?"

"Yeah, he fucking did," he said. "You've said it three times—that I know of. But you act like this is brand-new information—"

"May I speak?" His anger had gotten the best of him, and he was running me into the ground.

A flash of anger moved over his eyes, but he gave a nod and conceded.

I tried to piece together my emotions, to build them into a story that would make sense. "I don't know how long I've felt this way. Makes me wonder if I've always felt this way. Since the night we met. Since the first time I touched you…" I swallowed, struggling to hold his gaze because the anger was still visible. "I fought it for a long time, but then I fought it less, and that's when it started to creep into my words and actions without my even realizing it. Because it's just so inherently right that I knew it was true before I even admitted it."

His eyes began to soften, his anger fading away like clouds on the wind.

"It scares me because…I know this is it. When I married Adrien, I thought it would last forever, but this is so different, I can't even compare the two. I wasn't the same person then that I am now—and this is who I'm supposed to be."

He showed no anger at all now. Just a soft gaze.

I looked away because it was too much. "I love you so much—" within a single breath, the tears were in my eyes, blurring my vision "—that it fucking scares me. I drowned in a coffin, and I still want to stay. I've watched men try to kill you, men who would have killed me if they'd succeeded with you, and I still can't imagine my life with anyone else. This is not the life that I wanted—but I don't fucking care because you're the man I want." My voice rose louder as I continued to talk, continued to cry. "And I can't believe this is it, that this is my life. Because even though I trust you, I'm still fucking scared because I love you more than I ever loved him, and you could fucking break me into pieces if you ever walked away." My cries turned to sobs, an ugly cry, but I couldn't stop the dam that had opened and the flood that rushed out. "I've never been so scared in my life. I would rather drown in that coffin again than watch you leave me for someone else." I knew he would be angry with me for what I said, for comparing him to Adrien, for suggesting he was capable of such deceit, but those were my true feelings. I didn't believe he would ever hurt me, but just knowing the power he had if he chose to hurt me was fucking terrifying.

"Sweetheart." He moved over to me, his knees on the rug, sliding his hands into my hair to pull it from my face. He swiped his thumbs over my cheeks to catch the tears that dripped to my lips.

I looked at him, his face blurry from the moisture that coated my eyes. My breaths continued, labored and shaky, and I felt stark naked in a blizzard, vulnerable to the cold, with a sharp dagger to my heart.

I blinked a few times, his face becoming clear.

He continued to stare at me. "I have the power to hurt you, but you have the power to bring me to my knees, to make me fall stupidly and desperately in love when I thought I was incapable of feeling a damn thing. Now I have something I love more than anything, something I must protect like my life depends on it, because it does. I'm wrapped around your finger, trapped under your thumb, so hopelessly in love with you that I would burn this city if you ever left me." He slid his hand farther into my hair and cradled my face. "But I know you won't, not when I'll never give you a reason to. Not when I'll suffocate you with my love and desire. When I'll never make you question what you mean to me, when I'll never make you wonder where I am or who I'm with, when your call is the one I'll always take. When a minute doesn't pass before your text gets a reply."

He wasn't angry with me. Instead, he showered me with love that I didn't know he felt.

"We're in this together, sweetheart."

I stopped crying, holding on to his wrists for the strength I didn't possess.

He continued to stare at me, my face cradled in his hands, with his eyes soft but determined. "I love you." It was the first time he'd said it to me, and he said it so calmly and so sincerely, like there was no doubt in his heart. "You're the first, the last, and the only."

"Bastien…" I felt my eyes water again before I pressed my forehead to his. "Fuck, I love you."

FLEUR

We'd made love before, but this was different.

I used to hide my heart behind my eyes, lock my soul in a cage so it couldn't touch his, but now, everything poured out like sand from a bottle. My focus was no longer on protecting myself, but on letting myself be open to him, feeling everything that I'd been afraid to feel.

He was on top of me, my knees squeezing his torso, my ankles locked together in the center of his back, bending and tilting to accommodate him as he rocked into me, his muscular arms holding his body above mine, his hungry lips kissing mine with sexy slowness, really feeling my lips, savoring them.

My hands scooped behind his shoulders, and my nails dug into his flesh, feeling him worship me with kisses to the neck, to the corner of my mouth, his tongue in my mouth before he stole my breath away.

I'd already come at the start of this, not because it was the best sex I'd ever had, but because I was so fucking in love with this man. I admitted it to myself, felt it in my broken heart with a painful throb.

"I love you," I said it against his lips, feeling the twinge of pain burn inside me, giving myself fully to him to do whatever he wanted. My fate was in the palm of his hand— and he could crush me.

He moaned against my mouth like I'd said something dirty. His cock twitched inside me like I'd said the perfect words to get him off. He continued to rock into me, but his thrusts slowed as he gave his final pumps—and then he filled me. He filled me as he rested his lips against mine, his muscular chest like a cloud over my sky, the smell of his sweat and the rain all around me.

He finished then rubbed his nose against mine, his blue eyes endless in their depth. He kissed me then kissed me again, looking at me like I was the only thing that mattered to him. Still hard, like he didn't need a break or a moment to catch his breath, he started to rock again, sliding through my cream and his come. "I fucking love you, sweetheart."

***

I'd fallen asleep, and when I woke up, it was dark outside.

I looked at the time on the clock on the nightstand and saw that it was almost eight, so I'd taken an hour nap. Bastien wasn't there, so he must have already showered or gone into the living room.

I lay there for a bit before I got out of bed, helping myself to one of his shirts like whatever was his was mine.

He was on the couch in his sweatpants, the TV off, the lights dim.

My stomach gave a loud rumble and announced my presence to the room.

He smirked before he looked away from his phone and stared at me. "You and me both, sweetheart. How about a pizza and strawberries in the tub?"

"I thought baths weren't your thing."

"I'm open to new things."

I sat on the couch beside him, and he immediately hooked his arm around me and pulled me close, planting kisses on my neck and my exposed collarbone, making me feel like his favorite person in the world.

I knew he was mine.

He fired off a text to Gerard like it was room service. "I'll start the water." He began to get up, but I kept him down.

"It's okay. Let's just stay on the couch."

He studied me, clearly picking up on everything I didn't say. "Sweetheart, it'll be okay."

Sitting in a tub full of water reminded me of my watery grave. "I'd rather stay on the couch."

"I know how much you love taking baths. Don't throw that away—"

"It's too soon."

"I'll be there with you."

I looked away.

He cupped my face and directed my eyes to his. "I'll be there with you." A calm confidence was in his gaze, not a sharp sternness. It wasn't him telling me what to do, but him encouraging me to do it.

With every passing day, I felt better. Felt that memory drift further to the back of my mind. It was something that would stay with me for the rest of my life, a part of who I was now, but it didn't have to define me. I stared into his eyes for a while before I gave a slight nod. "Okay."

He kissed the corner of my mouth before he walked into the bathroom. The water came on a moment later, the faucet audible.

I'd taken a couple of baths in there as a guest. Reading in the bath every day while Bastien was asleep or at work would have been my favorite activity after I moved in, but I'd never even considered it after what had happened. Now I went to cafés and listened to music on my headphones so I wouldn't have to hear the chatter of people nearby. The tub wasn't even an option.

Bastien seemed to realize that and wanted it to change.

He came back to me on the couch, his arm moving around my shoulders as he pulled me into his side. He brushed a kiss against my hairline. "You've lived here a while, and never once have you used it. Time for a change."

I swallowed, thinking about the cold water against my feet and shoulders, the way it pressed against the back of my neck as it continued to rise. It had been on my mind the first time I'd taken a shower after. Still crossed my thoughts when I waited for the temperature of the shower water to turn from cold to hot.

Bastien stared at the side of my face. "You're the bravest woman I've ever known."

I gave a quiet scoff. "Your mother was married to a drug kingpin for however long—and I can't take a bath."

"She knew my father had mistresses, and she stayed. She was fortunate enough never to be a pawn in someone's cruel game. In the face of adversity, she'll choose to ignore it. But not you."

"Leaving a cheating husband isn't brave."

"If it's not brave, then why do so few women do it?"

I stared at the table.

"I know you can do this."

"What does it matter—"

"It matters because I don't want you to live your life in fear, afraid to enjoy something that used to bring you joy. You give power to your enemies—power they don't deserve."

"Bastien, no offense, but you've never died."

He stared at me for a long time, like the words dismantled

his argument. "No. But you're a hell of a lot braver than I am."

Gerard brought dinner, drinks, and dessert, and Bastien got into the bathtub first. It was big enough to fit four adults comfortably, but Bastien was bigger than the average adult, so he took up two spots himself.

The bathtub wasn't long and narrow, far rounder than a coffin, so at least they were aesthetically different. The pizza had been placed on a riser so it wouldn't get wet from our movements, and there were several bottles of champagne for us to enjoy. A couple weeks ago, this would have been the most romantic night of my life, but now, it felt like a challenge, one that brought me a shit-ton of anxiety.

"Sweetheart, you got this." He reached his hand over the edge of the tub so I could grab it and use it to step over the side and into the warm water. He wore his look of confidence, staring hard into my gaze with transparent calm.

I didn't want someone else to dictate my life. Didn't want a dead person to have such power over me. But it was hard to be brave. If it were easy, then everyone would be brave. I stared at the water then looked at his hand again, giving a quiet sigh before I grabbed his fingers.

The smile on his mouth and the pride in his eyes lit up the whole fucking sky. "Attagirl."

One foot hit the water and then the next. I stood there with the water to my knees, the bubbles on the surface from the bath gel he'd added. The overhead lights had been dimmed, and I stood in a bathroom that was more expensive than an average apartment. It was nothing like a coffin in a muddy grave. The only commonality between them was the water that swirled around my feet.

After a beat, I lowered myself into the water across from him, letting the warmth submerge me to my shoulders. Nightmares still struck me, despite the weeks that had passed. Bastien didn't know any of that because he was out working. But having the walls of his home surrounding and protecting me was enough to make me feel safe again.

He leaned against the edge of the other side of the tub, his arms stretched out along the sides, looking like someone who enjoyed a bath even though he never took one.

I sat there with my arms around my knees, looking at the bubbles that floated on the surface of the water. It took me a couple minutes to accept it, to rationalize the situation and convince myself I wasn't in danger, that this moment was nothing like the other. My heart started to slow, and the smell of the pizza was suddenly noticeable.

He watched me the whole time but didn't say a word, giving me time to adjust to the situation on my own. He picked up his champagne flute and took a drink before he grabbed the bottle and refilled it.

I looked at the pizza. "Smells good."

PENELOPE SKY

The smirk on his face was so handsome. It'd melt my panties if I wore any. "There's my girl." He grabbed a piece off the platter then took an enormous bite, eating half of it in a single go.

I grabbed one for myself and took a bite, the cheese fresh like it was just grated, the sauce homemade like Gerard whipped it up on the stove before he'd poured it on the dough. It was covered in mozzarella and veggies— mushrooms, tomatoes, olives, and artichoke hearts. "Let's hope Gerard doesn't quit and open his own pizza place."

He smirked. "I pay him too much to even think about it."

"Does he live here?"

"Yep."

"Does he get time off?"

"He does. He has an assistant cover for him, usually on the weekends because I'm out of the house."

"That's dedication."

"It's a dream job in the hospitality world. Makes two hundred thousand euros a year and has no rent or bills and eats for free."

My jaw almost dropped. "That's an insane amount of money."

"I think he's worth it."

"How do you know he won't just work for a couple years then quit when he can retire?"

Bastien grabbed another piece and took a bite. "If that's his prerogative, I'll hire someone else. But I doubt he will. I'm pretty easy to work for."

"That's what *you* think."

He chuckled before he downed the rest of his slice. "He's never complained."

"Because he'll get fired."

"I'd only fire him if he betrayed me to my enemies or tried to fuck you. If the laundry isn't done or there's dust on the counter, I don't give a shit."

"Then maybe I should have taken you up on that offer to be your whore a long time ago."

He gave me a long stare, a ghost of a smile on his lips. "It's got a lot of perks. Great pay and a free place to live. But the job itself is a little challenging…"

"Isn't it what I do now?"

He gave a slight shrug. "Close, but not quite."

The conversation took my focus off the past entirely. Now, I didn't associate the tub with the coffin at all. "Is there something you'd like to do that I'm not doing?" I thought our sex life was pretty great. I'd slept with a lot of men during my ho era, but I wasn't exactly kinky. Bastien, on the other hand, seemed like he'd be down for anything.

"That's not what I said."

"But you just said it would be different."

"It would be different," he said. "But I don't want it to be different."

He said what he meant, but I was lost. "I'm having a hard time following this."

"It doesn't matter, so we should just forget it."

"I want to know. Say what you mean."

He smirked slightly, his own words thrown back at him. "Alright, sweetheart." He grabbed his glass and took a drink. "If you were my whore, we'd have a very different relationship. I'd boss you around, tell you what we're doing and how we're doing it. But I don't want that kind of relationship with you because I'm in love with you."

My insecurity started to slip away.

"I wouldn't pay a whore to do vanilla. But I'll gladly do that with you. I'd fuck a woman in the ass, but I wouldn't do that with you. That's the difference."

A surge of jealousy suddenly filled me but I wasn't sure why. He didn't care about all the guys I fucked around with, so it seemed immature to care about his past. But he spoke about prostitution like he was well-acquainted with it. "It sounds like you've paid for sex a lot."

He responded honestly, like he always did. "A lot isn't accurate. *Some* would be more appropriate."

"But you're so hot. Why would you need to pay someone?"

He would normally have smiled at the comment, but he didn't this time. "Sometimes it's nice to get down to business with no bullshit. And you can do things that you wouldn't do with a woman you met at a bar or whatever."

"Like?"

"It doesn't matter."

"So…you wouldn't fuck me in the ass?" I was almost offended by it, that he would do stuff with strangers but not with me.

He looked me dead in the eye. "No."

"Why not?"

"Trust me, you wouldn't like it."

"You don't know—"

"I do," he said firmly. "It hurts like hell. I don't mind hurting a woman who's being paid to be hurt, but I don't have any desire to do something like that to you. You're taking this offensively when it should be the opposite."

"I just didn't realize you were into…other things."

"I'm a man. Of course I am."

"But if you won't do those things with me—"

"What we have is so much better than anything I've ever paid for. You can't put a price on this."

He smacked my insecurity away like a buzzing gnat.

I felt better, but unease still lingered in my chest.

He saw it on the surface of my eyes. "What's bothering you, sweetheart?"

I wanted to hide from the truth, lie and say everything was fine, but he didn't lie to me, so I didn't want to lie to him. "I guess…I'm jealous. Knowing you were paying whores to do whatever you wanted… I don't know."

"There were far more women I didn't pay, if that makes you feel better."

"It doesn't," I said with a sarcastic laugh. "Just hard to wrap my mind around it."

He stared at me for a while. "You said you've been with a lot of guys. It doesn't bother me."

"But I didn't pay them."

"Why does the exchange of money matter?"

"I don't know…it just bothers me."

"Prostitution is the oldest profession in the world. You don't strike me as the kind of woman to look down on it."

"I don't look down on it. I just don't like the fact that you turn to other women for something that you'd never want from me. Makes me feel…like I'm not enough or something."

"That couldn't be further from the truth, sweetheart," he said. "And this was before you, before I met you, before I walked into that bar and you set my heart on fire." He stared me down with that intense expression, like he could grip me without even touching me. "Before I became insanely and dangerously obsessed with one woman."

He defeated my insecurity once again, and I felt foolish for letting it bother me in the first place. "Was this one of the secrets you mentioned earlier?"

He cocked his head slightly when he absorbed the question. "No. The purpose of a secret is to conceal shame. I have no shame in paying for sex."

Then, I didn't know what secret he wanted to protect. He killed people all the time, so I assumed it had nothing to do with that. He didn't seem like a thief or a cheat, so that didn't make sense either. I was curious but didn't ask. "It's hard to imagine a scenario where you would feel shame." Perhaps it was something he'd done a long time ago, before he became a man, when he was still a boy trying to find his way in the world.

His eyes finally left mine, looking at nothing in particular, staring at the wallpaper on the wall. The quiet was amplified by all the tile and porcelain, reflected by his brilliant blue eyes. His gaze eventually came back to me. "I've only shared this with one person—Luca. But I should share it with you too, because you deserve to know the man you love and decide if you still want to love him."

"If love was a choice, I would have left a long time ago." I had no control when it came to Bastien. From the moment we met, I was sucked into his magnetism like he was a black hole that could grab hold of something as transparent as light. "Whatever you say won't change anything, babe."

He stared with vacant eyes, looking at my face like I was a painting rather than a person. His closed fist was against his temple as he rested his face against it for support. The shine in his eyes was gone, like a cloud had moved over his sun. "I killed my father."

I wasn't sure what I'd expected him to say—but it wasn't that. From what he'd shared about his father, he sounded like an asshole, but he must have done something really sinister for his own son to kill him. I didn't press for more information, treading carefully around this subject because I could see how sensitive it was.

"We hadn't spoken in two years. I told him I was ashamed to call him my father, and then he pretended I didn't exist for the final years I lived in the house. I received shit marks in my final years of school, so university was out of the question. I moved out at eighteen and didn't hear from anyone but my mother. No call. No text. Nothing. Then my father came by my apartment when I was twenty…and it happened."

"Why?"

He took his time choosing an answer to that. His eyes were guarded like they were bulletproof. "Because his love was conditional. It had to be earned on his terms and under his regime. If I wasn't a soldier in his army, then I was the enemy. He said some things he could never take back—and I did something I could never take back." He didn't give me specifics, like even after all this time, it was still hard to talk about. "It wasn't premeditated, but it wasn't self-defense either. I snapped."

I didn't know what to say to that. Didn't know how to handle something so delicate. "Does your mother know?"

He gave a slight shake of his head. "No. If she did, she would never speak to me again. There are times I want to come clean because she deserves to know who killed her husband, but I know it would kill her. And I mean that literally—she would swallow a whole bottle of pills to make the pain stop."

She was better off not knowing, in my opinion. "Does your brother know?"

He nodded.

"And he's never told her?"

"For the same reason. He knows she couldn't take it."

I struggled to find the words to say, to comfort him when I didn't have the story or the facts. "I'm sorry that you had to go through all of that."

"He's a lot sorrier than I am since he's dead." He looked away, grabbed his glass, and took another drink.

"Whatever the reason you did it, I love you just the same." His father's love had been conditional, but mine wasn't. If it were, I would have left the second our lives became tumultuous. I'd be dating some guy who ran a restaurant or something. A normal life with normal expectations.

His stare landed on my face with invisible heft and stayed there, rooted in place for what felt like forever. "I know you do."

7

BASTIEN

Thirteen Years Ago

I sat at the table in my apartment, rain hitting the windows as the droplets caught on the wind. It was a warm winter day, and we were getting rain instead of several more feet of white snow. I sat there with my laptop, my apartment a mess because I'd had a party over the weekend, and I still hadn't cleaned. Some of the guys were shooting up and snorting cocaine. I joined them, but I wasn't addicted like they were.

Night started to creep into the city, but I had a cup of coffee beside me because I'd just started my day. My nights were mornings and my mornings were nights. I'd wanted a life different from my father, but I'd ended up there anyway.

Because I'd basically flunked out of school and was rejected from every university I applied to. My father could have bribed or threatened my way into a program, but I didn't have a father anymore, not as far as I was concerned.

A knock sounded on the door.

I turned away from the laptop and stared across the room to the door but didn't move to answer it. I chose to stay quiet so whoever the fuck it was could just go away.

But they knocked again. "I know you're in there, Bastien."

My heart plummeted into my stomach because I recognized that voice.

It belonged to my father.

I stared at the door again, visualizing him on the other side, standing there in all black, his boots wet from the rain. I hadn't seen him in two years. Didn't know what he looked like these days, if he'd gained weight or lost it, if he continued to wear that cross around his neck like some kind of martyr. Whenever Mother called me, she didn't talk about him and she rarely mentioned Godric. She tried to act like everything was normal by talking about the new restaurants she had tried and what she'd seen on TV, but it just irritated me more.

Because she was a spineless coward.

She let my father cheat on her. Let him treat his sons like hired help rather than family. Let him destroy the family she so desperately wanted to have. Like it was the eighteen hundreds and he only had children to help run the farm.

I hated her more than him sometimes.

I finally walked to the door and opened it.

He was exactly as I remembered, his face just a little more sunken from the cigars and the booze and the stress of running an immoral drug empire. Our features were similar, and I hated to admit I looked more like him as I became a man. The sight of him should instill a sense of fear, but it was hard to fear someone you didn't respect.

He stared me down with the same ruthless expression, probably full of disappointment because of how useless I was. Godric rose to his expectations, became the right-hand man who would inherit the business when my father was killed or retired.

I stepped away and left the door open, turned my back to him even though it was possible he might shoot me in the back. He'd made me, so he could put me back in the ground where I belonged.

I heard his boots against the hardwood floor as he stepped farther inside. The door clicked shut behind him.

I turned back to face him.

He surveyed my shitty apartment, his eyes trailing over the old needles that didn't belong to me, the open bag of coke on the table that also didn't belong to me. It was dirty, and I still had boxes against the wall because I'd never really unpacked, even though I'd lived there for years now. The girls I brought home didn't seem to care because it was just for the night.

He stopped several feet away, his hard expression impossible to read.

I didn't know what to say. After years of estrangement, I hadn't expected a conversation to ever take place between us. When he spoke about family to his people, I just assumed he pretended I'd never been born and no one was stupid enough to ever say my name. I was certain my mother hadn't mentioned me either, called me only when he was out of the house and deleted the call from the log when she was finished. She remained connected to me because she loved me, but she didn't love me enough to actually stand up to him.

He stared me down for a long time, his eyes slowly rising in anger. "You walked away from the business just to be a shit imitation? I sell lobster and you sell garbage."

Hostility was exactly what I expected. "Would have gone to university if I didn't essentially flunk out of school."

"And it's my fault you were too stupid to count to ten?"

After two years of silence, he'd come all the way here for this? To be a fucking asshole. "It's your fault that you were a piece-of-shit father—and still are."

His eyes narrowed at the insult, and he gave a slight nod. "You haven't changed either, Bastien. Still blaming everyone else for your shortcomings. Sitting in this shitty apartment, shooting and snorting. You think you're better than me?" he yelled, his voice probably carrying to the other apartments in the building. "You're nothing without me. Useless and pathetic. A boy alone in an apartment that smells like piss and pussy. Wish you'd been a girl so I could have married

97

you off to an ally. But no, you have a dick that you don't even know how to use and a brain too stupid—"

"Why are you here?" His words bounced off me like bullets against a steel plate. I felt no love for this man, none whatsoever, so he was just a crazy stranger hurling insults like a clown tossing pies.

His face flushed red like I'd pissed him off. "No respect—"

"What do you want?" Now, I was the one to yell, wanting him out of my apartment as quickly as possible. "You haven't seen or spoken to your son in two years, and then you decide to come by and start shit? I'm fully aware of what a grand disappointment I am to you, *Dad*. But you're a far bigger disappointment to me."

I'd clearly hit one of his buttons because he stepped toward me like some cheap trick to intimidate me.

I'd lived a hard life these last two years, so I couldn't be intimidated. I stood my ground and faced off against the man I hated more than any other.

He snapped first and slapped me, slapped me like we were girls.

His palm struck me first before I twisted his arm around then shoved him hard into the boxes near the wall, needles and garbage flying everywhere, his heavy body thudding against the wall. He released a grimace when he landed hard on his shoulder then got back to his feet, looking at me like I was responsible for all of this. But this was how he'd always been, treating every reaction like it was the action that set everything in motion.

"I wanted one son, and your mother just *had* to have another. A worthless son I wish I'd never had—"

I punched him hard in the face, using all the muscles in my arm to send him to the floor. "And I wish you were dead. I wish you were rotting in the ground so I could piss on your fucking grave." I slammed my foot right down on his face.

His nose broke and he screamed. He reached for my ankle and tugged, sending me to the floor so he could crawl on top of me. He was much older than me but could still pack a punch. He hit me in the face with a closed fist. He grabbed me by the neck and slammed the back of my head into the floor. "Pompous. Arrogant. Son of a bitch." He punched me again.

My head turned, and I saw stars for a second, the lights turning off in my eyes.

He pulled his gun but didn't have the chance to point it at me.

I twisted his arm and pointed it into his chest, and then I squeezed the trigger, all of it happening in a split second.

He could have tried to get rid of the gun so I couldn't use it against him. Or he could have been prepared to shoot me right there, in the fucking head, and that was the reason he'd come in the first place.

But now I would never know—because he was dead.

He went limp against me, his eyes shifting away before they went still.

I rolled him off me, the gun dropping to the floor because his grip had died with him.

I lay there, seeing the blood pool on the floor and inch closer to me until it absorbed into my clothes and coated my flesh. I lay there in my father's blood, my eyes full of tears, not from what I'd done, but because of how this had ended.

He hadn't come here to reconcile.

He'd come to kill me.

8

BASTIEN

I drove us to one of the warehouses outside the city, a couple miles from the international airport. I rarely drove myself, so my collection of cars seemed wholly unnecessary. I'd picked out the Bugatti, custom-made with bulletproof windows and doors, and drove the two of us out of the city.

Our conversation in the bathtub last night had seemed to chase away her fear, so even though I'd confessed I was a coldhearted killer, at least some good had come out of it. Baths still weren't my thing, even with a sexy and soapy lady across from me. It was too hot, and I felt like I was boiling. But I did it for her, wanting her to get back something an asshole had taken from her.

She'd told me her feelings for me hadn't changed despite my secret, and despite the fact that she'd been quiet ever since, I believed her. She had no context for the situation because I didn't explain it to her. I'd never told Luca either. He probably assumed I'd hunted down my father out of spite and revenge, but it was actually the other way around.

We pulled past the gates and into the warehouse compound, which looked quiet and abandoned since there were only two cars there. The guys hid their cars in the hangar on the property across the road, completely out of sight.

I pulled into a spot and killed the engine.

She looked around, stared at the steel fence and the barbed wire on top. "It looks like a prison."

"It used to be a prison." A prison where girls were kept like chickens in a coop. I got out of the car first, and then she followed, wearing a thick coat that was zipped up to her chin because it was a cold morning.

I pounded on the rusty door then looked up into the camera in the corner.

Fleur stayed behind me, arms crossed over her chest.

The bolts and locks turned, and then the door opened. The guy nodded at me, clearly knowing who I was even though I couldn't remember his name.

"Come on, sweetheart." I walked in first, seeing the guys working at the tables, measuring the product before placing it into their airtight containers to maintain the quality. None of them looked up from their work.

Fleur came to my side and surveyed the scene, wearing her best poker face.

I nodded to the opposite side of the room. "This way." I crossed into the other area where a long table was set up, where I usually sat with Luca when we crunched numbers.

Guns, ammunition, and magazines were mounted on the walls.

She stood there, arms crossed over her chest, and she swept her eyes across the display of weapons.

"That room used to be full of underage girls working fourteen-hour days."

Her eyes came back to me. "Why are we here?"

I walked to the wall and grabbed a couple guns, a Glock, a pistol, a shotgun, and a rifle. I came back to the table and laid them out, along with the clips and the bullets. "Need to teach you a couple things."

She stared at the guns for a long second before she looked at me, eyebrows raised. "I don't understand."

"If you're going to be my girl, you need to know this stuff."

"Why?" Her eyes hardened in fear.

I recognized the unease that traveled across her face, the way her entire body clenched before it tried to become as small as possible. She wasn't the kind of woman to wear her trepidation on her sleeve—she had too much pride for that, but I could see it as clear as day. "I'll always protect you, sweetheart. But you should know how to protect yourself if you ever need to."

Her eyes flicked away, and she swallowed. "I've never touched a gun before."

"Nothing you can't handle."

"I just hope I don't shoot myself in the foot or something."

"Give yourself more credit." I lifted the Glock and displayed it to her before I showed her the chamber. Then I grabbed the bullets and loaded them into the clip. "Bullets go here. Here's the safety." I clicked it so it was on then I emptied the bullets and returned them to the table. "Now you try."

She stared at me for a second before she grabbed the gun like it was a grenade then opened the clip. When she picked up the bullets off the table, she pointed the tip of the barrel at herself because she wasn't paying attention.

I redirected it forward. "Never point the gun at yourself."

"But there are no bullets."

"Doesn't matter."

She kept the gun pointed forward before she dropped the bullets into the clip and closed the weapon. "Safety is still on?"

I clicked it and unclicked it, showing her the difference. "Alright, put it down."

She put it down, facing away from us.

I walked her through the other guns, showing her how to load them and unload them and make sure the safety was on. "The shotgun can only hold two bullets—but they count. Shoot someone at close range, and they're done." I showed her the rifle. "Use this if you have many opponents. This is a little different because it uses a magazine rather than bullets." I showed her how to add a magazine and take it away. "A Glock is good to have in your purse or in your nightstand, easy to carry if you've got one target. But if you're ever under threat, always go for one of these two."

"Do—do you think I'll be under threat?"

"No." I put the rifle on the table. "But like my father always said—be prepared." I cocked the shotgun and returned it to the table. "Let's start with the Glock."

"Start what with the Glock?"

"Target practice."

"You want me to fire this?"

"Yes."

"Uh…"

"Sweetheart, you've got this."

She stared at the gun before she picked it off the table. She kept it pointed to the floor like I taught her, but she looked awkward holding it.

I pulled the strap of the rifle over my shoulder, tucked the pistol into the back of my jeans, and gripped the shotgun before I headed to the back door.

Fleur followed me, and we stepped out into the cold, under the overcast sky.

Targets were mounted to the steel fence, practice for the guys when they had nothing else to do. I set the shotgun on the old, rickety picnic table there, where the guys smoked their cigars and played a round of cards when it got too stuffy inside. I set the rifle beside it and turned back to her.

She looked at the target, her breath coming out as vapor. "Won't someone hear us?"

"Probably."

She stared at me but didn't question me further.

"Aim."

She grabbed the gun with two hands, one hand supporting the other, and stared at the target that was at least thirty feet away.

Her stance wasn't perfect, but she wasn't training to be a soldier or combat operative. She just needed to shoot someone if the situation ever arose.

"Fire." I checked to see if she remembered the safety.

She squeezed the trigger, and nothing happened.

"The safety is the most important part of the gun. Always know when it's on and off."

She looked at the gun and clicked the button before she aimed again. She went still with focus and then fired, the gun kicking back and knocking her off-balance for just a second. The bullet hit the target, at the very edge.

"Not bad, sweetheart." I came up behind her and helped her get into position. "Use the nose of the gun to aim. Line it up with the center. Keep your strong foot back and tighten your core for the kickback." I stepped back. "Try again."

She aimed for the center, fired, and her body barely moved with the kickback.

I remembered when my father had taught me how to shoot. Not a memory I recalled fondly. Anytime I messed up, he didn't hesitate to say how weak and stupid I was. Now, I felt like a father myself, protecting the person who mattered most to me.

Did I ever matter to him?

She nearly hit the center of the target, so she fired a couple more times, trying to best herself. Then the gun made a clicking sound because she ran out of bullets.

"Reload." I reached into my pocket and pulled out a handful of bullets.

She grabbed them then inserted each one into the empty clip before she slid it into place.

She already looked like a pro. "Good job, sweetheart." I pulled out the pistol tucked into the back of my jeans and held out my palm to her, seeing if she'd put on the safety before handing the Glock back to me.

She did then placed it in my palm.

I grinned. "Attagirl." I was far prouder of her than my father had ever been of me.

She took the pistol, turned off the safety, and got into position again. She fired, her bullets hitting the same places as before. The gun had slightly more firepower than the Glock, but she handled it.

When she ran out of bullets, she turned on the safety and handed it to me.

I put both guns on the table then grabbed the shotgun. "This is what I use when I wanna blow heads off."

Her eyes widened noticeably at my honesty.

"Hold it like this." I showed her how to handle it before I handed it over. "It's heavy."

She took it without complaint, but it was obvious it was heavier than she was used to holding.

"Hold the butt of the gun to your shoulder." I placed my hand over my shoulder so she could see where it should sit. "When it kicks back, it's gonna hurt." I tapped the top of the gun. "This is where you line up the shot, but you shouldn't have to aim if you're that close." I moved us toward the target, bringing her fifteen feet closer to the target. "Aim and fire."

She put the gun into position, the butt of the gun against her shoulder like I taught her, and then she fired. She clearly didn't expect the force of the kick because she took a couple steps back in surprise. But she'd hit the target.

"Again."

She cocked the gun and fired, blowing off half the sign.

I beamed in pride. "Reload."

She opened the barrel like I'd taught her, took the bullets from me, and reloaded the gun before she cocked it back into place.

"Alright, time for the rifle."

She clicked the safety before she handed the shotgun to me.

"This is heavy too." I handed it off, and she held it like she'd seen enough American action movies to know how it should be handled. Without waiting for me to fire, she directed her gun toward the targets and sprayed them with bullets, left to right, denting the steel fence with all the ammunition.

She fired until the magazine was empty. "Ooh, I like this one."

I smirked then handed her another magazine.

She reloaded effortlessly then clicked the safety before she handed the gun to me.

"That's my girl." I pulled her in for a quick kiss then gave her a playful smack on the ass. "Alright, now I'm going to teach you a couple maneuvers."

"Like, fighting?" she asked.

"More like self-defense."

All the excitement she'd shown a second ago disappeared. "Is there something you aren't telling me?"

I stared her down and let my confidence comfort her. "No. You'll probably never need any of this, but I would be an asshole if I didn't teach my woman this stuff when I had the chance. There may come a time when I have to fight and you need to run, and I want to know you can get away if you need to."

"Like I'd ever leave you…"

Whatever pride I would have felt was masked by anger. "You bet your ass you'll leave me."

She stilled at the venom in my voice, clearly stunned I could be so affectionate and then so ruthless in a split second. Her eyes flicked back and forth between mine, treating me like an opponent at that very moment.

My words had clearly made an impact, so I let the topic die. "Ready?" I set the guns on the table before I turned back to her, seeing her breath continue to come out as vapor even though she was bundled up in her coat.

"Yeah."

"These are the three ways a guy will grab you. I'm gonna show you how to get out of all of them, alright?"

"Okay."

"I'll be easy now, but then we'll practice for real." I faced her head on then grabbed her by the upper arm so I could drag her away. "Always twist away and then hit." I moved her arm to show her what I meant. "My hand will have to release. Otherwise, I'll break my wrist. While this is happening, hit the nose with the heel of your palm. This all happens at once." I guided her hand to my face, showing her the way the heel of her palm should strike. "Okay, let's try this for real."

"I'm not gonna hit you."

"Pretend you are." I grabbed her by the arm hard, as hard as I would if I were truly trying to capture her.

She panicked at first, clearly surprised by my grip.

"Twist."

She turned her arm, hooking her forearm around and breaking my hold.

"You're supposed to hit me at the same time."

"Oh shit."

"Again." I grabbed her again and watched her twist. This time, she struck her palm up, tapping me on the shoulder rather than hitting me in the face. "Good." I showed her a couple more moves, making sure she knew how to handle herself if she were attacked from the front or behind. I also showed her how to get a gun out of her face or take it from an opponent. Without regular use and practice, I feared she would forget the instructions. Maybe she wouldn't need it for five or ten years, and by then, she'd forget.

But hopefully, she wouldn't need it ever.

When we finished, she didn't seem cold anymore. Even unzipped the front of her coat to let the heat leave her body. "Does your mother know this stuff?"

"I doubt she remembers it now, but she did at some point."

"Where did you learn it?"

"My father." Everything I was, everything I'd learned, had come from him. Sometimes it was hard to look at myself in the mirror and accept that I was his son, that every part of me was rooted in greed, blood, and evil.

She gave a slight nod with no judgment.

"Let's go home."

"Good. I'm starving."

I smirked. "What do you want to eat?"

"I don't care—as long as I have you for dessert."

I walked into the church in my suit and tie while Fleur hung on my arm. She was in a little black dress with sky-high heels, still a valley in the shadow of my mountain. She wore a gold necklace and bracelet, gold hoops in her ears, looking like a model who'd stepped straight out of a catalogue.

The church was already packed with people, but since guests were anxious to get to their seats before the wedding started, there wasn't a lot of small talk. Luca caught my attention to the left side. He had a girl with him, a girl I'd never seen before.

When we came close, Luca gave Fleur a kiss on each cheek.

She hesitated before she reciprocated the gesture.

I knew he liked her, but he wouldn't have done that if it wasn't more than that, if she wasn't family.

"This is Amelia," he said. "Bastien and Fleur."

I greeted her with a nod, and Fleur shook her hand.

I put no effort into Luca's women because I would never see them again.

We took our seats in the row then waited for the ceremony to begin.

My hand went to Fleur's thigh, and if we weren't in public, let alone a church, I would have slid it under the material and inched much higher. The ceremony started, and it was a bore-fest because I didn't know anyone but my business partner, who gave his daughter away before he took his seat at the front of the church.

The ceremony finally ended after what felt like an eternity, and then we headed to the Four Seasons, a few blocks from the church. The ballroom was drenched in luxurious décor, dimmed lighting, and flower centerpieces that flowed with elegance.

All I cared about was the bar.

I went to the bar with Luca and stood in line to order our drinks.

I felt bad leaving Fleur to make small talk with Amelia, but when I glanced at them, they seemed to be doing alright. "Who's the girl?"

"Met her last week during a night out."

"Met her at a bar or a brothel?"

"You think I'd bring a prostitute for a date?" he asked incredulously.

I shrugged. "I've done it."

He gave a shake of his head like I was ridiculous. "Does Fleur know that?"

"I told her." Not that I'd taken a whore to a party, but that some of the women in my bed had been paid to be there.

"She was cool with it?"

"Why wouldn't she be?"

"Remember Cynthia?" He stepped forward when we moved farther up the line. "She lost her shit when I told her."

"Sounds judgmental."

He shrugged. "She was just one of those jealous psychos."

"Good thing it didn't work out."

He smirked then took another step forward. "The guys told me you took Fleur to the warehouse."

"Taught her how to shoot."

"Why?"

"Because she needs to know this stuff if she's gonna be around."

"Fleur doesn't seem like the shooting type."

"Well, she is, and she's pretty good at it," I said with pride. "She said the rifle is her favorite."

He looked like he was about to chuckle. "I can picture that. Sounds like it's gotten more serious…" He didn't outright ask me if anything had progressed, but he definitely dropped a line to see if I would take a bite.

"It has." I smiled.

He studied my expression before his smile mirrored it. "Happy for you, man."

"Thanks. That means a lot." I wasn't the kind of man to have a best friend because that was pussy shit, but if I did, it would be Luca.

"She's a good woman."

"She is."

Luca made it to the front and ordered drinks for him and Amelia.

I did the same, getting myself a stiff drink and Fleur a glass of wine.

Luca walked with me back to the table. "And she really is a good woman if she's willing to learn all that, especially after what happened."

"She's braver than most men I've met."

"Damn right, she is," he said. "Too bad she doesn't have a sister."

I chuckled then let the conversation die because we'd returned to the table. I took my seat beside Fleur then dropped my arm over the back of her chair, making it clear to the room that she was mine.

She drank from her wineglass, smearing her lipstick on the rim just the way she did when her lips were around my dick.

I stared at her harder than I should in public, and then some of the guys came over and disturbed the moment. I knew a lot of people at the wedding so I was sure it would turn into an unofficial meeting when we should be relaxing for once.

Rudy sat directly beside me. "First Regis and then Oscar... it's been a rough couple months for you."

"Just doing my job." I'd known this would be a boring night for Fleur, just sitting there with her hand on my thigh, drinking her wine, while she was pretty much ignored. But she was my girl, and she was the one I wanted beside me. I wanted her to be a part of my world, for the guys to know who I shared my life with.

"The Aristocrats have always been a bunch of cult freaks," he said. "But dangerous cult freaks."

"I'm not worried about it."

"Word on the street is you should be worried."

I smiled like it was nothing to be concerned about. "I'll handle it." I was aware there would be some kind of retaliation for Oscar's death. Even though their organization was sizable, they still didn't have enough power to challenge me.

"I'm sure you will, Butcher." He raised his glass to me then took a drink.

I talked with the other guys, and it was more of the same, talk about Oscar and business. I never told anyone how Oscar had crossed me. Didn't want to mention what had happened to Fleur because it was still too raw to talk about —and it was too raw for her to hear.

Music blared over the speakers, appetizers were passed around along with flutes of champagne, and the ballroom had nearly four hundred guests at round tables. I'd never been to a wedding that wasn't big and grand, that didn't include nearly the same guest list as the last one.

But there was one guest that I didn't expect.

I felt his stare long before I saw him.

He was far across the room, a beautiful woman at his side whispering in his ear.

He gave a nod like he was listening, but his stare was focused on me. He grabbed his glass of champagne and took a drink, eyes still connected to mine.

This was the first time we'd crossed paths in public because he avoided my presence as much as possible. But now, he didn't seem to care so much.

That could be bad—or good.

"I'll be back, sweetheart." I kissed her before I finished off my scotch and left the table. She was surrounded by people she didn't know, and everyone would be too afraid to talk to her, but she had Luca there if she needed a friendly face.

I crossed the room, and Godric seemed to know he was my target because he preemptively left the table, hands in the pockets of his suit, and met me in the no-man's-land between the tables.

The chandeliers that hung from the ceiling were dimly lit, and the music from the string quartet was in the background, not the party music everyone would dance to at some point. He stopped, and he shifted his weight to one leg, staring me down in public.

I stared back, eyes identical to mine, his height just an inch shorter. "Do you know the bride or groom?"

"I know everybody, Bastien."

The same arrogant son of a bitch. I smiled slightly in amusement. "And I thought you came to see me."

"I never want to see you."

I gave a slight nod in mutual agreement. "Guessing you still don't have any names for me?"

His stare seemed to last forever, even though he lacked any distinct expression. His indifference was potent, like I was a beggar off the street rather than his own flesh and blood. "No."

I gave a slow nod, somehow disappointed even though I'd gotten the exact answer I expected. "I'm actually glad I ran into you. Something I've been meaning to tell you…for thirteen years."

His eyes narrowed.

"You've never asked me why I did it. How I did it. Where I put the body…"

His gaze hardened in preparation for whatever I would say next. His indifference was washed away. "Because I know you would never tell me."

I shook my head. "You were wrong, Godric. So, ask me."

He continued to stand there with his hands in his pockets, staring me down like this was a silent room rather than a wedding with hundreds of guests. Anyone who gazed upon us must have been able to see the visible tension between us.

"Ask me."

Godric wouldn't take the bait, afraid he would step into a trap I'd laid out.

"All these years, you and everyone else believed some ruthless killer plotted the downfall of one of the biggest kingpins in Paris. That they planned that moment with great detail, either for revenge or greed. And when you realized it was me…you finally feared me the way you should."

He didn't blink, hung on every word, like he believed I would say what he'd wanted to know all these years.

"But the truth is, I'm not some mastermind who planned the death of my own father. He came to my apartment on a Tuesday afternoon alone. Didn't tell anyone where he was going, probably to make sure it didn't get back to you or Mom. But that was a mistake. Told me I was unwanted, that he wished I'd been a girl because I would have been more useful with a pussy between my legs. Then he tried to kill me—but I killed him first."

He did his best not to react, but his eyes gave him away. They widened slightly like he couldn't control his silent shock.

"I cut off his ring finger to send to you as proof of his death, dumped his body, and cleaned up the mess. No one came for me."

His breathing picked up. Whether it was in anger or emotion, it was unclear.

"I waited for someone to accuse me, to realize I was the person who hated him the most, but not a single person even *thought* it could be me. Like I'm some spineless pussy just because I didn't want to shoot an innocent girl. Dad said I was weak and worthless, but who's in charge of this city now?" My eyes flicked back and forth between his. "It's not him. It's not you. *It's me.*"

His eyes were impossible to read, but there was no doubt he was glued to my tale, probably wanting more details but was still too proud to ask for them.

"You know what's most ironic about all of this?" I hadn't expected to come to this wedding and run into my brother, of all people. And I certainly hadn't expected to dump all my daddy issues on him either. "If he knew what I'd become, he'd be proud of me—and the fact that that makes me smile is the sickest thing I've ever heard."

Godric finally did something, pulled his hand out of his pocket and rubbed his jawline like he needed a second to process everything he'd just learned. It was hard to hear little details over the music, but the breath he released was so loud I noticed it. "Why didn't you tell me this sooner? Thirteen years ago. Five years ago. But you decide to tell me now in a crowded room at a fucking wedding."

I dug deep inside and tried to find the answer, but it was like trying to find something in a thick pool of mud. My mind usually protected me from what I failed to tolerate, but that mechanism seemed to have stopped. "Because I wasn't ready—and now I am."

He took another slow breath, his chest visibly rising as he felt those words all over his body. But his eyes dropped, like he didn't know what to say, how to feel. "The Aristocrats are planning something big in three days. Make a deal or hit them first."

For the first time in eighteen years, I didn't look at my brother like an enemy.

He prepared to turn away, like this conversation had run its course. "And I didn't know Fleur was your girl. I would have stopped Oscar if I'd known."

So, he'd known about the hit and didn't lie about it. He had more honor than most men who looked me in the eye. "I believe you."

He stepped away and headed back to his table, his girl watching him as she waited for him to return to her, as if they'd been in the middle of a conversation when he'd gotten up and walked over to me.

I left the ballroom and entered the hallway to find the bathroom, needing a break from the music and the people and the laughter and the bullshit. I'd been in a good mood before I spotted my brother across the room. Talked shop with the guys with my hand on my woman's thigh. But that all went to shit, and I confessed to Godric like he was my goddamn priest.

"Bastien."

My eyes had drifted to the carpet below my feet because I was so deep in thought. It was something I never did. I lifted my gaze and looked at a woman in a dark blue dress, leaning against the wall and smoking a cigarette.

I knew her face but not her name. Maybe if she'd caught me on a better day, I would have recalled it.

"Didn't expect to see you here." She let the smoke escape her nostrils before she extended her cigarette for me to share.

I gave a slight shake of my head.

"Trying to cut back?"

I didn't share cigarettes or drinks with anyone but Fleur— and occasionally Luca. "Bride or groom?"

"Neither. My boyfriend invited me."

At least she'd moved on.

"I saw you with that brunette." She held the cigarette between her fingertips, all attitude. "She's pretty."

I knew a backhanded compliment when I saw one. "Why do you think I'm fucking her." I wasn't sure why I continued to stand there and talk to her. Guess it was a nice distraction from what had just happened. I could pretend that conversation had never taken place.

She sidestepped the comment. "Remember that time in the Louvre? When you took me there after it closed, and we did it right up against the sculpture?" She took another drag from her cigarette. "That was fun."

I'd taken a couple girls there. Something about art history made them kinky. "I wish I remembered. Excuse me." I walked around her and headed to the bathroom. When I stepped inside, I moved to the counter and stared at my snow-white face. My eyes were angry—even when I looked at myself.

I wasn't sure how long I stood there, but I appeared to be the only one in the room, everyone else at the bar or mingling at their tables. I'd always been a sucker for weddings, not for the romance, but for the energy and excitement for what lay ahead. But every time I tried to look at my future, I somehow looked at my past instead.

I washed my hands just so my trip wasn't completely pointless then returned to the hallway. The girl in the blue dress was gone, but the smell of her cigarette smoke lingered. I walked through it and then noticed Fleur in her little black dress and sky-high heels. She must have used the restroom herself and assumed that's where I was.

She turned to look at me, and when the smile didn't bloom on her face like it always did at the sight of me, I knew she'd witnessed my exchange with Godric.

I stopped before her, chin dropped so I could look into her face.

She studied mine before she spoke. "That was your brother, wasn't it?"

She'd figured it out across a low-lit room. Figured it out even though our conversation was muted. "Yes."

"You look so much alike."

We were practically carbon copies of each other. All our soft features from our mother and the rigid masculinity from our father.

"Just wanted to see if you were okay." Her eyes shifted back and forth between mine. "Because it seemed like you weren't."

She'd gauged all that from just the back of my head? "My relationship with Godric has been complicated for a long time. Seeded with hatred and resentment and distrust...but the soil will always be watered with the blood we share."

She didn't ask for details or specifics. She never pried, never overstepped boundaries. Her love and affection were subtle when they needed to be and then overwhelming when I asked for them to choke me. "I'm sorry."

"I know you are, sweetheart." She was a relatively new addition to my life, but it felt like she'd always been there, the person I trusted most. The person I loved most.

Her eyes dropped down for a second before she looked at me again. "I saw you speaking to that woman…" Her eyes flicked away again, like she was uncomfortable pursuing this conversation. "Seemed like you knew each other well."

Not well enough, because I didn't remember her name. "What's your question?"

"Just wanted to know if she was a friend or an acquaintance?"

It was an odd question, and it seemed like she was testing me. She'd probably overheard our conversation when she'd come after me and wanted to know if I would admit I fucked what's-her-name before. Fleur was the last person who should feel jealous or insecure, especially sexy as hell in that little black dress. If only she saw what I saw, she would never feel intimidated by another woman that I'd been with. "Neither. I slept with her a while back." I passed the test, but I would have passed it even if I hadn't known it was a test.

She gave no distinct reaction, like that was exactly what she'd gathered herself.

"Let's head back. Probably going to serve dinner soon."

9

BASTIEN

I went to Basilique Sainte-Clotilde, a church that had been standing since the seventeen hundreds. But I didn't walk through the front door. Instead, I took the back entrance, all the way next to the Seine, and took the underground passage, past the homeless and the amateur drug dealers pushing low-grade products idiots were stupid enough or broke enough to buy.

I walked down the dark tunnel and made my way to the church, based solely on memory, sidestepping the rats that scurried from their corners. Sometimes I spotted human bones down here, but I walked right past.

I took a set of stairs deeper underground and then a couple of tunnels before I reached a large room with double doors that were twenty feet in height. They'd clearly been installed from above because there was no way to get something so large into these caverns. Given the color of the stones and how it was dimly lit by the sconces high on the wall at the top of the stairs, they obviously marked the entrance to something important.

There were no guards on patrol, probably not to draw attention to what was on the other side. The caverns from the Seine and the Catacombs that stretched underneath the streets were practically a city of their own, with their own laws and regulations for those who lived there. The police didn't follow criminals into the depths, so it was essentially a lawless land. Only those who were brave—or stupid—came down here.

At the bottom of the stairs, I grabbed the copper knocker and clapped it against the door, a knock that reverberated on the other side. I stepped back and waited for the doors to open or a panel to slide apart.

A section of the door came away, and a pair of eyes looked into mine.

"The Butcher."

He verified my identity instantly and then opened one of the doors to let me pass. He was dressed in all black and held a rifle, security armed at the perimeter.

When I stepped inside, I saw the other guard. They didn't normally pat me down and check for weapons, but this time, they did. But they didn't find anything because I'd come unarmed. They didn't say a word to me, but hostility was present.

They escorted me across the room to another set of double doors. They opened one and let me pass into the underground cathedral that the Aristocrats had claimed for themselves. It looked like the church up above, rows of seats on a red rug that faced a large organ and a dais, like they offered sacrifices. In the next room was their grand storage of collectibles, ancient paintings, and sculptures that they deemed belonged to the French Republic and no one else. It was safer underground, where it couldn't be touched by fire or the sun. As long as the Seine didn't have an apocalyptic flood, everything would remain untouched.

I found it ironic that they hoarded all these cultural masterpieces to themselves, when they weren't even on display because they had so much shit to store. It looked more like a treasure room in an enormous vault. The French Republic couldn't enjoy it because it was stashed underground in a place no one knew existed.

I stepped inside and looked at the paintings leaned against one another, the golden goblets, and the old coins. Centuries of art and artifacts all packed together without rhyme or reason.

Now that Oscar was gone, another had replaced him, and he stepped toward me in his gold robe and matching hat, looking like a goddamn idiot. I recognized him as Marcus, one of the other members of the Aristocrats and clearly Oscar's replacement. I was unarmed, so he didn't seem concerned about arming himself. They claimed to be a peaceful religious group, but they killed anyone who didn't give them the answer they wanted and didn't worship any god, so they didn't seem religious to me.

Marcus stopped several feet away from me and stared me down. "How dare you come here?" He spoke quietly, but his voice still echoed off the walls. His anger was conveyed in his restraint, the long sleeves of his robe touching the floor.

"You killed my woman."

"She lived—"

"*After she died*. You buried her in a coffin, and she drowned in the rain." I kept my voice level, but I was about to explode in rage. "The law of the Fifth Republic has been clear since I became the Butcher. You violated the law when you took an innocent woman as collateral. Be grateful that I only hold Oscar accountable for that and not the rest of you."

He held on to my words with absolute stillness, his anger packed behind his eyes.

"You will receive no apology from me. I would burn Oscar from Notre-Dame again if I could because one death wasn't enough for what he did to my woman."

The back doors opened, and more of the Aristocrats joined us, wearing their robes like members of the clergy, when they were just a fanatical group of freaks. They came up behind Marcus and then stood at his side in a line.

Was that supposed to be intimidating?

Marcus spoke. "You've declared war upon us—"

"You took my woman, and I retaliated. We've been allies for years, and I'd prefer to continue that instead of killing you all. I took my revenge against the man who killed my woman, and I'm prepared to move on if you can do the same. So, can you?"

Marcus didn't need to confer with his disciples. They seemed to have already made up their minds, something I knew because of the information Godric had provided. But I kept that hand close to my chest and didn't show my cards.

"Adrien has defied us for too long—and it's time he's paid the price."

"Do what you want. That has nothing to do with me."

"You intervened once."

"I saved my girl. That's all I cared about. Adrien isn't my problem, so if you want to dump his body somewhere in the Catacombs so the cannibals can feast, then be my guest. I told him to yield to you on multiple occasions, and it's not my fault he failed to listen."

Marcus continued to observe me.

"I did not come to plead for that asshole's life. I came here to resume our allyship. I hold no ill will toward you as a group, but if you give me a reason to, I will burn your church above ground and then demolish the vault that lies beneath."

"Casting lies isn't the best negotiation tactic."

"It's just a reminder that I will destroy you if you come for me—in case you forgot."

Marcus turned to the man on his right, and their eyes met for a brief moment. It seemed like they wanted to discuss their next move aloud, but neither of them would speak in my presence. Marcus came back to me. "If you want peace, then you will not intervene when we come for Adrien."

"I don't moderate conflicts between the organizations. As long as you abide by the law, you're free to do whatever you wish. Put his head on a spike on the Eiffel Tower for all I care."

"And if you want peace, then you will make amends to us."

"You came for my girl, and I came for Oscar. We're even as far as I'm concerned."

Marcus stepped forward. "You humiliated us on the world stage, and you know it. You made an example out of the Aristocrats and spat on our name. You burned one of our own alive—and not in privacy, but at one of our most cherished churches to be shown live on the news. It was barbaric—"

"Burying an innocent woman alive with a camera on her is far more barbaric. I told you I would not apologize for what I did because I'm not sorry, and you bet your ass I would do it again. You speak like I'm the one who started this whole thing when I was the victim."

"Oscar didn't know that Fleur was your girlfriend."

"Well, that was his mistake, and he paid for it. I'm not gonna let any man who touches her go free. Just accept it. So, are we going to make peace, or am I going to kill you all right here, right now? Because you know I'll fucking do it." I didn't need a gun. I could break skulls under my boots and snap necks with my fingertips. There was lots of heavy shit around us. Lots of weapons to use.

Marcus stepped away. "Give us a moment to confer."

"Sure. Take your fucking time."

Marcus stepped away with his disciples, and they spoke in quiet voices, the content of their conversation inaudible to me.

Instead of looking at my phone or texting Luca, my eyes remained trained on them in case they tried something. There was obviously a disagreement because the discussion continued for more than a few minutes.

I gave an irritated sigh because I had shit to do.

Marcus eventually came back to me. "You say you won't intervene on Adrien's behalf."

"Yes."

"Then bring him to us, and all will be forgiven."

A sarcastic smirk crept over my lips. "I already said I don't manage the conflicts among organizations. That goes both ways. This is your dirty work—so you handle it."

Marcus didn't hide his disappointment. "He has the Eye of the Seine. The most prized relic of the French Republic. He must be stopped."

"Then stop him," I said. "My peace offering to you is this— *peace*. I should destroy all of you because you were aware of Oscar's plan, but I've chosen to pardon your crimes. Do the same for me, or you'll have two enemies to fight—both Adrien and me. What will you decide?"

Marcus didn't need to confer with the others this time. Something about my words finally got through to him. "As long as you don't intervene in our hit on Adrien, then we will have peace, Butcher."

"Good," I snapped. "We've both got shit to do, so let's move on."

"What'd they say?" Luca said when he picked up my call.

I walked out of the cavern with the phone pressed to my ear, the homeless and weirdos watching me walk by. None of them was stupid enough to cross me. "A lot of bullshit. But I got them to get over it."

"And you believe them?"

"They know they don't have a shot without the element of surprise." I took the stairs to the next level and saw the Seine visible ahead, the lights reflecting off the dark water. "And even with the peace established, they know I'll watch them for the next six months."

"Sounds like Godric did you a favor, then."

He did.

"Did you guys talk about anything else? Because it seems a little random that he gave you that information. Almost feels like a trap."

I didn't tell him, but I wasn't sure why. "No, we didn't."

Luca didn't press it. "At least that's done."

I made it to the surface and headed up the stairs to the street. "They are going after Adrien."

"I'm surprised they haven't done it already."

"I must have been their focus," I said. "They said I'm not to intervene."

"To be fair, it's not your problem."

"I know it's not." But the guilt still gnawed at me like I'd done something wrong.

"I can tell it bothers you just by the sound of your voice."

I stopped at the street, staring at the lampposts next to the Seine that stretched out into the distance. I was right across from the Louvre, the building bright in the light. Fleur's old apartment was nearby. I wondered if they'd already found a new tenant to take her spot. "I'm not sure if I should tell her."

"You know you're going to."

"I said I wouldn't intervene."

"Then hopefully she doesn't ask you to."

———

It was seven in the morning when I got home.

She was still asleep in one of my t-shirts, the blankets tugged all the way to her side of the bed because I wasn't there to keep her warm. I stared at her for a long second before I changed into my workout clothes and hit the gym, doing my cardio first before I hit the weights hard.

I watched the sun rise in the reflection in the mirror on the wall, watching it burn through the open windows because they didn't have curtains to block out the light. I preferred to work out at the start of my day rather than the end, but when I woke up, Fleur was eager to spend time with me, and it felt wrong to leave her just to get in some cardio. I was dead tired after being up all night, but it was better to do it now than try to fit it in later.

When I returned to my bedroom to shower, she was still asleep, but she'd turned the other way like she was slowly waking up to a new day. I showered and did a quick towel-dry before I returned to the bedroom.

She was awake, sitting up in bed with tired but rested eyes. Even when she was groggy and still slightly out of it, her features lit up at the sight of me. "Hey, babe." She patted the bed beside her, wanting me to join her.

I got into the sheets beside her and pulled her close, hugging her in bed and kissing her, loving the way she looked when she first woke up. Her eyes were slightly wet from being closed all night, and she appeared so relaxed and calm. She cupped my jawline then my cheek before she kissed me. "How was your night?"

I didn't want to ruin her morning when she'd just opened her eyes, so I kept the truth to myself. "Fine. Yours?"

"I was asleep the whole time, so it was great."

I smiled.

"But it's even better now that you're home." Her eyes softened in affection, the look she gave when she wore her heart on her sleeve, told me she loved me without saying a word. "I know you must be tired...but I missed you." Her eyes moved down to my lips, like she wanted me to kiss her good and hard, to make her come at the start of her day.

"I'm never too tired for you, sweetheart." I rolled on top of her and tugged down my boxers before I removed the little white thong she wore. I let her keep her shirt on before I moved between her soft thighs. Like she'd been thinking about me all night long, her channel was so slick and smooth. I moaned as I sank, moaned like it was the first time I'd ever had her, when we'd been doing this for months.

She was even more enthused than I was, her ankles locking together and squeezing the top of my ass like she already wanted more. She explored my arms with her hands, like she could feel the twitch of my muscles from my workout.

I was drunk on this pussy, so fucking addicted that if I tried to get sober, it would kill me. After a long night running a city from the shadows, I longed to bury myself deep in the most magical pussy I'd ever fucked. It turned this man into a teenage boy. Turned this sober man into an addict all over again. "Fuck, sweetheart."

She gripped my arms as she moaned in my face. "I love you, Bastien."

Those words sent a shiver down my spine. It was the dirtiest thing I'd ever heard a woman say. It was my fantasy, hearing this woman give herself to me completely. I'd hunted her and chased her, gotten her into my bed, my life, and then into my house. I wanted to make her my wife next. "I love you, Fleur." I'd never told a woman I loved her, never thought I'd ever want to, but now that I had her, my heart started to beat differently, started to race whenever she was in the room, like I was always about to die...and I wanted to die.

When I woke up, it was four in the afternoon.

As always, my phone had blown up with calls and text messages during the night.

The double doors that led to the rest of the house were closed, and the light that should be visible at the bottom of them was absent, like Fleur had put down a towel to block it out so I could sleep in complete darkness.

I grabbed my phone and checked her location to see if she was in the house or out and about. I saw her dot in the house but not in the bedroom, so I zoomed in to see that she was in the kitchen, probably baking something.

I went through my other calls and texts to see if anything important was going on, and when I found there wasn't, I got out of bed and started my day. I put on sweatpants and a t-shirt and headed downstairs. The building was three stories with guest rooms and sitting rooms and studies, but I never used anything but my bedroom. Honestly, the rest of the house pretty much belonged to Gerard.

I just needed something bigger for protection, to make it difficult to get to me. If I lived in a regular apartment, it wouldn't be hard to blow up the building or shoot out the windows. I headed downstairs and stepped into the kitchen, a place I never went, and saw Fleur and Gerard at the counter together.

"Like this." Gerard appeared to be folding an egg inside a mixing bowl. "You have to be delicate. Otherwise, you'll break the yolk." He finished then let her try the next one. She didn't notice me because she was so focused on what she was doing. She took over, and Gerard watched from beside her. "Yes, just like that."

She finished her work then wiped her hands on her apron. "Just need to mix it, and it'll be ready."

Gerard took the stand mixer from one of the cupboards.

I approached the kitchen island and took a seat on one of the barstools on the other side. "What are you making, sweetheart?"

She gave a slight flinch when she realized I was there.

Gerard nearly dropped the mixer before he set it on the counter. "I'm sorry, sir. I didn't realize you were there."

"It's fine, Gerard."

Her face lit up like it always did when she saw me, like every time was the first time.

I hoped she did that for the rest of our lives.

She came around the island and wrapped her arms around my neck before she kissed me, our mouths level because I was seated.

I grabbed her ass with both hands and pulled her into me as I kissed her, not caring that Gerard was right there. When she pulled away, I repeated the question. "What are you making?"

"Chocolate cake. I found this recipe online, and I haven't stopped thinking about it."

"Would you like breakfast, sir?" Gerard asked.

"Dinner is fine," I said without looking at him. "Chef's choice."

"Of course." Gerard left to speak with the chef in the other kitchen, which was for the chef's exclusive use. This one was for entertaining, not that I ever did that.

Fleur mixed the batter before pouring the contents into a round pan. Then she placed it in the oven and set a timer on her phone. "Fingers crossed."

I was glad she spent her time baking and reading instead of working for a stiff suit in a stale office. It was nice to wake up and know she would be there. If she went to work every day, we would be back to our previous arrangement, where we only had the weekends together. "I'm sure it'll be great."

She came back around and took a seat on the other stool. "Not that it matters to you...since you don't really eat sweets."

"Oh, you know I eat sweets." I stared at her as I leaned my elbow on the counter.

Right on cue, her cheeks flushed because she understood my meaning perfectly. "How'd you sleep?"

"Like a rock."

"Good." Her eyes drifted away, and slowly, her blush did as well.

Now that I was face-to-face with her in the light of day, the guilt started to simmer underneath the surface. I'd assumed I could keep Adrien's plight to myself, but Luca was right. The second I was with her, I felt the burden on my shoulders. Felt like I betrayed her when I hadn't committed any treason.

She tapped the screen of her phone to see the time left for the cake. "Are you working tonight?"

"Yes."

She didn't complain or look disappointed. "Amelia was nice. You think we'll see her again?"

My eyebrows furrowed in complete bewilderment. "Who?"

"Luca's date."

"Oh." I didn't even remember her name. "No."

"How do you know that?"

"Because I've never seen him with the same girl more than a handful of times."

She gave a slow nod. "You think that will ever change? Or is he the lifetime bachelor-type?"

"Well, I thought I was the lifetime bachelor-type, and then I met you."

The smile was instant. It took a second to grow, for the affection to reach her eyes.

"Don't make plans, because life will change those plans."

"So, your plan was to be single forever?"

I gave a shrug. "I was always open to the idea of monogamy if I ever found someone worth the commitment. But I didn't ever expect to find anyone, not when all women were the same, at least it seemed that way to me."

"Maybe Luca is the same as you."

"He's a bit more stubborn than I am."

"Why is that?" she asked.

"I don't know. He'd never tell me if I asked."

"Why not? You're best friends."

"Because men don't ask each other that—and we aren't best friends."

"You have a closer friend than him?" she asked incredulously.

"No. But a grown-ass man doesn't go around saying that."

"Why?" she asked. "It's cute."

I gave her a hard look. "I'm not cute, sweetheart."

She held my gaze for a while before she tapped her phone again. "I just want some cake."

"You could ask Gerard to grab some for you."

"I wanted to make it. But you should never bake on an empty stomach."

"Is this a new hobby of yours, or have you always been into baking?"

"It's new," she said. "I used to cook all the time, so I was never in the mood to make something *fun*."

She referred to her time being Adrien's wife, and the mention of him added more weight to my shoulders. If I kept this information to myself, my implication in the matter would never come back to haunt me, but I felt deceitful, nonetheless. "There's something I need to tell you."

She turned away from her phone, her eyes guarded like she already knew it was bad news.

"I made peace with the Aristocrats, but they're coming for Adrien." Perhaps she had already realized that. Perhaps she'd been worried about it the entire time but didn't want to mention her ex-husband to me. "They said they would make peace with me if I didn't intervene."

Her stare didn't change, like she needed more time to let the situation sink in.

I waited for her to say something, but nothing seemed to be forthcoming. "I debated telling you."

"I knew the problem hadn't been solved."

So, she had thought about it. "Is there something you would like me to do?"

"Like what?" she asked.

"Like stop it."

Her elbow rested on the counter, and her chin was propped on her closed fist. She busied herself with a vase of flowers that sat on the corner of the kitchen island along with a grouping of white candles, like she hadn't noticed them until now. "They warned you not to intervene, right?"

"But you know I would intervene for you, sweetheart." Did I want to solve problems for my woman's ex-husband? No. But I would do anything for her if she asked. I loved her unconditionally, would put my life on the line for the man she'd loved before me if that's what she wanted.

Her eyes flicked away and stayed that way. "I'll always care for Adrien. I wish nothing but the best for him. But you warned him multiple times, and he chose to disregard your advice. I'd appreciate if you told him what's coming…if he doesn't already know…so he can leave the country or something. But I don't want you involved in this in any other way. I can accept Adrien's death because he brought it on himself, but I could never accept yours for any reason or circumstance." When she found the courage to look at me again, she met my gaze and focused on me.

I would go to war for this woman, but it meant the world to me that she didn't ask me to. It probably wasn't easy to desert the man she'd promised to love for a lifetime, but she did to prioritize me. "I'll let him know."

———

My driver was taking me to my next stop when I called Adrien.

It rang and rang.

The Aristocrats would probably consider a phone call an intervention, but Fleur had asked me to, and it was a small enough ask.

He finally answered. "How is she?" He always asked about her first, and he did such a good job of acting like he cared for her I almost believed he did. I should feel sorry for him, even though he'd fucked around on her a dozen times.

"She's my responsibility, not yours, so stop asking."

"I just want to know if she's okay."

"She's great. Went to a wedding with me last weekend, baked a cake this afternoon, and now she's dead asleep in my big-ass bed. What else do you want to know?"

Adrien didn't push back. "What do you want, Bastien?"

"I don't want anything. But I spoke to Marcus and the Aristocrats yesterday, and they want your head on a fucking platter. They told me not to intervene, but Fleur asked me to warn you. And what my woman says goes. So, consider yourself warned."

"I didn't kill Oscar."

"They don't care, Adrien. He would still be alive right now if you'd just given in to their demands."

"Why do I have to change my business model just because they think they own all of French heritage?"

"It's pretty rich of you to condemn their ideologies when you're a thief who steals art history from your own people."

"I'm Italian, not French."

"And I think that pisses them off even more, asshole."

He sighed his frustration into the phone.

"You've got two options. Give them what they want and disappear. They won't hunt you long if they have what they want. They'll give up after a couple weeks. Or hit them before they hit you. But that would be the stupid choice, because you don't have the manpower, and I'm not helping you with this."

"I didn't ask for your help, Bastien."

"You're right. Because if you did, you wouldn't be in this position in the first place, like a dumbass."

Adrien stayed quiet.

I waited for him to say he was going to run for it, but he didn't. I should just hang up and leave him to his problems, but I stayed on the phone out of some ridiculous obligation to the woman who didn't love him anymore. "Adrien."

"What?"

"Jesus Christ, why are you so fucking stubborn?"

"Because it's bullshit. They think they own everything because of some pure bloodline. It's insanity."

"I think they're a bunch of weirdos too, but they're powerful and well-connected weirdos who won't hesitate to feed your body to the cannibals in the caverns, alright? It is what it is. You have enough money to retire, start over somewhere on a beach with a warm pussy on your lap. Do not get yourself killed over this."

"You don't understand—"

"Adrien. I need to make this abundantly fucking clear—*I will not come for you*. Fleur will not ask me to come for you. You're on your own."

He was quiet over the line.

I'd done my best to make him see reason, to value his life over his pride, and I couldn't do much more. "Good luck, Adrien."

10

FLEUR

I got into the back of the SUV, and the driver took me away from the gates. I was in a black dress and heels with my buttoned-up coat on top. Bastien had asked me to meet him and the boys because they'd decided to go out for a couple of drinks.

I assumed they drank all the time and wasn't sure why Bastien would even want me there, but he didn't ask if I wanted to go—just told me it was happening.

Ten minutes later, the SUV pulled up to the bar, which was packed with people I could see through the window. I walked inside, the sound of music hitting my ears and the cigarette smoke hitting my nose.

The hostess took my coat, and then I looked across the bar.

Bastien stuck out, not like a sore thumb, but like the hottest guy in the world. He sat in a big round booth that fit at least twenty people, girls on men's laps, all of them smoking and drinking. Bastien was in the middle, like he was the center of attention, and he looked so hot just sitting there with his arm over the back of the booth, talking to one of the guys without seeming to care about all the gorgeous women around him with their tits nearly popping out.

I headed over, moving through the crowd of people standing near the bar and the full tables.

Bastien noticed me when I was halfway there. He immediately tuned out the guy talking to him and gave me his bedroom eyes, like I was the only woman in the room, the moon on a starless night.

Adrien never made me feel like that—like I was literally the most important thing in the world.

Bastien nodded to the guys piled in on the side. "Get up. My woman is here."

The girls shuffled out of the booth, and the guys stood up, continuing their conversations like there hadn't been an interruption.

I scooted in, making my way around the curved seat toward him.

The back of his hand rested on the leather seat like he wanted me to plant my ass there so he could squeeze it then lift me to him.

I finally made it there, and he did exactly that. Squeezed my ass then cradled me into him as he kissed me, his tongue coated with booze so strong it burned my tongue. Then he put me on his lap, everyone sliding back in and retaking their spots.

He relaxed into the booth as he moved his hand into my hair, his fingers lightly grazing the soft skin of my cheek. His dick was hard underneath me, as if he liked what he saw. "Guys, this is Fleur. Fleur, these are the guys."

I'd met a bunch of people at the wedding, but these were all new people I'd never seen before. "Nice to meet you all."

Bastien picked up his conversation again while he rested his fingers between my closed thighs right at the hem of my dress. They talked about absinthe and then drugs, and then they discussed the heroin market in London. It was business as usual, but mixed with a bunch of alcohol.

I didn't notice that Luca was there right away. Probably because the woman making out with him had blocked him from view when I'd walked in. I didn't have anyone to talk to and I wasn't sure what the purpose of my being there was, but Bastien seemed to want me to be included.

Bastien finished his conversation then got the waiter's attention. "Sweetheart, what do you want?"

"Vodka cranberry would be great."

He projected his voice to her. "Vodka cranberry for my girl."

She walked off, clearly disappointed that Bastien was already claimed for the night.

Claimed for all the nights, as far as I was concerned.

He pressed a kiss to my shoulder then squeezed my thighs. "You're looking fine in this dress." He stared at my body, his eyes lingering on the deep V in the front that showed my cleavage.

"Not as fine as you look in anything—and nothing."

He smirked like he found that amusing, but I could tell he appreciated the compliment. He'd probably been hit on a dozen times before I'd arrived, so his ego was practically fatter than an inflated blimp. But he only seemed to care for what I had to say. "I'm gonna fuck you in the bathroom."

"I'm not screwing in the men's restroom."

"Why?"

"Because that's disgusting."

"You won't have to touch anything."

"How's that possible?"

"It's just like the shower. And I know you love the way we fuck in the shower."

When he held me with his thick arms, strong enough to move me up and down without any sign of fatigue. I was a full-grown woman, but he handled me like a pocket pussy.

He smiled in victory. "Knew that would change your mind."

I got hot and bothered just thinking about it, how strong he was, the way the tendons over his muscles popped as they flexed. He was the sexiest man in this room, but I was the only one he wanted—and that was a turn-on too. Before my face got too red, I changed the subject. "Who are all these people?"

"Partners. Some are producers. Some distributors. Mainly in arms."

"Arms?"

"Guns."

"I don't remember them from the wedding."

"They weren't there."

"So, you just know everybody?"

"Pretty much."

"And you party with them?"

"Business and pleasure go hand in hand." He slid his fingers farther between my thighs, as far as he could go when I was clenching them tightly together.

"Why did you want me to come?"

"Why?" he asked. "Because everyone's got a girl, and I want mine."

He could fuck around with any of the women there, and I would never know about it. But he'd invited me down there to be a part of his world, to show everyone he knew that he had a girl at home who he didn't keep at home.

"Let's go to the bathroom."

"We just sat down. I haven't even gotten my drink yet."

"It'll be here when you get back."

"If you only wanted to fuck, you could have just stopped by."

"That was before I saw you walk in here looking like a hot piece of ass." His hand left my inner thigh then moved over the top of my leg to slip underneath my dress, feeling the material of my thong hidden away. "Come on."

"I'm not making these people get up again—"

"Then we'll go the other way." He turned to the group before I could say anything. "Up. Gotta get by."

They all scooted out of the booth and stood up, taking their drinks with them like they couldn't part with their booze for a second. Bastien got out first and took me by the hand, walking me into the hallway where the bathrooms were located.

But instead of going into the men's room, he stopped in front of another door and tried the handle. It was unlocked, so he opened it, revealing a decent-sized closet with cleaning supplies like brooms and mops and extra toilet paper. Then he pulled me inside.

"Someone could open the door."

He grabbed the mop, snapped it in half at the perfect length, and then wedged it under the door handle so it wouldn't turn until he removed it. Quick on his feet, like he'd done this a million times, he could pull anything together.

He was on me right away, light coming in from the cracks around the door to silhouette him in the dark. He pinned me against the wall and kissed me as he yanked up my dress and pulled down my thong.

I was hurt that he'd done this a hundred times with a hundred different girls. That was why he was so good at it, so quick on his feet. But then I pushed the jealousy aside because he loved me and not them.

He helped me out of my panties then stuffed them in the front pocket of his jeans before he unbuttoned them. He got ready in just a few seconds, his fat dick coming out with an agenda.

He scooped me up into his thick arms then lowered me onto his dick, not even wetting his tip because he assumed I would be gushing for him. And he was right, because he slid right in like a perfect fit. "Jesus Christ." He left me on his dick as he savored the union of our bare bodies, as if he'd never felt me like this before, the first time without a condom, even though we'd never used a condom. "This pussy, I swear to fucking god." He started to move me up and down, pounding me onto his dick because he wanted to fuck me so bad.

My arms were hooked around his neck, and I felt my body rise and fall, sheathing his dick over and over, having the best sex of my life when I didn't have to do anything but enjoy it. His shirt covered his strong chest, but his arms were on display, enormous and muscly with rivers of tendons.

"Tell me you love me." He lifted me with incredible speed, like I was a pair of dumbbells when he was used to lifting the bar stacked with weights.

"I love you." I loved this man with my whole heart, loved this man enough to want to stay when I had every reason to go. Wanted to be by his side, whether it was in the rain or the sun.

"Tell me you want to marry me."

Now, I didn't know if he was drunk…or if he really wanted me to say that. Most men were afraid of marriage, and we'd never talked about it. I'd just moved in with him a couple weeks ago. But I wanted him forever…so I would marry him. "I want to marry you."

He somehow fucked me harder, got a surge of energy out of nowhere. "You want to be my wife?"

"Yes…I want to be your wife."

"Fuck." He moaned as he filled me, getting off on something that would freak out most men if they heard it during sex—or at any time. He gave his final pumps, shoving his whole dick inside me even when it was too much. But he barely took a couple breaths before he started up again, fucking me just as hard in the broom closet, jeans around his knees with his dick covered in my cream. "Your turn, sweetheart."

***

We left the broom closet and did the walk of shame back into the bar. Bastien didn't bother to go back for his drink at the table and instead walked right up to the bar and ordered us something new.

The material of my little thong wasn't much, so I was afraid two loads of his seed would become too heavy and streak down my inner thighs at some point. I had to make sure I didn't sneeze.

He handed me a drink, and when he got his, he pretty much downed it in a single gulp.

"Are you drunk?"

"I don't get drunk," he said. "But this is pretty close."

I took a drink of the vodka cranberry, the alcohol like gasoline because it was so strong. "Why me?"

"Why you, what?"

"You could be doing that in the closet with any girl here. Every night of the week, if you want. But you picked me, and I still don't understand why."

He set his drink on the counter and gave me a hard look. It started off lighthearted and easy, but his gaze slowly became penetrating and serious.

"You've given up a bachelor life. That's not easy to do."

"It was so easy with you. It's so fucking easy, sweetheart." He continued to stare me down. "If you could see yourself from someone else's eyes, then maybe you would understand."

"I'm not saying I'm ugly or something. You're just...a whole different level."

He didn't smile at the compliment. "Really? Because I think the same thing about you."

I woke up the next morning with a small headache. When I looked at the clock, I saw it was almost noon. We'd gotten home around four in the morning, and like the sex-in-the-closet hadn't happened, he'd fucked me from behind, my face in the sheets and my ass in the air.

He'd collapsed in bed and didn't wake up until after noon.

I knew he was hungover because he didn't hit the gym. Just took a quick shower before he joined me in the main room, his eyes tired and bloodshot. I watched him take two pills and swallow them down with water, something I rarely saw him drink.

He was definitely hungover.

"How are you?" I asked as I sat across from him.

He never answered the question, just looked at me with those dead eyes.

"Do you remember much of last night?"

"We went out with some of the guys to the bar. Had a few drinks, fucked in the closet, and then headed home."

I knew well enough to know he was putting on a front. I thought he recalled the major points of the nights but probably couldn't remember the smaller details, like when he'd gotten off on the idea of me being his wife.

I decided to keep that to myself. It wasn't a real proposal. Just a fantasy.

A fantasy that had turned me on too.

He ran his fingers through his hair in the sexiest way then looked out the window, still not fully awake.

"Will you work tonight?"

"No."

"So, you're all mine?" I asked in delight.

His bad attitude started to fade, and his smile grew. "Yes, sweetheart."

"Ooh, what should we do?"

"What would you like to do?"

"Dinner would be nice," I said. "Then maybe we can find a nice broom closet…"

Sometimes he wore this boyish grin that was such a turn-on. He was all man, but he had an infectious joy that was contagious. "You're my kind of woman."

11

BASTIEN

I hadn't drunk like that in a long time. Even around dinnertime, I still felt the effects of all the rounds that kept coming to the table. It was the first time I felt like I was in my thirties instead of my twenties. I guessed I was getting older.

Fleur didn't call me out on it, at least not directly. But she looked me over like she was worried about me. She sat across from me at the dinner table, wearing a low-cut top that showed her plump tits for me to enjoy. She took a drink of her wine as she looked at her menu.

I'd ordered wine even though I would have preferred to have water tonight, but I was too proud to admit that all the vodka had nearly knocked me off my feet last night. Vodka had always fucked me up differently than everything else.

"What are you getting?" she asked.

"The steak."

Her eyes flicked up to mine, and she looked like she was about to admonish me.

"I used to eat it every day. I can have it once in a while."

She stared at me for a moment before she returned her attention to the menu.

"What about you, sweetheart?"

"It's between the beet salad and the pasta."

"Those options couldn't be more opposite," I said with a quiet chuckle. "Why don't you get both?"

"I can't eat both."

"I think you can." I'd seen her inhale a whole stack of pancakes first thing in the morning.

"If we really are going to end up in a broom closet, I should stick with the salad."

I tried not to smirk. "It's not going to make a difference."

"But my stomach gets all puffy when I eat pasta."

"I've never noticed."

She looked at me over the top of her menu. "That's very gentlemanly of you to say."

The waitress came over to take our order. I ordered my steak rare. "She'll have the pasta."

Fleur shot me a small glare, but it was playful.

The waitress gathered the menus and left.

She rested her fingers on the stem of her wineglass and regarded me. "You're so hot. I could look at you forever."

Words like that would normally make me smile, but this time, they didn't. I was the one who was supposed to worship her, but she said things that made me feel like the prized stallion. The other women in my life were too busy playing a game to capture my heart that they never spoke their minds. Played hard to get. Like the less they cared, the more I would care. None of that shit ever worked because not a single one of them made the impact that Fleur did. I wasn't a romantic guy, but I swear to god, it had been love at first sight with this woman. I loved the fact that she made me feel good, that she never played games with me, that she made me feel wanted because she was the only woman I wanted to want me.

The moment was interrupted by the vibration of my phone in my pocket. I pulled it out and checked the name, seeing that it was Luca. I'd call him back later, so I slipped the phone back into my pocket.

After it stopped vibrating, he fired off a couple texts. I could tell by the way the phone shifted in my pocket. I pulled it out and checked the screen just to make sure it wasn't important.

Asshole, pick up the phone.

They got Adrien.

He was trying to leave the country, and they got him.

"Shit."

"What?" Fleur asked, her tone completely different.

I gave a sigh of frustration before I returned his call.

Luca cut straight to the chase. "Erik told me. It happened a couple hours ago, in broad daylight. Looked like he packed up his shit and was about to take off. It's not your problem, but I knew you'd want to know."

Fleur continued to stare at me, her face turning as white as her wine. She'd either heard what Luca said, or she could read the disappointment on my face.

Luca waited for me to say something.

But I didn't know what to say. I'd told Adrien this wasn't my problem, but it looked like he'd tried to take my advice and get out of there before they came for his head. He just didn't leave quick enough. "Do you know where they've taken him?"

"No, but I can call around." He hung up and got to work.

I returned the phone to my pocket.

Panic continued to burn in her eyes. "What is it? What's happening?"

So, she didn't hear. "I warned Adrien about the Aristocrats. Told him he should leave the country. Guess he took that advice, but he didn't take it quick enough because they got him."

"Oh no." Her hand immediately cupped her mouth as the emotion swept over her face like the incoming tide. She didn't dull her emotions for me, wore her heart on her sleeve because that was how she was, always transparent. It was a testament to her goodness that she cared for someone who had disrespected her so many times. A lesser woman would have said he deserved what he got. But not her.

I had been prepared to let Adrien suffer his fate, but I knew I couldn't after seeing her reaction. Her eyes were coated with tears that she didn't shed, and her breathing was erratic because of the panic. She would never ask me to do it, but she didn't have to. "I'll get him back."

"No, I don't want you to—"

"I know you don't, but if I don't do this, he's gonna die." And no one else could pull this off except me. The rest of the organizations in Paris would question my leadership by getting involved, but I knew Adrien's death would affect our relationship. His ghost would haunt us and chase away the joy that we'd found together. She would grieve like a widow.

"Bastien." She turned emotional right in the middle of the restaurant. "I can live without Adrien, but I can't live without you." She chose me. Put me first. Showed her loyalty to me. That meant the world to me.

But I would always put her first too. "You don't have to live without either one of us." I dropped the napkin next to my wine and left the table.

She scooted her chair out and followed me. "Bastien."

I walked out of the restaurant and stepped onto the sidewalk as I texted my driver.

She yanked on my arm even though I was standing still. "Bastien, I don't want you to do this. Please, just stay. He made his choice."

"I'll be fine, Fleur."

"It's not worth the risk."

I saw my driver round the corner and pull up to the curb in front of us.

"He'll take you home. I'll call when it's done."

"No." She dug her boots into the sidewalk like a stubborn horse. "I want you to stay."

"Sweetheart." I cupped her face. "If I stay, he'll die a gruesome death. I'm not going to tell you the things they've done to others in the past because you'll never sleep again. I understand you've chosen me over him, but I also understand you'll never be the same if this is how he dies."

Her eyes continued to water and she blinked to fight them back, but that just made them release like rivers down her cheeks. "I'll die if you die, Bastien. I will..." The tears started to roll down like an avalanche, and she cried right on the sidewalk.

"I won't die, sweetheart. They don't know I'm coming. It'll be quick."

She breathed and panted, a mess in the cold but a beautiful one. "Promise me you'll come back. Please."

I didn't make promises, not in this line of business, but I wanted to give her the reassurance she needed so she could go home and wait for me, so she wouldn't waste more time. Every second was a second closer to death. "I promise."

———

The SUV pulled over onto the side of the road, and Luca threw the door open so I could hop in quickly. The vehicle took off before I even fully shut the door, and then Luca opened the barrel of his shotgun and filled it with bullets.

"My contact says they have him at the church. Going to offer him as a sacrifice."

Of course they were.

He rested the gun across his knees. "You sure about this?"

I stared at him.

"It's not a good look for us. We don't get involved in the affairs of our partners."

"My girl almost died because of them. That can be our excuse."

"Let's hope it's enough."

The driver sped through the streets, our vehicles in a line like a motorcade to protect President Martin.

Luca handed me a vest, and I strapped it on.

I shoved a knife into my belt sheath then loaded my pistol before I cocked it. I'd take a shotgun as well. A rifle was too dangerous, especially when we were trying to avoid shooting Adrien. "Marcus admitted they knew about the plan, so they're all culpable in their violation of the rules. They deserve the same fate as Oscar."

"But you made peace with them."

"Yeah." I felt a little guilty about that, going back on my word. "Hopefully they didn't tell anyone."

"Yeah."

The cars arrived outside the church, taking up the entire block. The pedestrians who happened to be on the sidewalk immediately booked it because they knew shit was about to go down. It'd become an unspoken rule that if you stayed out of the way, cop or civilian, you would be spared from gang warfare.

We hopped out of the vehicles and converged on the church. Didn't bother trying to break down the door. The doors were fifty feet high, so the guys lined it with explosives and prepared to destroy a piece of French history.

We all stood back and then blew the doors. They broke from the hinges as soot marked the outside of the grand church and desecrated its history.

"They aren't gonna like that," Luca said.

"They'll be dead in ten minutes, so whatever."

Shotguns in hand and with a line of my guys around us, we moved through the smoke and stepped into the church. Adrien was the easiest to spot because he was staked to a cross like Jesus Christ. He was soaked in his own sweat and writhing in pain, pierced through his hands and wrists and clothed in a blood-soaked robe. Music from an organ continued to play like it was coming from a sound system that they hadn't turned off.

The back wall was lined with their guards, men with rifles and shotguns who were as prepared to blow us to smithereens as we were to do that to them. They already had their guns aimed, but they wouldn't fire until Marcus made the call.

Marcus was in the center in his golden robe, and he gave me a look packed with more rage than he could express with words.

Adrien looked like he was going to pass out. But his eyes widened in surprise at the sight of me. He didn't speak, but he looked livelier when he realized there was a chance he would escape this.

Marcus's stare went ice-cold. "The Butcher is not a man of his word, it seems."

I stepped forward, my gun held across my chest. "As the First French Emperor of the Fifth Republic, I declare that every member of the Aristocrats violated the code. You knew Oscar took an innocent woman, and you supported that decision. You're just as guilty as the man who snatched her from her bed."

"You asked for peace—"

"I changed my mind." I cocked my gun, aimed the barrel at his chest, and fired.

Marcus was blown away, the bullet hitting him square in the chest and killing him instantly. He hit the floor next to one aisle of seats and lay still.

The second he was down, it was open warfare.

Luca ducked into one of the aisles and aimed for the gunmen who marched forward. Bullets shattered the stained-glass windows, broke the chandelier that hung from above, desecrated the altar.

Adrien was stuck in place. Hopefully he survived this.

I took down one of the guys who came for me then ducked behind a seat. "Don't let the robes get away," I called to my guys. I came out again and fired another shot before I had to reload. I shoved the bullets inside, but one of the guys jumped over the seats and came at me straight with a knife. He cut me on the arm and drew a line of blood, but I punched him so hard in the face he flew back and collapsed on the floor.

I grabbed him by the throat and snapped his neck then moved on.

The rest of it was chaos, blood on gold, glass everywhere, bodies at the foot of the altar. The shooting finally came to a stop, and only one enemy remained. A speck appeared and disappeared in the corner.

"Luca, he can't get away—"

"I'm on it." Luca sprinted across the room, and one of our guys followed.

I had to make sure none of the Aristocrats lived to tell the tale of what had happened here. I trusted Luca to handle it and moved to the stake that the robes had nailed Adrien too. He was still alive, still sweating profusely like he was about to faint.

The guys cut him down and laid him on the floor, and I quickly yanked all the nails and knives out of his skin.

He screamed every time, blood gushing out and dripping everywhere.

If I didn't get him to a hospital soon, he'd probably bleed out.

"Why—why did you come for me?" He was barely conscious, his eyes bloodshot and glazed like his mind was slowly slipping away.

I took the gauze from one of the guys and bundled his wounds tight. It was unclear whether he would make it, his face whiter than snow, whiter than cream in coffee. "Ask Fleur when you see her."

12

FLEUR

I sat there alone in the living room, looking at the cold fireplace with the phone sitting in my palm. A watched pot never boiled, and a watched phone didn't ring either. But I continued to wait, continued to pray, continued to hope that the love of my life would come back to me.

Then he called.

"Oh my god." I took the call and nearly dropped the phone as I tried to put it to my ear. "Bastien?"

"I'm okay. Head downstairs. My driver is going to bring you to the hospital."

"Why the hospital? Are you okay—"

"I'm fine. But Adrien isn't."

"Oh."

"We're a couple blocks away."

I was quiet as I absorbed that, that Bastien may have gotten there too late. "Do you think he's going to make it…?"

He held his silence for a while. "I won't lie to you. It doesn't look good. He's lost a lot of blood."

"Is he with you now?"

"Yeah, he passed out a couple minutes ago."

"Fuck."

"I'll see you in a bit."

"Okay. I love you."

He didn't hang up, just sat with the phone to his ear. "I love you too."

I hung up to head downstairs, and I got into the back seat of the SUV. His driver took me across town, driving in the dark, the streets still full of people because it wasn't midnight yet. Now that my biggest fear had been alleviated, that Bastien hadn't been killed, I could breathe again.

But I also didn't want Adrien to die.

I hated him for the way he'd treated me, but I believed Bastien was the man I was supposed to be with all along, so it was hard to hold a grudge. I didn't believe in fate or destiny, but it seemed like those things might be real. Maybe all those bad things were supposed to happen so I would find Bastien…and he would save my life.

Twenty minutes later, I arrived at the hospital. Bastien wasn't in the waiting room, but Luca was. Other than an ugly bruise on his face, he looked unharmed. He rose from his chair and came to me when he saw me walk into the room.

On instinct, I hugged him, gripped him hard, and squeezed. "You okay?"

He flinched at my touch, his arms at his sides like he didn't know how to reciprocate my affection. But then his arms moved and closed around my body. "Yeah...I'm okay." He gave me a squeeze before he pulled away.

"Where is he?" Bastien was the first person I'd expected to see, but he wasn't there. Maybe he was in the restroom or the cafeteria. But I couldn't imagine him leaving until he saw me first.

"He's getting stitched up."

"*Stitched up?*"

"Guess he didn't tell you that."

"Tell me what?"

"He got stabbed in the arm. But he'll be fine."

"He got stabbed?"

"He's been shot, so this is nothing."

"*What?*"

"Not now, but a couple years ago—"

"*Luca.*"

I heard his voice behind me and immediately turned to see his face.

He gave Luca a cold stare. "You have the worst bedside manner I've ever seen."

"I told her you were fine," he argued.

"You told her I was shot," Bastien snapped. "She did not need to know that."

I moved into his chest and hugged him tight, smelling the rain that had dampened his clothes. He was alive and well, and I squeezed him as I treasured that fact.

His arms circled my shoulders, and he held me there, let me hold on to him like a life raft. "It's alright, sweetheart."

Luca silently excused himself.

I pulled away and looked at Bastien's arm, seeing the thick bandage that had been wrapped tightly around his bicep. "You kill the asshole who did this to you?"

He gave a slight smile. "You know I did."

"Where have you been shot?"

The smile disappeared. "That was a long time ago."

"Where?"

His hand moved to the back of his head, and he rubbed an area behind his ear. "It grazed me. It's the one spot where I can't grow hair."

"You were shot in the head?"

"I said grazed."

"Jesus." He was right in front of me, alive and healthy, probably healthier than he'd have been if none of this had happened and he'd been able to eat that steak. But I still felt winded, like the action continued even though the end had arrived. "Where is he?"

"With the ER staff."

"No updates?"

He shook his head.

"What did they do to him?"

Bastien never answered the question. "You want to wait for him here or head home? I can have my guys call with an update."

If I went home, I would just pace the room and wish I were at the hospital. "I'm going to wait here. I understand if you want to go home and clean up."

"I go where you go, sweetheart." He guided me to one of the chairs and sat down. "It's probably going to be a while, so get comfortable."

I sat there and crossed my legs, still in the same outfit I'd worn to dinner, a low-cut sweater with tight jeans and boots. The ER was packed with people who were waiting to be seen or waiting for an update about their loved ones. The TVs in the corners showed sports or soap operas.

Having to sit there and wait was anticlimactic after all the fear that had gripped me for the last hour.

Luca took a seat beside Bastien.

"Did you get him?" Bastien asked in a quiet voice.

He shook his head. "Disappeared into the crypt...like a cockroach."

Bastien said nothing else.

I wasn't sure who they spoke of.

Luca continued. "By the time I reached the caverns, it would have been too late."

Bastien remained quiet.

Luca slouched in the chair and stared at the TV.

"You don't have to wait here," Bastien said. "You don't have to pretend to care about this shithead."

"I don't care about him—but I care about you and Fleur."

I was scared for Adrien, but Luca's words broke through the fear and made me smile. "Best friends..."

The doctor finally gave us an update.

Adrien had lost a lot of blood but was able to get a transfusion soon enough to survive the ordeal. It sounded like he'd been stabbed all over his body. We were invited to visit him in his room, but I was the only one who went in because Bastien didn't seem interested in seeing him.

I walked into the empty room and found him asleep in bed, the monitors beeping quietly, the streetlights shining through the closed blinds. It was a private room, so he was the only one in there.

I approached the bed and looked down at him, his skin so pale, his body so lifeless. He looked like he'd lost ten pounds even though he'd been fit the last time I'd seen him. It was either the loss of blood or the stress…or he really had lost that much weight since the last time I'd seen him.

As if he knew I was there, he opened his eyes slowly. It took him a second to focus on my face and another second for him to recognize me. "Fleur…" His voice cracked like he'd been asleep for a long time, when it'd only been a few hours at most. He slowly moved his hand across the bed and inched closer to mine to take it.

I crossed my arms over my chest. "I'm glad you're okay."

Hope disappeared from his eyes quicker than the flame of a lit candle in the wind. He swallowed, his disappointment palpable. His wrists were bandaged, and he looked like he'd been hit by a shipping truck, his skin bruised like he'd taken a frying pan to the face. "Why did you ask him to save me?"

"I didn't, actually," I said. "He just did it, because he knew I didn't want you dead." I grabbed one of the chairs and pulled it closer to his bedside, even though I had no intention of taking his hand, of ever touching him again. Tragedy brought people closer together, but this tragedy wasn't enough, not when he wasn't innocent in this story.

He didn't exactly move mountains to save me, so I shouldn't move mountains to make him feel wanted.

"Does my family know?"

"I haven't told them."

"Good. Let's keep it that way."

I looked at the window instead of his face, unable to bear the sight of his beaten expression. "What happened?"

He didn't answer me for a long time. "I got what I deserved."

"I don't know what happened to you, but I'm sure no one deserves that."

"I tried to get out, but I wasn't quick enough."

"Bastien told me."

"At least Bastien killed them, so I don't have to."

"You're going to continue the business?"

"I don't know," he said quietly. "I thought I was going to die last time I was conscious, so it's hard to think further ahead than the next hour."

I wouldn't be the one to take care of him. I wouldn't get him home and into bed. Wouldn't bring him his meals and handle the house so he could rest. He'd thrown all that away when he'd stuck his dick in someone else. It seemed even less worth it now because we both knew none of those girls would come to the hospital if they knew he was there. "You'll need to tell one of your brothers…so someone will come get you."

His mood dropped further, like he'd expected me to do more for him. "Yeah. Call Anthony."

"Sure, I can do that."

I continued to sit there even though I didn't have a reason to stay. I guess it was pity that kept me there. He'd thrown me away, and I was still the only person he could count on. He'd betrayed me, and I was still there when I shouldn't be.

"Thank you for coming."

"Yeah."

"And thanks for...saving my life."

I couldn't take the credit for that, not when I didn't have to ask. Because Bastien loved me enough not to make me ask. "You're on your own now, Adrien. Take care of yourself."

"I'll try."

I got to my feet then returned the chair to the wall.

"Fleur?"

I turned back to him, unsure what else there was to say.

"I'm sorry...for everything." His eyes burned in their own darkness. "If I could take it all back, I would."

I used to dismiss his apologies. Used to discount them as pleading. But I could see the sincerity like a beacon of light that called the ships home. "I know, Adrien."

"And..." He didn't grimace in pain as if that was the cause of the interruption. Didn't seem to lose his train of thought either. He just struggled to get the words out. "And I'm happy for you…he's a good guy."

I'd never needed his blessing, but it was nice to receive it. The final page had finally turned, and the book had closed. It was a novella, more of a footnote compared to the story of my life. Just as winter ended the year, I felt the closure I'd sought for many months. The guilt-free acceptance of the end. I'd loved Adrien with all my heart, but those feelings had faded faster than the setting sun. Now, my heart burned white-hot for someone else, a torch I would carry for eternity. "I'm going to marry him."

There wasn't a wince or a look of surprise. Instead of turning the page back to the start, he let the book come to an end. Let the winter winds blow our past over the countryside and disappear. "I know."

———

By the time we got home, it was nearly three in the morning.

Our dinner had been interrupted, so we hadn't eaten. My appetite kicked in once we walked into his bedroom, now that all the fear and uncertainty had passed.

Bastien seemed to have the same thought because he pulled out his phone and fired off a text, and I assumed it was to Gerard. I supposed it could have been to anyone, but I knew Bastien well enough to suspect he was starving.

That man was always starving.

He changed out of his clothes and put on his sweatpants. He was shirtless, so the gauze around his arm that concealed the stitches underneath was visible like a commemorative medal. He poured himself a drink from the bar then took a seat at the table, eyes heavy like he was tired but too hungry for sleep. Then he grabbed a cigar, lit it up, and just let it sit between his lips.

I changed too, choosing to wear his clothes instead of my own. They were more comfortable, and they smelled like him. Smelled like romance and rain and the City of Light. I sat across from him, one knee bent with my foot against the seat, his shirt like a baggy dress.

He didn't usually smoke his cigars around me, and now that I saw him do it, I realized I hadn't seen him smoke in a while. And when he came home, he didn't smell like it either. Made me wonder if he'd been trying to cut back on that too.

He let the cloud of smoke escape from his mouth, relaxed in the chair with his arms slightly crossed. He looked out the window and over the dark water to the lights of the buildings across the way, the Eiffel Tower the beacon of the city.

"How are you?"

He took another drag and then released the smoke. "Fucking hungry."

I could tell he was in a bad mood, and now I knew he was *hangry*. All it took was one skipped meal, and he was beside himself. The stab wound and almost getting killed was no

179

problem at all. I stayed quiet and drank the wine he'd poured me and let the silence go by, knowing he would be the man I remembered once the food came.

Twenty minutes later, Gerard delivered the meal.

Bastien didn't even wait until Gerard placed my plate in front of me before he started to eat. It was a steak and potatoes and greens, so he was determined to get his steak tonight, regardless of what went down.

I didn't mind that he'd dropped his manners. He deserved to eat.

Gerard left, and we ate in silence. I had a bowl of penne pasta with a side salad, as if Bastien had told him to make that specifically. The hot food hit the spot after the crazy night. I hadn't realized how hungry I was either until I'd walked in the door. My last meal had been at lunchtime, and it was just a cup of soup.

He smoked his cigar between bites, something I'd never seen him do. When he finished inhaling his food, he put out the cigar right on his dinner plate then drank the rest of his glass until there was nothing left.

Life came back into his face, and he looked like the man I knew and loved. "Are you okay?"

"Yeah, I'm okay," I said. "It was hard seeing him like that, but he'll be fine. He's got his brothers and parents and stuff."

"He's not your problem."

"I know he's not. Now, you're my problem." I gave him an affectionate smile before I glanced at the gauze on his arm.

He didn't smile back, but his eyes softened subtly.

It was a rough day, a day that could have ended quite differently. But it ended in the way that I needed it to end, a final goodbye that wasn't teary, but kind. "I finally got the closure I've been looking for…and that was nice."

"Good. You deserve peace."

"Yeah, just wish it could have happened differently." Without Bastien being stabbed and Adrien… I wasn't sure what exactly had happened to him.

"We both lived to tell the tale. All that matters."

"Yeah." I finished half of my food and left it there, my focus entirely on Bastien now. "I don't even know how to thank you for what you did. Adrien is my ex-husband, and you still helped him. And you didn't even make me ask." It took an extraordinary man to be that secure, to risk his life for a man who used to call me his. But he felt no jealousy. Never showed a single sign of it.

He crossed his arms over his chest fully, and he stared at me hard, almost like he was angry. His eyes were focused with a lethal precision. It was hard to know what he was thinking in that moment, if my words moved him or annoyed him.

"I'm not sure how I can ever show my gratitude." His love felt unconditional, as if he would truly do anything for me, no matter what it was, even if it was putting his life on the line for an ex who deserved what was coming to him. I

181

would never understand why he'd chosen me to love, when he could have literally any woman he wanted with those devastating blue eyes...but he did.

The silence was heavy, as if whatever he was about to say had enough substance to put a hole in the wall. His eyes were sharp like the knife that had cut his arm, and he seemed to slice straight into my soul. "I know how."

Bumps formed on my arms as the excitement prickled. After the night we'd had, I expected a quiet evening on the couch, but it looked like he wanted to throw me on the bed and tie my wrists to the headboard.

He cocked his head slightly, still giving me a look that hit harder than a bullet. "Marry me."

I blinked, unsure if that was a serious statement or some kind of a joke. But given what had just happened over the last few hours, it seemed like a shitty time to make a joke. I almost asked but I changed my mind, and that was probably for the best.

His stare didn't change, and that told me he was dead serious. "You want to thank me for what I did? Then marry me."

All that stuff in the closet was dirty talk—but it was also true. It'd clearly been on his mind, but for how long, I didn't know. It gave me a rush of adrenaline, of excitement and fear packaged together into a swirl of emotions. I'd just told Adrien that I would marry Bastien, but I meant someday, and the question still put me on the spot.

He waited for me to say something, not blinking since he'd begun this showdown.

I swallowed. Melted in the heat of his stare. Felt cornered like an animal. "Are you actually asking me—"

"*I'm telling you.*"

Jesus.

"That's what I want. Now, give it to me."

I was hot all over, a strange mixture of being turned on and fucking scared. No other man had ever wanted me so desperately, had ever been obsessed with me from the moment our eyes met. But it wasn't a passion that flamed out as quickly as it started. It continued to burn, continued to grow, and he never seemed to grow tired of me.

"You said you had closure."

"I did—"

"Then let's do it." He was so pragmatic about it, like this was a business negotiation rather than a romantic gesture. Every time I gave Bastien an inch, he demanded a mile. And now, he demanded all of my miles.

Jesus, my heart was beating so hard.

He abruptly rose to his feet and walked off. He headed to the bedroom.

I gave a quiet gasp in fear, afraid that I'd pissed him off and chased him away, but I was rooted to my chair, still grappling with the fact that he'd just asked—*told*—me to be his wife.

He returned as quickly as he left and placed a small box in front of me.

The lid was already open—revealing a big-ass diamond ring. "Oh my fucking god..." A brilliant oval diamond started up at me, reflecting the light that came from every corner and angle, the clarity unmistakable. The diamond had to be about twenty carats, the kind of ring only a queen would wear. Like, an actual queen. It was so big that its intention was more than to denote marital status, but rather the status of the man who'd given it to me. I wasn't a jeweler or someone who knew anything about engagement rings, but this one had to be worth at least a couple million. "Bastien..." How long had it been sitting in his drawer? How long had I been sleeping right next to it? When did he buy it? When did he plan on giving it to me? Because I didn't believe this was the moment he'd been waiting for.

"Do you like it?"

My eyes flicked up to his, and I released a strained laugh. *"Do I like it..."*

"Then put it on."

"Is this too fast—"

"No."

"Bastien."

"I know what I want, and I'm not afraid to say it." His arms moved to the table, and he leaned forward. "Are you?"

"No…"

"Then put on the damn ring and be my wife."

I sucked in a breath before I looked at the ring again. My last wedding ring had been a completely different cut and style, and I was relieved to see something new, something that was unique and breathtaking but still me. I loved it the moment I saw it, and I loved it more because of who had given it to me.

I took the ring out of the box and slid it onto my finger, and of course, it was a perfect fit. The diamond was enormous compared to my slender finger. Anyone who saw it would know that a very powerful and rich man was behind it, that I belonged to someone ruthless…and romantic.

When I looked up at him again, he didn't look pissed off anymore. Now, his eyes had softened slightly, and a wonderment was in his gaze. His eyes shifted back and forth between mine before a slow smile crept on to his lips. Then he slammed his hand hard onto the table, so hard it made the plates and glasses dance and clatter against the surface. "Fuck yeah." He came around the table and dropped to his knees between my legs, kissing me hard, both hands cupping my cheeks, his tongue already in my mouth. His hands were in my hair, and he ravished me like I'd only been a fantasy until this moment—when he finally got to have me.

He lifted me from the chair and put me on the table, my legs wrapping around his waist. He grabbed my baggy shirt and pulled it off until my tits were out. My thong came next, yanked over my ass and thighs until it slid to my ankles then dropped to the floor.

Bastien breathed quick and hard as he shoved down his bottoms and revealed his rock-hard dick. He tugged me to the edge, tilted my hips enough to shove his fat dick inside, squeezing into my tight paradise. He forced his way in and gave the sexiest moan when he claimed my lands in his name. "Fuck." He tugged on the back of my hair with his hand, and he fucked me more like a whore than a fiancée.

But I fucking liked it.

He was vicious, pounding into me hard and fast, not caring if it was too much or too deep.

I clung to his arms, saw my brilliant diamond against his beautiful skin, felt claimed by him in a deeper way than before. I would be more than his woman. I would be his wife. The woman of the house. The mother of his children. He wanted me for all his life, and he wasn't afraid to say it. He didn't play games. Didn't run away from commitment like a boy with too many options.

"Say you'll marry me." He breathed into my ear as he continued to fuck me.

"I'll marry you." I squeezed his hips with my thighs as I took the ruthless pounding.

"Fucking marry me."

"Yes." I was already going to come, starting at nothing and going to a hundred in a second. "I want to marry you." I clawed at his arms, even at his injury, but he didn't react to the pain. "I want to marry you…"

"Fuck yeah."

I started to come around him, the tears shedding, my body on fire. "God…yes."

He rammed into me harder as his skin blotched red, coated in sweat. He gave a moan as he released, dumping his seed inside me as I came with him, the two of us moaning and grunting and crying out as we exploded in fire.

We didn't stop until sunrise.

We started at the dining table, then hit the couch, and then made our way into bed. After the third time, we were both spent, tired from the long night but still high on each other. I lay beside him, my leg hiked over his hip, tracing the rough outline of his stubble with my fingers.

His eyes were tired, but he didn't close them, still staring into my depths.

When I'd left Adrien, I'd expected to be single for at least a year, to take my time before getting back into the dating world. Instead, I ended up engaged less than six months later, and it felt right. "The ring has been sitting in your nightstand this whole time?"

"Yeah."

"How long?"

"I bought it six weeks ago."

Six weeks ago. That was before he'd asked me to move in. Before we'd said we loved each other. When we were trying to take it slow. "You knew all the way back then?"

"I knew it even before. Went after I had drinks with Luca."

"Why then?"

He gave a slight smile. "I'll let Luca tell you the story."

I continued to outline the hard bones in his jawline with my fingers. I was smothered by his scent, the smell of man and sweat and cigar smoke and rain...all the things I loved. "It's beautiful. I love it."

"I love the way it looks on you when you're naked."

"Of course you do."

His hand went to my ass, and he squeezed it with his big hand.

"Will you wear a ring?"

"I prefer to wear ink rather than jewelry."

I suddenly remembered that conversation from long ago, when he'd said he saved room to ink his wife's name on his arm. Based on that, I'd assumed he would also ink a wedding band on his finger if he ever got married. Was he thinking of me when he said that? Had he bought the ring then? "That's pretty hot."

His handsome smile emerged. "Black. Permanent. Forever a part of me."

"It's sweet."

He pulled me close then sprinkled me with kisses, on my shoulder, my neck, my collarbone, drenching me in his love. He returned to the pillow then continued to stare at me, the sun slowly rising and moving between the cracks in the curtains. They brightened his eyes, making them look like tropical ocean pools.

"I love you." With all my heart. With everything I am.

He didn't blink. He didn't say it back. Silence stretched, and it was clear something was on his mind. He'd been happy a moment ago, but slowly, the sadness started to creep into his bones and then his flesh. "My father and I hadn't spoken for two years when he came to my apartment one night..."

All the warmth left me when I heard those words, when I understood whatever he had to say was important...and heartbreaking.

"He came alone and unannounced. I don't know what made him do it. If he was in my neighborhood and it was a spur-of-the-moment decision. Or if he planned it, which was why he drove himself instead of having his driver bring him. So many questions and I'll never be able to ask him because that night ended with me killing him."

I didn't know why he told me all this. "You don't have to explain, Bastien."

He ignored what I said. "My father had never been good at putting a full sentence together, unless it was three words or less. *Do this. Go here. Kill so-and-so.* So, when he came to my apartment, he said a lot of shitty things. Like he wished they'd never had me...or that I'd been a girl he could use as a pawn." His eyes flicked away, and he swallowed.

It was the first time I'd seen Bastien seem unsure of himself, take a moment to feel and reflect and writhe in silent pain. So afraid to spook him, I didn't move or speak, just hoped he would finish the horrible tale.

"My father wasn't a good man, but even then, I don't understand how anyone can just barge into someone's apartment after not speaking for two years, only to say the most unspeakable things. There must have been a better reason for him to come. Must have been something else that he'd never said. Or maybe that's just me wanting to believe in a fantasy because reality is too fucking harsh."

I did my best not to cry. Did my best not to provoke him. Bastien was never vulnerable, and I knew once this moment was gone, it would be gone forever. He would return to his rock-hard callousness, back to his sly jokes and indifference.

"Back and forth, we insulted each other. He hit me first and I hit him back. We fought on the floor, and he reached for his gun inside his jacket. To this day, I still don't know if he grabbed it to shoot me...or if he grabbed it so I wouldn't shoot him. It all happened so fast, and I didn't think it through at the time. He said he hated me, and I said I wished he were dead, so I turned the gun on him and squeezed his finger over the trigger...and killed him."

I nearly gasped in shock but somehow kept it back.

"He bled out...and I lay there in it." His eyes weren't on me anymore. They were looking into the distance, living in the past while I stayed with his body in the present. "It's hard enough to listen to your father say you're unwanted...but then having to kill him when you didn't want to...and having to carry that guilt these last thirteen years...to hate your brother and watch him hate you...and to lie to your mother every day because she has no idea that she birthed the monster who killed her husband... Sometimes it's too much." A buildup of moisture had coated his eyes, but he blinked and it was gone. He took a couple breaths, pushed back the avalanche of sorrow that had started to roll down his mountain. "But it doesn't feel like too much with you."

13

BASTIEN

The butler escorted us into the sitting room, the equivalent of a lobby in an office building, and we waited a few minutes before my mother emerged in a white button-up blouse with midnight-blue trousers and ballet flats. Around her neck, she'd tied a little scarf. My mother always lit up at the sight of me, lit up in a way my father never did, even when I did something right or impressive.

"My baby, what a surprise." She came over to me and kissed me on each cheek before she gave me a squeeze. Then she turned to Fleur. "Lovely to see you again." She kissed her on each cheek and blanketed her in motherly affection. "You look beautiful. I love this—" She spotted Fleur's engagement ring and cupped her mouth with both hands. "Oh my lord, look at that!" She clutched her hands to her chest before she moved back to Fleur and hugged her hard. "You've made me so happy."

I hadn't seen my mother in the throes of joy in a long time. She smiled politely and appeared engaged in her life, but never anything like this. Nothing that made her shriek in unbridled happiness.

My mother finally let Fleur go and turned to me. "I'm so happy for you, baby." She hugged me again, Fleur's size, so also a foot shorter than me. "I did not expect this when you dropped by for a visit. I can't believe it, but I can very much believe it. So, when is the wedding? It has to be within at least a year—"

"Mom." I pulled away and gave her a gentle squeeze on the arm. "We're still in the moment right now. We'll figure it out later."

She turned back to Fleur, took her hand, and examined the ring under the light of the chandelier. "Bastien." She clicked her tongue against her teeth. "This ring is marvelous. You have impeccable taste."

"I know," I said with a smirk.

"Did you tell him you wanted this?" she asked Fleur.

"No," she said with a smile. "He did this all on his own."

"This has to be twenty-four carats," Mom said as she continued to examine the ring like a jeweler. "The clarity is truly remarkable." She finally let go of Fleur's hand and looked into her face. "So happy for you. I can't believe there will be another Dupont soon. And little Duponts running around, carrying on the family name and legacy."

Any children we may or may not have wouldn't be included in the Dupont legacy. They would do something better with their lives than what Godric and I had chosen. Something respectable, commendable.

"This calls for a celebration," Mom said. "Champagne and caviar in the drawing room." She stepped into the other room to speak to her butler and tell him all the details.

"I'm glad your mother is excited," Fleur said. "I wasn't sure how she'd react."

"She loves you."

"I was afraid she would say it's too fast, that we're in a rush."

"She trusts my judgment. You're the only woman of mine she's ever met, let alone heard of."

That seemed to make her feel warm because she smiled and looked down at her ring again, lightly grazing her finger over the large diamond in the center. After a long gaze, she looked at me again, her eyes so bright they were like moons. "I love you."

I savored the look on her face, the way she wore her heart on her sleeve and it beat just for me. So caught up in the stare, I almost didn't say it back. "I love you too."

I sat in the warehouse with a cigar in my mouth. It was pouring rain outside, the drops like a stampede of cats on the roof. I'd spent the last few days in bed with Fleur, fucking like rabbits in spring, but unfortunately, I had to go back to work.

My phone vibrated with a text. *Can we meet?*

It was Godric.

He was the last person I expected to hear from. I wanted to fire off questions about his intentions and the purpose of the meeting, but that could scare him off. *When?*

Now.

I'll be in the city in 15 mins. I left the warehouse without a word, having driven myself, and returned to Paris. By the time I was surrounded by the buildings and lights of the glorious city, he texted me a location, a bar that he must own because nothing was open at four in the morning.

I parked on the empty street then entered the dimly lit bar, seeing Godric alone at a table in the center of the room. There was no bartender, so he must have made his own drink. None of his men appeared to be with him, a gesture of peace.

I helped myself to the bar and made a drink before I sat across from him.

His drink looked to have been sitting there awhile, because most of the ice had melted and diluted the scotch in his glass. Condensation was on the outside, and there was a noticeable ring on the table around the base. He wore an expensive black jacket with an Omega watch on his wrist. He'd always cared about nice things—clothes, cars, jewelry.

The only thing I cared about was women. And now, I had a woman worth more than all the cars in my garage and all the watches in Godric's closet.

He stared at me as he relaxed in the chair, his guard dropped, unlike how it'd been at the wedding. He opened his coat to reveal the stash of cigars before he grabbed one and extended it to me.

"Can't say no to that." I took it and lit up.

He did the same.

Soon, we were surrounded by a cloud of smoke. The two of us sitting there in comfortable silence like we hadn't been enemies these last few years. With our blond hair and blue eyes, our relation was impossible to miss. He was lean and toned like he ran on a treadmill instead of lifted weights, like a fucking pussy. He put his faith in guns rather than himself. I had a different philosophy, because an enemy could take away your guns and knives, but they could never take your strength.

Minutes passed, and neither one of us spoke, just smoked and drank, the large window that faced the street coated with rivulets of rain that continued to fall.

I knew Fleur was dead asleep right now in my bed in my t-shirt. I wondered if Godric went home to anyone. When I got tired of the silence, I broke it. "Thank you for the warning." I didn't want to show appreciation to him for anything, but I knew it would be poor taste if I didn't.

He swirled his glass, even though there was barely any ice left. "I expected you to make a deal, not call for war."

"I did make a deal, and then I changed my mind."

He took a drink then returned the glass to the table. "For your fiancée's ex-husband."

"Mom told you."

He gave a slight nod. "Congratulations."

I didn't accept it, unsure if it was genuine.

"Why would you destroy your alliance with the Aristocrats for the man who used to fuck your girl?"

I didn't appreciate how he phrased that, but I didn't rise to the bait. "Love makes you do crazy things."

He took a puff of his cigar and let the smoke absorb on his tongue as he stared at me. Seconds later, he let it go as a cloud.

"They were all aware of Oscar's plan to bury Fleur. They're just as guilty as he is."

"Sounds like an excuse."

"It is—but it's still valid."

"You know they'll come back. And when they do, they'll come for you."

"I'll cross that bridge if and when I come to it." I set my cigar aside and took a drink. I hadn't done this with my brother for years, not since we were business partners, before he lied to me.

There was a long stretch of silence before Godric spoke. "This is the real deal?"

I regarded him, searching for his meaning before I responded. "Yes."

He stared at me for a while before he gave a slight nod. "Mom was so excited when she told me, I could barely understand a word of what she said."

"I'm surprised she told you."

He gave a shrug. "Every couple of years, she makes her plea for us to be brothers again. To put aside the past and start over. I think that your upcoming nuptials reignited that." He took another puff on his cigar. "She knows I'll never get married, so…"

"Never say never. Didn't think I'd get married either."

"Then she must be one hell of a woman."

"You have no idea, brother."

He stilled when I uttered the endearment, something I hadn't said to him in a long time.

I was somewhat embarrassed for the way I'd dumped my emotional baggage on him, in the middle of a crowded room when he had no warning of the missile headed his way. But it was done now, so I had to pretend I had no regrets about it.

Godric enjoyed his cigar a while longer, his eyes drifting elsewhere as he remained lost in thought. "His name is Ivan."

My full attention focused on him, the sound of the rain suddenly gone.

"Escaped from a Russian prison for crimes against his own government. Laid low in the Middle East for years. Now, he has his own organization in Paris. Says it's the mecca of wealth and power."

I didn't get anxiety, but I felt floods of adrenaline akin to waterfalls.

"Bastien." He took the cigar out of his mouth and let it rest between his fingers on the table, the conversation turning even more serious than it'd been a moment ago. "He puts the psycho in psychopath."

"Then why do you work with him?"

"I don't. We just have the same ideologies about business."

"If you share the same beliefs, and he's a psychopath, what does that make you?" I cocked my head as I penetrated him with my stare.

He stared back, smoke rising from the tip of his cigar.

"Just something to think about…"

He stared like those words bounced off him. "He's bribing all the groups in the city to roll on you. And those who don't accept the bribe are getting a threat to their family instead. But a lot of them support the old Republic, only adhere to the Fifth Republic because you force them to. They're looking for new leadership."

My skin flushed before it prickled. As if a gun was pointed at the back of my head, I felt a sense of imminent danger, even though it was just the two of us in an empty room.

"You don't have much time left."

I had the best poker face in the world, so I didn't react to what he said, but I'd be lying if I said I wasn't worried. A snake was in my garden, and it'd eaten all my fruit before I'd noticed it was there. He was powerful enough to threaten the gangs that reported to me, and he was powerful enough that they were too afraid to tell me about the threats. "Why are you telling me this?"

The smoke continued to rise to the ceiling from the tip of his cigar. He regarded me for a long time with guarded eyes. But slowly, the walls dropped, and the resentment faded away. "Because you're my brother, Bastien."

"It's late," Luca said, wiping his eyes like he was dead tired after the long night. "The sun is about to rise. Last time I was up this late was when we burned Oscar from Notre-Dame." He leaned against the table with his arms crossed.

"Godric asked to meet."

Luca perked up, like this information was enough to defeat the fatigue. "What'd he say?"

"Heard of some Russian asshole named Ivan?"

He shook his head.

"Neither have I. But he's bribing and threatening our guys to roll on me one by one. If Godric is telling the truth, and I think he is, that means the guys are lying to our fucking faces."

Luca absorbed all this, his stare slowly sharpening like a buffed knife. "How do we know this isn't a play—"

"Because it's not."

"Godric has had it out for you for years."

"He's telling the truth."

Luca studied me, his head slightly cocked. "Why are you so sure?"

Because I'd told Godric the truth. Spoke my truth and poured out my fucking soul to him. "I just am."

Luca seemed to see something in my stare, because he didn't push. "How are we going to handle this?"

"We tell the wrong person that we know, and Ivan moves in."

He nodded in agreement.

"Which means we need to hit him first."

"And execute all the assholes who supported this coup."

14

FLEUR

Over the next couple days, I rarely saw Bastien.

He was barely home. Barely slept. He always replied to my texts and called to check in on me, but he was clearly distant, like his mind was elsewhere. I knew it had nothing to do with me because he'd just asked me to be his wife, still made love to me during the brief periods when he was around.

But something bothered him.

He came home one morning and went straight to bed because he was exhausted. When he woke up, it was the late afternoon. He showered then came out in his sweatpants, like he didn't need to run off right away for once. But he didn't seem to be in the moment with me, his mind elsewhere.

We had dinner, breakfast for him, and he continued to check his phone like he expected news. He was distracted, not invested in me or our conversation like he usually was.

"Babe?"

He put down his phone when I addressed him directly.

"Is everything okay?"

He took a bite of his food as he stared at me, and he seemed to drag out the answer on purpose. "I've got a lot of shit going on at work right now."

"I know. That wasn't the question I asked." The fact that he tried to dodge it made me more concerned about whatever he was dealing with. "I asked if everything is okay, if you're okay."

"Everything is fine, sweetheart."

It was the first time he'd lied to me. I could tell because he was terrible at it. "You said you wouldn't lie to me."

He released a frustrated sigh, like a parent annoyed with their child. "I'm having to deal with a lot of shit right now. I know I haven't been home a lot—"

"I don't have an issue with that, Bastien. I just want to know you're okay."

He relaxed in the chair, no longer interested in his meal, and just stared at me. "I'm okay. Everything will be okay. I'm just in the middle of something."

"What's going on?"

"It's not your problem."

"I'm going to marry you, so it *is* my problem."

He released another sigh, backed into a corner the way he'd backed me into a corner so many times. "Please let this go." He said it quietly with a slight plea to his voice, a controlled desperation.

I wanted to know what was consuming him so deeply, but if he didn't want to talk about it, I wouldn't force it out of him. Like a vault, he locked away his secrets, and only at the most unexpected times did he punch in the code and open the door to me. "Alright."

"Thank you." He went back to his meal, his appetite returning once the interrogation ended. He shoved a big bite into his mouth, and his impressive jawline hardened as he chewed. He could do anything and look hot—ride horses, chop down trees. He could be a garbageman, and he'd even make that sexy. "Any thoughts on the wedding?"

I doubted he cared about the wedding, just wanted to change the subject. "I'm guessing you want a big wedding because you know literally everybody?"

He chewed his bite as he stared at me hard. "I want to marry the woman I love. I don't give a shit about the guest list. What do you want?"

"I don't know, honestly." I'd already had a big wedding when I married Adrien. Hundreds of people in a big church, a grand reception, the whole nine yards. It had been the best day of my life until the day I'd wondered if it was all a lie. "Something small is fine with me, but I feel like you should have a say in this since I've already had a wedding." I didn't want to bring up Adrien, but I did have experience where Bastien did not. It had to factor into the decision.

"You've had a wedding before, but you've never married me before." His blue eyes could be so breathtaking sometimes, like now when he was all serious and intense. "This one is gonna last—until I die."

I only had a handful of friends and no family, so the number of people on my side would be minimal. But Bastien was right. The guest list didn't matter.

"The only thing I want, the only thing I won't compromise on, is seeing you in a wedding dress. I want you to take my name as your own. Then I want to take off that dress and leave it on my bedroom floor. *Our* bedroom floor. As long as I have those things, I'll be happy. You can decide everything else."

He hadn't struck me as a romantic guy when we'd met, but he was by far the most romantic man I'd ever been with. "Last time I saw Adrien, I told him I was going to marry you. Then you asked me just a couple hours later."

His eyes didn't soften like I expected. They turned more possessive, like he was on the verge of taking me to the church and making me his wife at that very moment. "I guess we were both thinking the same thing that night."

"Yeah, I guess so." Except he'd been thinking about it longer, long enough that he'd had time to buy me a big-ass diamond ring that could knock a man out cold. "Since we're on this subject, I wanted to ask you about something."

He stopped eating his dinner, either because he was full and there were only a few pieces left, or this conversation was taking all of his focus. "What is it, sweetheart?"

I hadn't thought this far in advance, not when everything had happened so fast, not when I'd gone from a heartbroken divorcée to head over heels in love in a matter of seconds. But now, the moment was here, and it was time to face it. "I realize this conversation is premature because I'm not in this headspace right now, but...we should talk about kids."

He didn't blink or flinch. Didn't grow visibly uncomfortable by the subject.

Adrien had always dragged his feet on it. Anytime I mentioned it, he looked like he would have a full-on panic attack. But now, that was a blessing because I wouldn't have wanted to have kids with such a lying, spineless man. Now, Bastien...I would love to have his babies. Especially if they had his eyes... Oh lord help me.

After a beat, Bastien spoke. "We can have them if you want them."

"But how do you feel about it?"

"Do I look like the dad type?" he asked somewhat coldly. "It's not on my agenda. But if you want a family, just tell me when and I'll step up."

He didn't shy away from the topic, fully cooperative. I should be grateful, but I hoped to have a husband who wanted to be a father. But I couldn't ask him to want something he didn't, to be a different person than he was. "May I ask why?"

"Why I prefer not to have them?" he asked with slight incredulity. "For starters, my line of work is not ideal for raising a kid. I sleep during the day, I'm gone at night. If I show up to a parent-teacher conference, everyone will shit themselves. And my childhood was a shitshow of trauma and violence, so I don't know a damn thing about creating a warm, nurturing environment for a child to thrive." He cocked his head. "You know what the last thing my father said to me was before he died?" His voice was different—angry but contained at the same time.

It hurt me to listen to all of this because I could see his pain in his eyes, hear the unspent rage that burned in an inferno inside his chest. He commanded a room with his confidence, but inside, he was broken like the rest of us.

"He said I was—*and I fucking quote*—a worthless son I wish I'd never had."

I inhaled a painful breath, killed the tears before they had the chance to start. It hurt to picture that exchange, to picture anyone saying that to someone I loved so much. His mother was so loving, so motherly, and it was hard to imagine having a father who was such a fucking prick.

"Not only do I have no desire to be a parent, I'm also unfit for the job."

I needed a second to process what he said, to accept his heartbreak with a straight face. "I'm sorry that happened—"

"Don't pity me. I'm a grown-ass man who doesn't need sympathy."

It was as if his confession in bed had never happened, his vulnerability long gone. "It's not pity or sympathy."

"Whatever it is, I don't fucking want it." He turned vicious, treating me like I was some asshole who'd crossed him rather than his fiancée.

I normally would have snapped back, but given the fact that he continued to bleed from wounds he refused to see, I let it go. "I've seen the way you treat your mother. You're kind, respectful, and gracious to her. And you've made me feel more loved than anyone ever has in my entire life. You're at odds with your brother, whom I can tell you still care about, because you want to protect young women who are strangers to you. You say you're unfit for the job, but you're more fit than I am."

His stare remained rock hard and stoic, refusing to let my words pierce his flesh.

"And if we had children, you wouldn't be working anymore, so we wouldn't have to worry about all that stuff."

His eyebrows slowly furrowed at what I said. "I would never ask you to give up your dream of having children, so why would you ask me to give up my dream of running this city?"

"I—I wouldn't ask you. I just assumed that's what would happen."

"That was the wrong assumption."

The disappointment hit me like a wrecking ball. "So, we would have little ones while you're the head of this country's organized crime faction with a target on your back? I'm okay with being at risk because I'm grown enough to make that decision for myself, but they wouldn't be."

"I would never let anything happen to you. I've proven that."

"I know, but—"

"And I would never let anything happen to our children either. I will provide for you and protect you. Always."

"I understand that, Bastien. But you can't control everything."

"I won't give up my work for something I don't even want." He didn't raise his voice, but it somehow felt like he was yelling. "And it's wrong of you to expect me to."

"Bastien, do you even like your job?"

"What kind of question is that?"

I knew I'd hit his trigger, but I continued. "Sometimes I wonder if you're still trying to prove something." Prove that he was more than what his father had said. Prove himself to be a bigger kingpin than his father ever was.

Bastien was dead silent, and the longer that silence continued, the more suffocating it became.

Fuck, there was no going back now.

His expression hardened, and even though the change was subtle, he somehow looked fucking deranged. When he spoke, he managed to speak calmly, but he was right up against the border of insanity. "Don't. Analyze. Me."

"Bastien—"

"I'm talking now, and you're going to fucking listen."

Jesus, that felt like a slap across the face. He'd never spoken to me like that before. If this was restraint, I hated to picture how he spoke to men before he slit their throats.

"I've already compromised with you. I'm willing to have these kids that I don't want if it's what *you* want. Now, it's *your* turn to compromise. It's called diplomacy, negotiation, being a fucking adult. You have these kids and I continue my work, or you don't have these kids and I continue my work. Those are your options." He abruptly left the table and walked behind me, probably heading to the bedroom.

I stayed in my chair because I was too scared to move. I'd never seen him like this before. Never had him talk down to me. Never seen him attempt to restrain all the rage that was reserved just for me. He'd talked about ripping off my wedding dress, and then mere moments afterward, it was as if he hated me.

He came back a minute later, dressed in his street clothes like he intended to walk out.

I didn't stop him. Didn't ask him to stay.

When he walked out, he slammed the door—and he'd never done that either.

When midnight arrived and he didn't come home, I knew he wouldn't be back for the rest of the night.

I lay in bed, constantly on the verge of tears, hating how distant I felt from him.

I looked at his location often, something I never did, wanting to know where he was because the paranoia had set in.

But Bastien wouldn't do that.

His dot stayed inside a bar for a couple hours, like he needed some time alone to cool off. Then he moved to different locations across Paris, perhaps meeting with his other partners.

I lay there, unable to sleep, having the shakes because I was that scared.

Scared that he might leave me. That I'd crossed the line with what I said. That I'd forever changed the dynamic of the best relationship of my life.

I knew Bastien wouldn't call or text. He'd stay out until morning. Maybe not even come home then. I could tell that was how pissed off he was. But I knew he would ever ignore my calls or texts, no matter how much he might want to.

So, I called him, blanketed in the glow from the lit-up screen.

It barely rang once before he picked up. There were voices in the background, and then they started to recede, like he was walking away to another part of the building or perhaps to the sidewalk outside. He didn't say anything, like he knew I was okay because he'd been checking my location the way I'd been checking his.

I didn't know what to say, how to start. So I said the only thing that I could, the only thing that made sense. "I love you." I wished he were home, but I didn't want to ask. Didn't want him there if he didn't want to be.

He didn't say anything for a long time, let the silence sink between us like an anchor out to sea.

I was scared he wouldn't say it back.

He let out a quiet breath, and it wasn't clear if it was a sigh of annoyance or simply a calming breath. Or perhaps he'd been smoking when I called, and the cigar still hung between his lips. "I love you, sweetheart. Always."

I was on the couch when he walked inside.

It was four in the morning. I'd gotten so tired of trying to sleep with this anxiety in my heart that I just showered and got ready like it was morning and then sat on the couch in front of the fire, wearing his t-shirt and sweatpants.

He stopped and stared at me, like he hadn't expected me to be there.

I didn't look directly at him, like my stare would chase him away again.

He ran his fingers through his hair then moved into the armchair, crossing one ankle on the opposite knee.

I hated this. How distant he felt. How strained our relationship had become. It was a strange situation because an apology didn't feel necessary from either of us. No one had really done anything wrong, but the conversation had imploded our relationship, nonetheless. "I want to have children with you."

He shifted his gaze and looked at me, like that wasn't what he expected me to say.

I could picture a little boy with blond hair and blue eyes. Picture my heart a mess on the floor at the sight of him. Watching him grow into a man and leave the house would be so bittersweet. "But I can't do that if you're in this business. Not after what happened to me. Because if what happened to me happened to them…" I couldn't finish the sentence, not when just the thought would kill me.

He looked away again, like he'd just stepped into the ring for another round.

"But I can live without children." I could live without a reality that I'd never had. Live without something that hadn't come true. Because my love for Bastien and my life with him had completed me since the moment we'd met. "But I can't live without you."

He turned back to me, and just like that, all of his anger was gone. His stare had a depth he'd never shown before, visibly moved by what I said. There wasn't a blink or hesitation in his stare. He looked at me for what felt like forever. "You don't have to decide now. Perhaps in a few years, you'll feel differently."

Time had numbed my fear like an ice pack numbed a burn, but it was still there, haunting me like a ghost that continued to live in the attic. I would never forget the second before I was submerged, never forget the rawness of knowing I was going to die and it would be painful and horrible and dark…and there was nothing I could do to stop it. If I couldn't say there was no chance that would happen to my child, then I was unfit to be a mother. And if I wasn't willing to leave their father to give them a better life, then I definitely was unfit. "I won't change my mind." I accepted the loss of a different life, accepted a different path that I hadn't expected to walk. But it felt right.

He studied me like the confidence in my stare wasn't enough. "I expected to see your stuff packed up when I walked in. Expected to see your ring on my nightstand. Expected you to tell me it's done."

My eyes watered. "I've been a fucking mess since you left." Lying in bed, waiting for him to come home, scared that I'd destroyed the best thing that had ever happened to me. "If death didn't chase me away, then what could?"

He moved to his knees before me then swept up my hair with the way he cupped my face. He moved between my open knees as he held me, his callused thumbs catching the tears that rolled down my face. "Nothing—because nothing could chase me away either."

15

BASTIEN

The second the food came, Luca hunched over his meal and scarfed down his pancakes.

We were out late, so late that by the time we were done, it was almost lunchtime. Breakfast food was perfectly agreeable to both of us. I was dead tired because work had become my life, and then I needed to give my woman the attention she deserved when I came home.

My bachelor days were behind me. I didn't have my house to myself, didn't watch the game with a decanter of scotch as my only company. Now, there were vases of flowers in the bathroom and the living room that hadn't been there before. Sometimes when I opened my drawer to grab underwear, her thongs spilled over onto my side. Another nameless woman wouldn't be in my bed. I wouldn't leave cash on the nightstand for the whore who did her job.

But one single woman gave me more joy than all those things.

"How's the wedding planning?" Luca asked.

"Ask Fleur."

He took another enormous bite and needed several seconds to swallow it. "Do you know anything about it?"

"She wants to get married in Luxembourg Gardens then have the reception at the Four Seasons."

"Then it sounds like a big wedding."

"That's what happens when you know the entire city." I ate my eggs and bacon before my pancakes. Luca preferred to hit the sweets before the savory food.

"Is your mom helping her?"

"No, but I guess I should recommend that. They could get to know each other better."

He nodded with a mouthful of food. "Double-edged sword. Your mom could start pressuring her into grandkids and all that horseshit."

"Fleur and I aren't having kids."

"Really?" he asked. "Lucky you, man. Women are so obsessed with kids like there's nothing more to life. Fleur is cool, so I guess that doesn't surprise me."

I debated telling him the truth. Should probably keep it to myself because it was my business, but I told the guy everything. "Actually, she wants kids, but only if I leave the business. I told her I wouldn't do that, so she said she was fine not having them."

That was surprising enough that it made Luca stop eating. "Just like that?"

"She said she'd rather live without children than live without me."

He continued to look skeptical about the whole thing. "And you're okay with that?"

"Why wouldn't I be okay with it? That's exactly what I want. I've never wanted kids. A long life with Fleur with nice dinners and warm nights in front of the fireplace and expensive trips is what I want."

"But that's what *you* want. She wants that and more."

"Relationships are about compromise. You can't have it all."

"Really?" He didn't return to his food, and the conversation became far more serious than I'd expected it to be. "Because it looks like you got everything *you* want..."

I didn't let my anger rise, not when we were in a crowded room, not when I knew he always meant well, even when we butted heads. "I told her we can do the kid thing. I'm not the asshole, and I don't appreciate being treated like one."

"I'm just surprised, man."

"Why? I told her I would protect her and whatever children she wants to have. Not my fault she doesn't have any faith in that."

"Your dad always protected you, didn't he? But growing up in that situation fucked you up bad."

"I would never involve my kids in this life." I'd never put a gun in their hands and order them to shoot an innocent girl. I would never tell them they were unwanted, even if that was how I really felt.

He was quiet for a while, looking down at his food but not eating it. "You've loved this woman since the moment you saw her. I know she took off in the beginning because she was scared, but this woman fucking *drowned*, and she stayed. Now you tell her you won't give her a family in a safe environment, and she *still* stays. The loyalty she has shown you is unbelievable. She's got balls, man, and I'm just surprised that after all that, you could do this to her."

I'd felt no guilt for my decision, but Luca completely changed that perception.

"How can you love this woman as much as you do and refuse to give this to her?"

"I think you're just trying to take my job."

He immediately smirked at the taunt. "If I want your job, I'd just shank you, asshole."

I'd made a joke to dispel the tension, but the second I waved away the smoke, it wafted back in.

He turned serious again. "It's not like this is happening now. You've got at least five years, Bastien. I don't want kids, never have and never will, but if I loved a woman like you do, I couldn't do that to her, not when she's been one hell of a woman."

My food remained untouched and turned cold, and the rest of my body followed suit, like I was in the process of rigor mortis. It was hard to imagine a boring life of diaper changes and spit-up all over my clothes, especially when I didn't have the adrenaline at night, when I didn't thrive in the shadows after they went to bed. Adrien had been a big fucking disappointment for her, said he loved her and never proved it, never gave her the love and respect she deserved.

I didn't want to do the same.

When I came home, she was happy to see me, as if that horrible fight had never happened. She'd already gotten ready for the day like she intended to go out after I went to bed. Her hair and makeup were done, but she wore one of my long-sleeved shirts like a baggy dress.

She rose on her tiptoes to kiss me, her arms unable to wrap around my neck so she grabbed on to my shoulders instead.

I slipped my hands underneath her dress, and I took hold of that fine ass. I was dead tired when I walked in the door, but the second she was in my grasp, I was wide awake. I gripped her thighs then lifted her up into me, her legs automatically wrapping around my waist.

Now, her arms could circle my neck, and she kissed me like she'd been thinking about me all morning. "I missed you."

Her neediness turned me on—that was how much I loved her. No amount of clinginess could deter my obsession with her. Sometimes, less was more, but other times, more was more. When a woman grabbed my hand, that was all it took for the night to come to a screeching halt. But there was nothing Fleur could do to make me feel that way. "I missed you too, sweetheart." I carried her to the bed and dropped her on the edge before I took hold of her panties underneath her shirt and tugged them down. I pushed the shirt above her tits and dropped my bottoms before I grabbed her hips and lifted her into place to take my dick.

I slid through her slickness that drenched my dick, and I already wanted to come. "Fuck, you really did miss me."

When I woke up, she was on the couch reading, in a different one of my shirts. As far as I could tell, she didn't have any loungewear because she'd never worn it in front of me. She preferred my clothes, and that was just fine with me.

I showered then joined her on the couch.

She immediately closed her book and left it on the coffee table before she crawled to me and got on my lap, the excitement in her eyes like a torch she carried just for me. "How was work?"

My hands went to her thighs. I could feel the change in her legs, the muscles she'd built just from running on the treadmill every day. Her waist was a little tighter, and I could feel her abs against my thumbs whenever I squeezed her. Her ass was tighter too—and I definitely liked that.

"Same shit." I didn't know how to answer such a routine question, not when I was a criminal rather than a guy working in an office. "How was your day?"

"I had a blueberry muffin that was to die for, so it was pretty great." She was all over me again, her hands on my chest, her ass right in my lap, obsessed with me like I'd been with her since the moment I saw her.

I had no doubt that she was really past our fight, that she felt no resentment toward me for what she had to sacrifice. I could just let it go, let myself have what I want and let her take the hit.

But now, I felt so much guilt. "I've changed my mind."

"About what?" she asked, her eyes narrowed like she really had no idea what I referred to.

"If you want to have kids, I'll leave."

It took her time to absorb that statement, her expression going through various stages of confusion, deeper confusion, and then shock. She'd been happy a moment ago, and now she looked devastated, like I should have just left it alone. "What do you mean, Bastien?"

"I'll retire from the business. We can start a new life."

"But you said—"

"I know what I said. I changed my mind."

"But why?" Her affection retreated. She left my lap and moved to the couch beside me. She seemed overwhelmed with emotion rather than joy, which was the opposite effect I'd intended.

"Because I love you, Fleur. Because I asked you to marry me, and you deserve everything you want. You deserve a man who puts you first. You shouldn't have to compromise on a damn thing." My life had changed when I'd met Fleur, but it had changed again when I asked her to marry me. All my priorities were different now. She was the single most important thing to me, and I'd feel like a worthless piece of shit, denying her what she wanted most. "So, whenever you want this to happen, we'll make it happen."

Her eyes drifted away like she needed time to come to terms with what I'd said. "I—I didn't expect this." Her dark hair was pulled back over one shoulder, and her eyes had an emotional depth that I hadn't seen before. "I don't want you to give up what you love either, Bastien."

"But I don't love it, Fleur. I love you."

Her eyes came back to me.

My heart started to race as I felt it creep up my spine, the truth that I'd pretended was a lie for a decade. Broken shards started to fuse together once more, but somehow, the healing was more painful than the initial break. "You were right."

She continued her stare, not a blink in sight.

I thought about what I'd said to Godric at the wedding, how fucked up in the head I was. "I did all of this to prove that I'm not the spineless, weak, unwanted boy my father said I

PENELOPE SKY

was. But he's long dead, and I can't prove shit to a ghost. If I were truly a secure man, I wouldn't care about proving a damn thing. But I'm not."

Her eyes softened like she might start to cry.

"This job doesn't mean anything. It's you that means everything." I'd made my billions, I'd proven that I was a greater man than my father was, proven that I was more successful than his favorite son.

But I was just as empty as I'd been the moment my father looked me in the eye and said he wished he'd never had me. I'd changed in a lot of ways, put on a hundred pounds of muscle and covered my scars with tattoos, was unrecognizable to most people who knew me as a boy, but underneath, I hadn't changed one bit.

I'd been lying in my father's blood and staring at the ceiling all this time.

"Bastien…" Her hand went to my arm, like she knew I was on the verge of tears that I would never shed, not even in front of her. I hadn't cried since the night I'd killed my father, and I never would.

My eyes were on the fireplace when I grabbed her hand and cradled it to my mouth. I kissed her palm before I enclosed it in my fist and placed it against my heart. "You are my life now."

"You sure about this?" Luca sat beside me in the back seat.

"Yeah."

"Could be a trap."

"Even if it is, I'll be fine." I opened the back door and got out before Luca could say anything else. It had just started to rain, but I let my clothes grow damp and my hair wet as I took my time approaching the doors to the restaurant.

The lights were on inside, showing a dimly lit steakhouse with a checkered tile floor. The grand fireplace against the wall was on and blanketed half of my visitor's face in light and the other half in darkness.

No one else seemed to be there, and the table he occupied wasn't directly next to any windows.

I approached the table and saw him up close, blond hair and blue eyes, his Russian features obvious. He had the nose for it too. He had a distinct scar from his eyebrow to his chin, like a knife had gutted him badly years ago.

We stared at each other for a hard minute before I took a seat.

He didn't have a drink in front of him. Kept his hands above the table with his arms crossed—unspoken etiquette.

My elbows rested on the table, my hands together near my face.

Heavy silence passed, both of us staring at each other, trying to pierce the other's bulletproof exterior. He reminded me of the cosmonauts I saw on TV, launching from Kazakhstan.

With men like us, this staring contest could last days.

He spoke first. "You've been looking for me, Butcher." He cocked his head slightly, a man who was ten to fifteen years older than me but still bulky with muscle. "Well, here I am."

I was an arrogant man, but I was never arrogant about an opponent that could affect my city so profoundly. With his harsh ideologies, he campaigned for my job, and he was obviously a decent candidate because my own supporters were turning on me. "Good. No one likes to chase a rat in a sewer."

Instead of rising to the insult, he allowed a slow smile to creep over his lips. "You're a young, arrogant son of a bitch. I like it. You remind me of myself." He raised his hand toward his face then traced the scar from eyebrow to jaw. "Before I got this."

The threat was subtle, but I definitely got the message.

"I still remember the man who gave this to me. Was never the same after…"

"Did it feel better after your mother kissed it?"

His smirk returned. Most men were probably too intimidated to face off with him, and he seemed to genuinely enjoy the fact that I wasn't intimidated at all. "I've admired your work. From humble beginnings as the son of a simple dealer to President Martin's right-hand man and the first French Emperor, it's quite impressive for a young man. Which is why I'm going to offer you a deal that would be unwise to refuse."

I already knew what that deal would be.

"Step down and revoke the Fifth Republic—and I let you live."

"You know I can't do that, Ivan."

"Ivan?" He smiled again. "We're on a first-name basis now?"

"Aren't all people who want to kill each other?"

This time, he chuckled. "I like you, Bastien. Which makes this a little harder…but only a little."

"We won't go back. France's economy is the strongest it's ever been. Tourism is up over fifty percent. And all my partners are rich and operating with convenience. Working with the government rather than against it has increased productivity."

"Perhaps that's true, but margins are less favorable with paid labor, and with the taxes and tariffs they're forced to pay, they're working more and keeping less."

"But innocents are spared, and the country in which they reside is the most powerful in its history—and that counts for something."

"Over eighty percent of your partners disagree, Bastien. They don't care about patriotism or morality. They want the old Republic to be reinstated—and they want you gone."

I'd hoped in time that the men would accept the new policies, but apparently they were too greedy for that. "The Fifth Republic stays. When I discover the parties who have aligned with you, they'll be replaced."

"We both know that's not going to happen, Bastien. You seem like a smart kid who still believes in the good of people, very commendable." He sat upright and placed his elbows on the table. "But that shit is gonna get you killed."

I held my silence.

"If you want to do good in this world, be a cop or a teacher. Be a philanthropist. You're rich enough for it."

"In the years since I've been doing this, I've saved thousands, tens of thousands, of innocent lives, and I've strengthened my country's place within the world. I will never know the true impact of my work because it simply can't be quantified. That's more important than money, Ivan."

"Those who care about money the least are always the ones who have it."

"And you don't?"

"I was in a Russian prison for five years. I managed to escape and have had to start over. Eating out of dumpsters and robbing men for their clothes. When I came to Paris, I heard about the infamous Butcher...and I knew that was the job I wanted."

"I'm sorry to inform you that we aren't hiring right now."

"No," he said with a smile. "You're one of those pricks who loves to smell his own shit because it smells so damn good. But if you don't pull your head out of your ass and smell the fresh air, you're going to get that head cut off." His smile faded, and he turned dead serious. "You have no idea what you're up against. This is your last chance to take my offer. Think wisely because it won't come again—"

My patience had snapped. He was playing checkers with someone who played chess, and I was ready to wipe all his pieces off the board. "I won't let you destroy my country. I won't let you burn my city. And I won't let you rape and enslave my women."

His eyes narrowed with his frustration. "Then you have chosen death."

"My power and alliances reach much further than you know, Ivan. But you will know soon enough."

His eyes flicked back and forth between mine. "And if you're wrong, not only will you pay the price, but so will that pretty fiancée of yours."

I stilled at the threat, the line he never should have crossed.

"Too late, Butcher." He smiled. "My offer has expired."

When I got into the back seat of the car, Luca tried to hit me with questions.

But I cut to the chase first. "Fleur needs to go into hiding. Get a team together. Now."

"I guess that tells me everything I need to know." He started making calls and shooting off texts.

I started doing the same, calling in favors to allies near and far, one of them being the Skull King. I'd been taking his drugs through Paris to the Scandinavian countries. He didn't have a lot of power in Paris, specifically, but he had a lot of power, nonetheless.

When I arrived at the house, I walked into the bedroom and saw Fleur was dead asleep.

It was three in the morning.

I didn't want to wake her to this news, but I didn't have the time to waste. Perhaps Ivan knew that was how the conversation would go, and he already had a plan to hit me and Fleur within minutes after the meeting.

"Sweetheart." I stood at her side of the bed and gently rubbed her arm.

"Mmm?" She didn't open her eyes. They were clenched shut, trying to hold on to sleep.

"Sweetheart, I need you to wake up." I flipped the sheets off her.

Her legs immediately tightened toward her chest when she felt the cold.

I gave her a gentle shake.

She finally opened her eyes and looked at me, her eyes taking a moment to focus. "Babe?" She said it with a scratchy voice, a beautiful whisper.

I loved it when she called me that, and now I was afraid I

would never hear her call me that again. "I need you to get up and pack a bag."

"Pack a bag…?"

"Yes."

She seemed to understand that this was serious, that I wasn't waking her up because I missed her or I wanted to fuck, but because something had gone wrong. "What's happened?" Now she was out of bed and on her feet, her breathing uneven once she understood the danger.

"Shit is about to go down, and I need you out of here. The guys are going to take you to a safe house until it's over."

She blinked like she didn't understand a word of that. "But I want to stay with you—"

"You can't."

"I'm not going to leave you."

"You are."

"You said you would always protect me."

"And that's exactly what I'm doing. Get dressed and pack a bag. Now."

She breathed hard like she'd been on a run rather than sound asleep. She looked like she wanted to argue but didn't. Instead, she rushed off to throw her shit into a bag.

I got a call and answered immediately.

"The guys are downstairs for Fleur."

"She'll be there in a minute," I said before I hung up.

Fleur did as I asked, just threw a couple things inside and didn't try to coordinate outfits or take nonessential things. She zipped up the bag on the bed then put on jeans and a sweater. She didn't even brush her hair.

When she came back to me, she was winded from both exertion and anxiety. "I don't want to do this. I don't want to leave."

"Sweetheart." I cupped her face and held her close. "I'll get you as soon as I can."

"I don't understand what's happening."

I didn't want to tell her the truth. Didn't want to scare her when she was already scared. "I have to take care of something, and I can't do that and worry about you at the same time. It's only for a short while. You'll be okay."

"It's not me that I'm worried about." She looked at me with her teary eyes. "If I have to leave, then I know it's bad."

"I've had bad before, and it's always been okay." But not bad like this, when some asshole thought he could come into my city and take it from me. Could turn my allies against me and knock me off my feet. "But I have you now, and everything is different."

Tears sprang free.

I couldn't comfort her more than that. "We have to go." I grabbed the bag off the bed, took her hand, and we headed downstairs to the driveway behind the gate. Two SUVs were already there, the first one to take Fleur to the safe house. I opened the back door, tossed her stuff in the back, and then helped her inside.

She looked like she wanted to cry again.

I wanted to comfort her, but I wanted to protect her more, so I didn't linger. "I love you." I cupped her face, and I pressed a kiss to her forehead and kept it there, holding her for possibly the last time.

I didn't let go until I heard her say it back.

"I love you too," she said tearfully.

My hand slipped out of her hair, and I closed the door before I knocked on the back of the car, telling the guys to go.

They drove away, and I headed to the next SUV and got into the back seat. "The warehouse." The car left the roundabout. But in the rearview mirror, I noticed another SUV pull up behind me. They rolled down the windows, and the guards talked to the driver and passenger.

Maybe Luca was in there.

The car Fleur was in turned on the road and headed toward the edge of the city.

It was in that moment that I questioned everything. Instead of dealing with this maniac, I could have slipped into bed beside Fleur and watched her sleep. I could have woken up with her and taken her to breakfast. I could have a normal, peaceful life—but I chose this.

16

FLEUR

I was quiet in the back seat next to my bag, tears escaping even when I tried my damnedest to fight them. I was worried for him, but I'd be lying if I said I wasn't worried for myself too. Just a month ago, I'd taken my final breath and inhaled a pool of muddy water that killed me. I still remembered it vividly, how painful of a death it was. And then for the week afterward, I slept more than I ever had in my life, like my brain needed to heal from the loss of oxygen for however long I'd been dead.

And now here we were again…

I watched the city disappear as we headed farther away into the countryside, where it was just highways and billboards and then nothing of substance on either side. We turned on a road and left the main area and soon it was fields and the occasional building or warehouse.

It gave me heart palpitations because I felt like I was reliving the past, driving out to the middle of nowhere

where a coffin awaited. I'd expected to stay somewhere in the city, in an apartment or barricaded inside an office building, a needle in a haystack.

Something about this didn't feel right.

When I'd thrown my stuff in my bag, I'd grabbed whatever clothes were nearest, but I'd also grabbed a handgun from his closet and tossed that inside.

My eyes lifted when I heard the driver speak into his earpiece. "Yeah, we got her."

My blood burned and turned ice-cold at the same time.

Who was he talking to?

Bastien was the only one who would ask, and he'd already seen me leave.

My heart started to race faster, my gut telling me this wasn't right. None of this was right.

I opened my bag and found the gun inside. I checked that it was loaded just like Bastien had taught me and confirmed the safety was on so I wouldn't shoot myself by mistake. I looked ahead at the driver, wondering if I should just shoot him and hope I didn't die in the crash.

But what if I was wrong? What if this was all paranoia?

We slowed down and turned off the road, approaching a steel gate covered in barbed wire. It reminded me of the warehouse Bastien had taken me to, but we had traveled in a different direction to get here, so I knew it wasn't the same place.

We pulled onto the property and parked near the front doors.

I tucked the gun into the back of my jeans the way Bastien did, making sure my sweater covered it, and I tried to act normal. But when I looked out the window and saw the number of men there, all with guns, I knew this wasn't a safe house. A safe house was meant to blend in, to be inconspicuous. This looked like a military base.

My palms were so sweaty I almost dropped my phone when I grabbed it out of my back pocket. The guys approached to open the door, and I called Bastien as quick as I could, hoping he would pick up on the first ring.

The door opened, and the guy looked at me, seeing the bright phone in my hand and the name on the screen.

Bastien, pick up.

His realization quickly turned to panic, and he lunged at me to take it away. "Give me the phone."

Bastien picked up, his voice audible. "Sweetheart—"

"It's a trap!" That was all I could get out before he punched me so hard in the face that the phone went flying.

The guy dove for it, and another man opened the other door to grab me.

I could barely move because the blow had nearly incapacitated me, but I saw him turn the phone off so Bastien couldn't trace my location.

At least he knew I needed help. He would come.

He would come like he did last time.

He would save me.

He will save me...

17

BASTIEN

"Fleur!" Sheer panic gripped me by the throat and nearly suffocated me. The line went dead, and instead of wasting a precious second trying to call her again, I pulled up her location—but it was already gone. "This can't be fucking happening." I panicked, gripping my hair with both of my hands as I tried to think of my next step.

Luca watched me in silence, speechless for once in his life.

We were at the warehouse, hunkered down with guns and ammo as we made our next plan.

But it looked like all of our plans had been put on hold.

"The SUV behind me..." I looked at Luca, the pieces slowly coming together. I'd been in such a hurry to get her out of there, and I'd assumed the SUV that took Fleur was full of my guys, but now I realized they'd been watching the property, knowing exactly what I would do next, and then pulled in at the perfect opportunity. "I fucking gave her to them!"

Luca didn't waste time with questions. "I'll call around. Someone will roll if we offer enough."

For the first time in my life, I was in shock.

And I felt that feeling that other people had described, my mother, other women I'd slept with—anxiety.

I wanted to rush to Fleur, but I had nowhere to rush off to.

Then one of my guys gave me another dose of bad news. "We've got company."

Luca had the phone pressed to his ear when he walked over to the security system that showed all the cameras on the property. A line of Hummers and SUVs pulled up from the road, all taking various positions as they faced the warehouse where we were positioned.

We were fucking surrounded.

Luca ended his call and made another. "I'm sorry, Bastien." He abandoned Fleur and called for help. "Jeremy, we need backup. Get your ass here now." He hung up and made another call. "I'm calling Martin. He'll send the Foreign Legion under the circumstances—"

Gunfire erupted, and the bullets struck the walls of the warehouse, most of them bouncing off the steel, but with enough hits, the structural integrity would collapse. I knew he could launch explosives and grenades at us, so this was purely an act of intimidation.

But I didn't give any orders, incapacitated by Fleur's capture. It was literally impossible for me to save her. As if my wrists were bound in handcuffs, I just stood there and listened to the bullets rain down on the base.

"Bastien, what do we do?" Someone asked me, and I couldn't even think of his name.

Luca was still on the phone, his hand covering the other ear so he could hear.

I was stuck in this warehouse, but I'd let all these men die if I could get to Fleur.

"*Bastien.*" Luca shoved me in the chest. "We take 'em out, take Ivan alive, and get him to talk. That's how we find Fleur."

I nodded absent-mindedly. "You're right."

"Martin said he'll send everything he can, but we have to survive long enough for him to get here."

I couldn't let myself wonder where Fleur was or what was happening to her. My mind drifted to the worst-case scenario, unspeakable shit. But I pushed the thought away, because until I was done with this, I couldn't help Fleur.

I moved to one of the computers, punched in the code, and then the mounted guns slowly rose out of the ground outside the warehouse, automatic targeting locked on. I'd installed them years ago, and not once had I had to use them. It'd been so long, I'd nearly forgotten they were there.

"I forgot about those," Luca said in awe.

The mounted guns fired their rounds at anything that moved.

"They'll be distracted," I said as I left the seat. "At least for a minute or two. Take out as many as we can." We moved to the front, the wall still intact but the divots from the bullets visible in the steel. We slid open the panels to reveal the slots for the rifles to fire while keeping ourselves protected.

Everyone fired, shooting up the vehicles and the men using them for cover. It was a modern battlefield with hundreds of rounds fired, a graveyard of bullet casings. "Grenades!" We all pulled the pins and then tossed them hard through the holes before we slid the panels closed and ducked down behind the wall.

The explosions were so hot I could feel the warmth through the solid wall. Even with my ears covered, I felt like my eardrums were about to split. When the silence returned, the gunfire didn't follow it.

Luca looked at the monitor. "We took out a lot of the cars, but there are still men everywhere. Gun mounts are destroyed. We'll need to hit them a few more times."

"But now they know it's coming," I said. "Continue to fire."

18

FLEUR

They didn't even bother to bring my bag. Left it in the back of the SUV.

My head throbbed from the punch. I suspected my eye was all black and blue, because my vision was blurred on that side. With my arms pinned behind my back, they forced me into the warehouse then shoved me onto a dirty mattress lying there on the floor. The rest of the hangar was full of Hummers and even a small six-seater plane.

I hit the moth-eaten mattress and lay there for a second, the headache pounding with every beat of my heart. Six guys surrounded me, all with guns, all there to guard me. I was scared out of my mind, and the only power I had in that moment was the reassurance that Bastien would come for me.

I just had to stay alive long enough for him to get here.

That meant I should stay quiet, give them no reason to hurt me, and wait for this to be over.

But I quickly realized I wouldn't be afforded that luxury.

One of the guys spoke to the other in a quiet voice. "She's pretty sexy." He was an ugly guy with a squishy face, a guy who probably had to pay for sex because he couldn't get it on his own.

The other guy nodded. "Boss said she's fair game."

Oh fuck.

"He's gonna kill her anyway," he said back, like I was deaf and couldn't hear him. They didn't even handcuff me or pat me down for a gun because I appeared that helpless to them. "May as well go for it."

The pulse was so loud in my ears, it muffled the noise every few seconds. Bastien had taught me a few things, but my gun only had six bullets, so that meant I needed to shoot each guy in the head if I was going to get out of this.

My aim wasn't that good, and I wasn't that fast either.

But if I took out the rapist, at least that solved that problem.

The guy removed his rifle and handed it over. "I'll take her in one of the back rooms."

"Like fucking hell, you will." I didn't even realize I was the one who'd said that until I heard my own voice. It just came out because I was so appalled, it countered my fear. I was still on the mattress, leaned back on one arm so I could reach for my pistol if he came any closer to me.

He seemed shocked I'd said that too, because he blinked as he stared at me then looked to the guy who had punched me earlier. "Guess you didn't hit her hard enough." He stepped onto the mattress then reached for my ankle so he could drag me. He yanked on me hard and jerked me across the concrete floor.

I was about to take out my gun and fire, but then I realized I should let him pull me away from the other men. After I killed him, I might be able to find a key to one of these Hummers and get the fuck out of here.

He hauled me into an office with a couch then shut the door before he dropped his knee on my chest and punched me in the face, as if hitting me would make me submissive rather than pissed off.

"Motherfucker." I pulled the gun from the back of my jeans and shoved the barrel into his chest before I clicked the safety. Then I pulled the trigger, all of it happening in a split second.

As if I'd hit him with a shotgun, he flew off me and collapsed near the wooden desk.

There was blood all over me, but it wasn't mine.

My ears rang for a second because the gun had gone off right next to me.

I finally snapped out of it and moved his dead body before I searched him, looking for weapons or a phone. He did have a phone, but it was locked with a PIN, and there was no way I would guess that in a couple seconds. I found a sheathed blade on his belt, so I took that before I left the office.

The men were running toward me with their guns—and there were more of them than before.

"Oh fuck." I sprinted for the Hummers for cover in case they opened fire. I wasn't sure if they would keep me alive to use against Bastien or if they would just eliminate me as a liability. I made it to the other side, but I was cut off by a guy with a sniper rifle.

I didn't think twice before I raised my gun and shot him right in the face.

"Oh my fucking Jesus…" He was still alive but immobile, so I was able to rip the rifle out of his motionless hands. I continued to run down the line of cars until I got to the other end, where men were coming at me again. I knew then that they were coming from both sides.

I stepped out and held down the trigger, blowing a spray of bullets at all twelve of them. They wore tactical vests, so I aimed for their legs and kneecaps, making sure they couldn't come after me even if they were alive. Blood sprayed into the air, and the screams echoed off the steel that compromised the warehouse walls.

I'd already killed so many people, but I didn't feel a damn thing.

Fucking nothing.

More of them were coming the other way, but I knew my magazine was empty because the cartridge had popped out. I rushed over to the pile of dead bodies and others who

PENELOPE SKY

writhed in pain and took the magazine from the first rifle I could find.

"Stop that bitch!"

I shoved the magazine into place and fired up at the guy who had just appeared over me, sprayed him with bullets until he wobbled back and off me. A boot came from the side and hit me in the face, made blood squirt out of my nose.

The gun was yanked from me by someone else, and then another guy grabbed me by the ear.

"Fucking cunt." He tugged hard and made me scream. "You think you aren't going to pay for that?" He tugged again, ripping out a chunk of hair that made me scream again. He finally let me go, and the other guys forced me onto my stomach to zip-tie my wrists together.

"Let me go!" I tried to fight, but they just made it tighter, causing my shoulders to ache from being pulled back so far. It felt like they were about to pop out of the sockets. The men lifted me and carried me back to the mattress, dropping me face first onto it.

"Who's first?" one of the guys said.

"Me," the other said. "I'm gonna yank out more of that hair." His knees hit the mattress behind me, and he grabbed my jeans and underwear and tugged them over my ass to expose my bare flesh.

"No!" I tried to wiggle free, tried to bounce against the

246

mattress so I could get to my knees. "Bastien will kill you. He'll fucking kill you!"

Another grabbed me by the back of the hair and forced my mouth open to shove the barrel of his gun inside, his finger hot on the trigger. "Move, and my finger might slip." His eyes were so vicious that I had no other choice but to believe him.

All I could do was breathe, the metal of the gun right against the inside of my mouth. The mattress shifted and moved as the guy dropped his pants so he could fuck me on that dirty excuse for a bed.

I knew Bastien wasn't coming.

Not soon enough to stop this.

The tears started when I heard him spit on his hand.

I'd chosen to be with Bastien despite the risks, and now I was paying for that decision. A wiser woman would have chosen a nice guy with a nine-to-five, a guy who lived an unremarkable but safe life.

But I'd chosen this—and now I would be raped for it.

"What the hell is this?" A voice that sounded like Bastien's but was distinctly not his boomed through the warehouse.

The guy with the gun in my mouth turned to look but kept the gun in place.

The guy on top of me went still. His dick was probably out and hard and ready to go.

I couldn't move my head because I was afraid I would make the gun go off, but I looked up to see the man I recognized from the wedding, six-two with blond hair and blue eyes, a leaner version of Bastien but with the same ruthless aura.

Bastien said Godric hated him…but how much?

Enough to let this happen to me? Enough to do it himself?

He didn't look at me but looked at the rest of the guys who surrounded me, the ones who were waiting their turn. "Get the gun out of her mouth."

The man hesitated before he followed orders, slowly taking the gun away from my tongue.

When it was gone, I could breathe normally, but I hyperventilated, nonetheless.

Godric quickly pulled out his gun from the back of his jeans and shot the guy in the head.

He collapsed on the concrete beside me, the gun still in his hand.

I gave a quiet scream before he shot the guy who was on top of me, the one who was about to shove his dick inside me.

There seemed to be a commotion behind me, the sound of guns being drawn. But Godric was fast, somehow shooting them all dead with a single handgun.

I continued to pant, my wrists still bound, my bare ass out there for the world to see.

He returned the gun to his jeans and pulled out a knife from his pocket before he kneeled down and cut me free.

I got up so fast, pulled up my pants like my life depended on it, and then stared at the man who had almost raped me. Blood pooled around him on the floor, but he still breathed like he was alive.

I picked up the gun from the floor and pointed it right at his face before I fired.

And I fired again and again, kept squeezing the trigger until the gun was out of bullets. And then I threw the gun at his head before I released a scream. *"Motherfucker!"*

Godric watched me, his blue eyes so identical to his brother's that he had nearly the same expression, could replicate the same seriousness and intensity. He didn't come near me and kept his distance. All he did was watch me scream and cry, watch me pick up other guns that still had bullets and shoot the man who had tried to violate me until he didn't have a head anymore—until he was just a pile of brains on the floor.

19

BASTIEN

The shootout continued—and then the guys pulled out the rockets.

"This is about to go nuclear," Luca said.

"Where is the Foreign Legion?" I barked.

"I don't know," Luca said. "Maybe Ivan has another force they have to get through to reach us."

I was about to be blown into pieces, and Fleur…she was on her own.

I couldn't fail her. I fucking couldn't. "I promised her…"

All Luca could do was flash me a look of sympathy that barely lasted a second before he had to focus on reality again. "We get through this, then we go for her. We've got to head to the bunker."

"If we head to the bunker, then we'll be fish in a barrel," I snapped. "I'm dying with a bullet to my face, not my back."

"We're all gonna die if we don't do something—"

Ivan's amplified voice came from the speaker system of one of the Hummers, loud as a megaphone. "Butcher."

The gunfire ceased on both sides.

"They say to look both ways before you cross the street," he said. "And they say never get in cars with strangers. I guess your parents failed you."

I felt my neck tighten and the cords stretch. Felt my face burn red from the rage I couldn't express in any other way. I was hiding like a fucking rat, while my girl was who fucking knew where. I'd risen to the top, but now I came tumbling down to rock bottom—six feet under.

"All regimes fall, Butcher," he said. "Now it's your turn."

I looked at the room full of men who remained loyal to me, and that loyalty was about to get them killed.

"Surrender—and I'll let her go."

I sucked in a hard breath and felt my hands tighten into fists. I'd walk out there, and he'd shoot me in the head for everyone to see, to know that he was the one who had executed the Butcher and usurped his regime. He'd probably piss on my body once he was done.

And I would be okay with that if he really let her go.

Luca looked at me. "You know he won't do it, Bastien."

I swallowed.

"She might not…" He didn't finish the sentence, didn't make me listen to it. "Don't do it."

Ivan spoke over the speakers again. "Come on, Butcher. My patience grows thin."

I stared at Luca, but I saw Fleur's face. "I have to."

"You know he's lying—"

"Even if he is, he's going to kill us all anyway. At least I can save you and everyone else in here who's stood by me all these years. I go out there, and afterward, you get Fleur. Promise you will not rest until you get her back." I hated to think what Ivan would do with her if Luca didn't get her back. I couldn't bear it. Otherwise, it would bring me to tears.

Ivan spoke again. "Come out here, or I'll shoot her in her pretty little fucking head, asshole."

A flash of pain hit me, enough to make my eyes flood.

My phone rang in my pocket, and the only reason I fished it out was for the ridiculous hope that it would be Fleur telling me where she was. But it was Godric's name on the screen, someone I hadn't thought of since all this had started.

Luca stared at the screen. "What does he want?"

"I don't know. Too much of a coincidence." I took the call. "Godric."

Ivan spoke over the loudspeaker. "You've got ten seconds to walk out here, or she dies, asshole. Ten…nine…"

252

But it wasn't Godric at all. "I'm okay," she said as she cried. "I'm okay…"

Tears immediately flooded my eyes at her voice, and I clenched them shut.

"Eight…seven…"

"Sweetheart, Jesus fucking Christ…" I sniffled and swallowed the tears as best as I could. "Where are you?"

"Godric is driving me back to Paris. He saved me."

"He did?"

"Six…five."

"Yes," she said through her tears. "He—he saved me."

"Four…three."

"I have to go. I love you." I hung up before she could say anything else.

"What are you—"

I slid open the panel. "I'm coming out." I shut the panel again.

"What the fuck are you doing?" Luca snapped.

"I walk out there, and you throw the grenades."

"You'll die, Bastien."

"Whistle before you throw."

"This is suicide."

"Just fucking do it, Luca. I trust you."

"And I'm telling you not to—"

"Well, I still fucking do." I shoved him in the chest. "Now, come on." I went to the door and cracked it open while I still stared at Luca, telling Ivan I was about to come out. "You've got this." I stepped out and slammed the door, stepping into the low light from the sunrise because the darkest part of the night had passed.

When Ivan saw me walking toward him, he tossed the intercom aside and came closer to me, wearing that smug stare he'd had at the restaurant just hours ago. He stopped a couple feet away.

I stopped too.

I knew Fleur was alive, and that was enough to give me back the sense of calm that accompanied me in every situation. The adrenaline was like a drug, and I was higher than a kite, even when I was just seconds away from death. I really didn't care about myself at all, but I cared for her with my whole being.

But I had to pretend that call had never happened. He obviously didn't know Godric had betrayed him and taken her. My brother had probably killed all his men, so there was no one left to rat him out. "Let her go. She's got nothing to do with this."

"It got you out here, didn't it?" He was shorter than me, by at least six inches.

"I want proof that she's alive."

"You're already out here, Bastien."

"Just because I'm facing you like a man doesn't mean I surrender. Give me the fucking proof, or I'll come at you right now. If I go down, I'm taking you with me."

He crossed his arms over his chest as he considered the request, studying my eyes like I had a trick up my sleeve.

It was a fair assumption—because I did.

He finally pulled out his phone and made a call, holding the phone to his ear.

It rang and rang and rang.

He took the phone away and called someone else.

It took all my strength not to smile.

When no one picked up a second time, he didn't look nearly as confident.

Luca released a whistle from inside the warehouse, the sound quiet but noticeable if anyone was paying attention.

Ivan glanced behind me before he looked at me, and he opened his mouth to give an order.

I cut him off. "I guess people aren't as loyal to you as you think they are." Then I sprinted, running as fast as I could back to the warehouse, seeing the grenades flying over me in the opposite direction. Gunfire erupted, and right when I reached the small door that led to the warehouse, it flew open.

I was running so fast that I stumbled when I got inside, and I rolled several times on the concrete before I smashed into a table. The explosions were enough to make the ground tremble like an earthquake had struck.

Luca shouted orders, and the men continued to fire. "They're retreating."

I forced myself up and grabbed one of the rifles. "Ivan dead?"

"No, I don't see him."

I went to one of the holes and checked the road. The vehicles that were still operational fled the scene, leaving the cars on fire in the middle of the road. Dead men were everywhere, their bodies abandoned as the living got away.

Ivan's body was nowhere to be found.

The cars drove away, and the firing ceased.

The scene would be all over the news, and I wasn't sure what reporters would say about it. Because what had just happened didn't happen in countries like France. President Martin would have a hell of a time taking questions from the media.

But we were alive.

And Fleur was okay.

———

Luca dropped me off at the house, and I ran inside.

They were in the drawing room, a space with couches and a fireplace, perfect for entertaining—except for the fact that I never entertained. That would require me to have friends and a social life, and I had neither of those things.

Godric stood by the window, his back to me.

Fleur was seated in the armchair when I walked inside, and when she saw me, she gasped so loud and ran straight to me before she jumped into my arms.

I caught her and held her tight, savoring her smell, a scent I thought I would never breathe in again. I'd just seen her a few hours ago, but it felt like weeks and months when so much stress had aged my heart. My arms shook as I held her, and I felt tears burn my eyes because I was just so goddamn grateful that she was there. "I'm so sorry."

"It's okay," she said through her tears. "It's okay…"

It wasn't okay. It would never be okay.

I finally set her down and looked at her face—and I nearly threw up.

She had a black eye and a swollen nose. A cut on her cheek. Puffy lips like she'd been punched in the mouth too.

Tears flooded my eyes, and I cried like I never had, fucking broken. "No…"

"I'm okay." Her hands cupped my cheeks, and she cried, not for herself, but for me. "I'm okay."

Her beautiful face had been broken by fucking monsters, and I was going to kill Ivan and every motherfucker who had turned their back on me. It made me want to bloody their wives and kidnap their kids, just so they could see how it fucking felt.

"I'm okay," she said a third time because the other two hadn't been effective.

She was the one beaten and bloody, but she was the one comforting me. I was sick, truly fucking sick, at the sight of her. "He will suffer for this." I sheathed my tears and pushed past the burn in my eyes. I needed to be there for her, not be the mess that she needed to clean up. "He will die for this." My voice hardened as the blood lust came, as the all-consuming rage pushed out my despair.

She cupped my cheek. "I know."

Godric moved from the window and approached us like he wanted to speak with me.

She glanced at him over her shoulder before she turned back to me. "I tried to escape on my own, but there were too many of them. Then Godric came, and he killed them all. If he hadn't come…" Her eyes dropped like she couldn't finish the thought. "I'll let you two talk." She stepped away, and her hands slowly slid from mine until she was gone.

I needed a second to compose myself, a second to let myself accept her absence before I could look at my brother, a man I'd never known, a man I *still* didn't know.

He stepped in front of me, arms folded over his chest as he stared at the floor for a moment. He was neither arrogant nor angry. He seemed to be nothing at all, almost disinterested. But then he looked at me—and he looked different.

I didn't know how to find the words. I was painfully aware that I couldn't save Fleur, that even if I'd made it to her, it would have been too late. Now, I was forever indebted to this man I'd called my enemy just yesterday. "Thank you, Godric." Those three little words simply weren't enough for what he'd done for me. Didn't show the gratitude that I felt in my heart. "I owe you for the rest of my life. Whatever you need, no questions asked, I will be there." I would dispose of a murdered child if that's what he asked of me.

His blue eyes stayed on my face with no reaction. "That's not why I did it, Bastien."

"Then why?" I asked. "He'll know it was you."

"I'm sure he already knows."

"Then we'll kill him together," I said. "Now, tell me why."

He rubbed his arm gently as he looked at me. His gaze wandered for a bit before he found what he wanted to say. "Honestly, I wasn't going to intervene. I did my part when I warned you. And as a special favor to me, I asked Ivan to give you the opportunity to step down peacefully. I did what I could to look out for you, but you didn't take those opportunities." His gaze wandered again and didn't come back to me. "But then I saw her at the warehouse and saw what they were about to do to her—"

"Please, I beg of you…" I struggled to keep my voice even, to stop it from breaking.

He hesitated before he continued. "I thought about all the women you'd saved…and it was wrong there was no one there to save yours. It was a split-second decision. I killed them all and spared her from your greatest nightmare. Nothing happened to her."

I had been stuck in that warehouse while my girl had fought for her life and her dignity. No fucking way could I go on after this. "She's going to leave me, and she'd fucking better."

Godric didn't say anything to that. "That night Dad made you shoot that girl…"

I switched my thoughts from Fleur to the past. I gave a nod to tell him I remembered, because how the fuck could I ever forget?

"I shot her, so you didn't have to. It wasn't because I wanted to." His eyes remained averted, like he couldn't look at me. "I was always cold to you because I didn't want you there, not because I didn't like you, but because I wanted better for you. When I was fifteen, Dad pulled me into that world, and I hated every second of it. And I didn't want that for you. But then you turned fifteen…and I couldn't stop it."

I didn't say a word, afraid I would scare him off like a wild bird. I'd poured my heart out to him, and now he did it to me, told me something I'd never expected him to share, something that finally helped me understand.

"Dad was a fucking asshole." His eyes finally found mine again. "When I told him I wanted to be a veterinarian to help animals…" He took a breath and looked down, like he didn't want to relive it. "He laughed at me and then…said animals were meant to be eaten. So he shot Bear and tossed him into the woods so the vultures would eat him." He breathed harder, pained by the story of the death of our childhood dog even though he was a grown man now.

But he was still a broken boy...just like I was. "Mom told me he got hit by a car."

He shook his head.

"But you didn't want me to know..."

"No," he whispered, still visibly pained, like the memory haunted him all this time later. "I still wanted to be Dad, wanted him to be good to me, so I tried my hardest to be what he wanted. Then you wanted to be the opposite...and we drifted apart."

"Yeah..."

"I hated you for what you did to him, but then you told me what happened, and...it made me realize how fucked up it all was. The way he treated you. The way he treated us. If it makes you feel any better, he cared about me as much as he cared about you—which is not at all. He was just nicer to me because I did what he asked."

This was not how I expected my day to go. Head-to-head with my nemesis, getting my girl back from assholes, and having a heart-to-heart with my brother. I'd aged an entire year within a day.

He finally lifted his chin and looked at me again, his hardness back in place. "I'm sorry you had to go through that."

I didn't want or need an apology from him, not when he'd done nothing wrong, but it still meant the world to hear it. "I'm sorry about Bear."

"Yeah...it still hurts."

I stared at my brother with new eyes, seeing him as a quiet teenager who had grown distant from me. It felt like we were back in time, still possessing a fraction of innocence before we became the barbaric men we were now. "You've had my back...all this time."

His eyes averted in guilt. "I knew Ivan took her."

"And you went and got her."

His eyes hesitated before they found mine again.

"Why else were you there?"

He didn't answer.

"It wasn't a split-second decision, Godric. You were there to save my girl." My hand moved to his shoulder, and he flinched at the touch. "Because you've always had my back." I shook him. "*Always.*"

His eyes stayed on mine.

"And I've always had yours, even after all this time, even after all this bullshit." I felt the burn in my eyes, but I didn't let the tears fall. My fingers dug into his arm, and I felt his heat and his pulse, felt the blood that was the same as my own. "You're my brother—and I love you."

My father never told me he loved me. Not even in an obligatory manner. I waited and hoped it would come, but it never did. Those daddy issues had followed me all this time, even as a grown man. I didn't want to be like him. I wanted to show love rather than not feel it at all.

Godric didn't meet my gaze for a while, either uncomfortable by my words or overcome with emotion he didn't show. But he eventually looked at me again. "I love you too, brother."

I smiled for the first time that day, felt a peace I'd been searching for in the wrong places. "Let's kill this asshole together. You and me."

He nodded. "The Fifth Republic stays."

"Yeah?" Another thing I'd never expected him to say.

He nodded. "Hurt people hurt people. I'm done hurting people."

I stepped into my bedroom and found her standing near the window, too anxious to sit and wait.

Her back was to me, and I wanted it to stay that way, because the sight of her ugly injuries made me sick as hell. I wanted to kill the guys who'd done this to her, but they were already dead. So all I had left was Ivan.

She turned to me when she heard the door close, and she rushed to me like it was the first time we'd seen each other.

I hugged her tight and rested my chin on her head, squeezing her like she was made of stuffing and cotton rather than flesh and bone. The single most important thing in the world to me—and I was about to lose it.

I pulled away and looked at her, focused on her green eyes and did the best I could to ignore the bruises and swelling and the evidence of her horrible mistreatment. But it wasn't as bad as what could have come to pass, and that was all I had for consolation. "You should leave me." This was the woman I'd chased relentlessly, the woman I'd loved from the night we met, but I needed to let her go.

Her eyes turned wounded. "No."

"This is the second time it's happened—"

"*I'm not leaving.*" She stepped back slightly, clearly offended by the suggestion. "It's you and me, and that's it. I'm marrying you, and we're going to be together until we're old and die. So get over it."

Despite my stare, I felt myself crack a smile. Her ferocity was so fucking beautiful. "Then I'm done."

Her eyes shifted back and forth between mine. "What do you mean, you're done?"

"With this life."

When she realized what I meant, the emotion crept back into her stare.

"I swear to you that my life has been unremarkable for the last five years. And then you show up, and it's fucking mayhem. The first time was an anomaly, but now there's this, and I don't trust it anymore." No one tried to cross me. No one came after the people I loved. But now, my world was upside down, and I couldn't keep the one promise I'd made—that I would protect her. I'd fucking failed, and it was the most painful experience of my life. "I'm done."

She continued to breathe, her eyes shifting away as she considered what I said. "I don't want you to do something you don't want to do."

"Trust me, I want to do this." I wanted to walk away from the table while I still had a chance. I'd hit the jackpot with Fleur, and I wouldn't play another hand. Just take my winnings and walk. "Sometimes shit happens, and it changes you—and I'm fucking changed. I can't go back. I can't live another day when I'm not the only one with a target on my back." I shouldn't even let her stay, not after I hadn't saved her. My brother was her hero, when it should have been me. I would never forgive myself for it, but I was fucking weak and so damn in love that I couldn't do the right thing. "But I need to end this first. I need to kill Ivan, restore order in this city, and then hand the keys to Luca."

She stared at me for a long time. "Are you sure?"

"The only thing I've ever been sure of is you."

Her eyes flicked away as they softened, like the words pierced her heart when they left mine.

"I hate to do this, but Luca is on his way to take you."

Her eyes snapped back to me. "What? Now?"

"Yes."

"Why—"

"I have to finish this."

"But you mean *now*?"

"It has to be now. Ivan has retreated, the gangs have loosened their loyalty, it's chaos. If I wait, he might flee or hit me again." And his death was the only thing that would satisfy my blood lust.

"But you need Luca."

"He's the only person I trust right now. He'll die for you."

Her eyes started to water. "I just came back to you. I don't want to go. I don't want you to go—"

"Sweetheart." I cupped her face, and she immediately grabbed on to my wrists. "I know how brave you are. I know how strong you are. I need you to be those things for a little longer. Will you please do this for me?"

She tilted her head down, her eyes glistening and wet. She sniffled, sucking back the tears before they could fall. "Yes."

I didn't want to leave her again, but I wouldn't rest or eat or sleep until he was fucking dead. He would pay for what he'd done to my girl. For what he'd done to my city. "Attagirl."

Luca took off with Fleur. I told him not to tell anyone where he was going, not even me.

When I walked back into the house, Godric hung up the phone. "He knows."

"How long?"

"That, I don't know."

"You know where he is?"

"He's either calling in favors and headed this way—or he's fleeing."

"He doesn't seem like a runner."

Godric shook his head. "I know he's been using one of Sylvestre's buildings for a headquarters. I suspect that's where he is."

Sylvestre was one of my partners. I'd known him for years. I knew he wasn't thrilled about the change in order, but I didn't suspect him to be such a snake. "How many more of my guys have rolled on me?"

He turned his stare on me, and a beat passed before he answered. "It wasn't personal, Bastien. They always spoke highly of you, just disagreed with your ideologies. It's just business."

"Feels pretty personal to me."

"How are you going to handle this?"

I gave a slight shake of my head. "That's for my replacement to decide. I just need to remove Ivan from power and bring order back to the city."

He had no reaction to that, just studied my face with stoic calmness. "Alright."

"Call your guys, and I'll call mine."

"He'll expect us."

"Good. I want that asshole to know I'm coming."

We were in the back seat together, the driver taking us across town to where Ivan was located. We had a line of cars, and President Martin had evacuated the streets and cited a terrorist situation. It was already on the news, reporters saying a terrorist group had planned an attack on the city but was being neutralized. It was a decent cover-up and somewhat truthful.

That would be a dead giveaway to Ivan, but it didn't matter now. He was dead, regardless of whether he had a heads-up or not.

Godric glanced at his phone when a text came in. "He's injured."

I watched the buildings go by, the city hustling and bustling even though it was now late morning. We'd never done a hit like this smack in the middle of the day. We always waited for the cover of nightfall, but we didn't have a choice. Ivan probably assumed he was safe until he found a new plan.

But he was wrong. "Sounds like men are rolling on him now."

"When they found out he took Fleur, their loyalty wavered."

That iced my wrath—but only slightly.

Godric had this innate apathy to him as he stared out the window. He'd been that way since we were teenagers, like he was permanently numb to the world around him. But when he was a kid and we played with dinosaurs together and roughhoused in the snow, he wasn't. It made me wonder if our father's toll really had been worse for him than it was for me.

"She killed at least a dozen men on her own."

I turned back to him.

"Must have gotten one of their riles. Their bodies were on the other side of the warehouse, so she made it pretty far."

Pride swelled within me. "Attagirl."

"She suits you." He said all of it without looking at me, eyes still on the window.

"She does." That was the closest thing to approval I would ever receive from my brother.

The rest of the drive was spent in silence, but for a change, it wasn't packed with layered hostility and resentment. For the first time, I felt like I was sitting beside Luca, beside one of my guys, beside a friend.

When we approached the cordoned-off street, we pulled over in the middle of the road, the other Hummers and SUVs already there. There were police cars and SWAT vehicles, all dispatched by President Martin.

The building was surrounded.

Godric got out and strapped on his vest before he grabbed his automatic rifle from the back.

I did the same and walked with my brother toward the building.

Then gunfire erupted, bullets spraying the roads as shooters fired from the windows.

I shoved Godric to the back of a car for cover. The windows shattered from the bullets, and glass splashed across the ground.

"Not going down without a fight, is he?" Godric said without raising his voice.

"He's choosing to die like a rat. Not much of a fight to me." I crept around the side of the car and saw the Foreign Legion deploy out the back of one of the vehicles. "If we don't hurry, they're going to kill him before I get a chance."

"What does it matter? Let them kill him."

"It fucking matters." I watched the soldiers leave the van and break down the barricaded front door. More gunfire erupted. "I'm going for it—"

"Bastien."

I took off, sprinting between the cars, avoiding the gunfire that rained down because I was too fast. I zipped left then right, evading their aim until I reached the front with the other soldiers.

I took cover and caught my breath, squatted on the ground with my gun in hand.

Godric appeared from the other side, as if he'd taken a different path.

"You didn't have to come."

He watched the soldiers break down the door and kill Ivan's men. "Yes, I did."

They moved in and swarmed the building, and I followed behind them with Godric, clearing the building like we were other members of the team. There were three floors, but several different office spaces and conference rooms, a building up for lease that no one occupied.

It was like finding a needle in a haystack.

I wasn't on the comms system with the rest of the team, but I knew that wouldn't be the best way to speak with Martin, so I called him directly, standing in one of the hallways.

"Bastien, this is a government matter now, so you can stand down."

Godric stood with his gun lowered, watching the hallway in case we encountered company.

"I need to kill this guy, Martin."

"Luca briefed me. He'll be executed."

"You don't understand. I *need* to kill him."

After a beat, he spoke. "They've pinned him down to the northwest corner. Top floor."

"Thank you." I hung up then headed upstairs and caught up with the guys who were continuing to break down doors and get closer to the rat trapped in a corner. When they reached the last door, it was barricaded, so they broke it down with a battering ram and shoved aside all the furniture there.

But we got there too late.

Ivan had already hanged himself. He dangled from the chandelier in the center of the ceiling.

One of the guys cut him down, and he hit the floor. No life-saving measures were taken. No CPR or epinephrine. If he could have been revived, no one bothered.

I stood over him and watched him lying there, his eyes open and his skin pale, like he'd been dead for at least a couple minutes. I was robbed of my revenge, robbed of the sick pleasure I was owed.

I grabbed my pistol from the back of my jeans and shot him in the face.

Shot him again.

And again.

Shot him until he didn't have a fucking face.

The guys didn't stop me.

Godric just watched.

I fired until the barrel was empty.

He was gone and the fight was over, but I felt empty inside. I didn't save Fleur, and I didn't avenge her either. The rat chose to die like a coward rather than face me, rather than face my wrath like a man.

Godric came to my side and placed a hand on my shoulder. "It's over."

"For him," I said. "But it'll never be over for me."

———

Luca picked up on the first ring. "I saw the whole thing on the news."

"He hanged himself before I got there. But I shot his face off."

The news was audible in the background, like the TV was still on. "It's done. All that matters."

After the sight of Fleur's face, it wasn't enough. I'd planned to kill Ivan with my bare hands. Most organized crime and gangs worked against the government, not with them, so I had an unfair advantage in that respect. Without President Martin's intervention, it would have been harder and longer to capture Ivan, to scare off his supporters once he felt our wrath. It was an asset, but right now, it felt like a pain in the ass.

I could have gotten to him on my own—if I'd had the opportunity.

"How is she?" I asked.

"She's fine. Staring at me with puppy-dog eyes right now."

"Bring her home. I'm on my way."

"On it."

"And stick around. I need to talk to you."

Luca paused for a moment as he let the silence linger. "I knew this was coming…"

———

When I got home, Luca was downstairs waiting for me.

Fleur must have gone upstairs to give us a moment to talk.

He stood there with his arms crossed over his chest, his eyes guarded like he didn't want to have this conversation.

I stared at him and tried to find the words, but maybe the words were unnecessary. He knew my intentions just by looking at me, seeing the heartbreak in my eyes. My life was forever changed by what had happened, and that didn't need to be explained, not to Luca. "You've got this, man."

He gave a quiet sigh as he directed his stare elsewhere.

"We knew this would happen eventually. And at least it's not happening because I'm dead."

"I know. Just won't be the same."

"We both know you've been after my job this whole time." I forced a smile, trying to cheer him up, even though I needed to be cheered up myself.

He smiled too, but it was clearly forced. "You caught me."

I shook his hand and clapped him on the shoulder. "Thank you."

He offered a slight shrug.

"What will you do with the traitors?"

"Wait, you're done, like, now?"

"Immediate retirement."

"Jesus." He gave a sigh. "Just got the job, man. Haven't thought that far ahead."

"Good luck."

"Thanks." Power had been exchanged and the conversation had finished. But he stayed like he had more to say and didn't know how to say it. "We're still gonna go to Holybelly together on Sundays, right?"

I smirked. "Of course."

"And we're still gonna drink?"

"Absolutely."

"Good," he said. "Just wanted to make sure."

20

FLEUR

Bastien wasn't himself, even when a week had come and gone.

He didn't look at me the same, like the bruises were too painful to bear. Only when they started to fade did he behave more like himself. He was home with me every day, slept through the night beside me, worked out in the morning before he had breakfast with me. We didn't talk about what had happened. It seemed like he wasn't ready for that.

We lay together in bed, naked under the sheets, his skin fiery to the touch because he was still warm after doing all the work just moments before. But he was never hot enough to push me away and cool off.

I traced his jawline with my fingers, feeling the coarse hairs of his beard. "How are you?"

He hiked my leg over his hip, his hand on my ass. He didn't

address the question, sidestepped it with his silence like he didn't want to confront it.

"If you want to go back, you can—"

"I have no desire to go back."

He seemed distant and withdrawn, carrying a depression so heavy I could see it weigh down his shoulders. "Then tell me what bothers you."

"What bothers me?" he asked. "It fucking hurts to look at you. That's what bothers me."

"I'm fine, Bastien. It's already healed so much."

"Doesn't matter. I failed as a man when I let it happen in the first place."

"You did not fail me," I said gently.

"I did. If Godric hadn't gotten there, you would have been entirely on your own. I wasn't coming, Fleur. I was trapped in a warehouse fifty miles away, and it would have been literally impossible for me to save you. I promised I wouldn't let anything happen to you…and I broke that promise."

We finally had our lives together, finally had the peace that we desired, but it was destroyed by his disgust in himself. "That night we had dinner at Jules Verne…and I walked out. I left because I was scared of your world."

"As you should have been. I wish you hadn't come back."

That hurt more than when I'd been punched in the face. "I came back because I chose this life with you. I knew the risks but chose to stay. You put this all on yourself and forget that I was an equal participant. When I drowned, I still chose to stay. I chose to risk that all over again because the alternative was unthinkable."

He continued to stare at me, but his eyes were so hard and vicious. "I made you feel like shit for leaving."

"I forgive you."

"I don't deserve your forgiveness."

"*Bastien.*" I didn't want any more of this self-loathing. Didn't want any more of this distance and coldness. "We've made it to the other side. We're here now. I don't want to think about the past when I'm so excited about our present and our future. I know it's hard, but you need to let it go."

"I never let anything go."

"I know." I cupped his face. "But I need you to let this go. Because we finally have the life that I wanted, and I want to enjoy every second of it because forever will go by so fast."

He closed his eyes like I'd said the perfect thing to halt his rage. He released a quiet sigh, let out his frustration and despair.

"It's okay." I moved my fingers into his hair, wanting my man back with me, wanting his blue eyes and his smile and the warmth he gave me with just a look.

He inhaled a breath before he opened his eyes again, looking at me with a sharper stare, a hardness that wasn't angry, just focused. "At least I have the rest of my life to make it up to you."

———

I went to his mother's house several times a week, and together, we planned the wedding. A wedding normally took place a year after the engagement, but since we both wanted to be married now, and Bastien had a lot of connections with pretty much everyone in Paris, I was able to book everything I wanted with just six weeks' notice.

I didn't ask his mom for help because I needed it, just because I wanted to spend time with her, to deepen that relationship with her since she would be my mother-in-law. I'd been close with Adrien's parents, and I would always have love for them as long as I lived, but now, Bastien and his family would be my family.

My forever family.

Bastien had no interest in the wedding planning. Just gave me a list of all the people he wanted to invite, which included President Martin, several members of the Senate, and then all the criminals he knew from his time as the Butcher. I only had a few friends to invite, so pretty much the entire guest list was on his side.

One night, his mother invited us over for dinner, and when we walked inside, Godric was already there because he'd been invited too.

I'd barely spoken to Godric. He was definitely the strong and silent type, but I felt perfectly comfortable around him because of what he'd done for me. Instead of hitting him with a bunch of questions and forced conversation, I chose to mirror his energy so he would feel at ease around me.

His mother was so beside herself at the sight of them together in the same room that she broke into sobs before she pulled both of her sons in for a single hug, the two of them towering over her.

The brothers didn't hug each other, but Bastien gave him a pat on the shoulder.

"I just can't believe it." His mother pulled away, her hand over her heart. "Both of my sons here. One of my boys is getting married. I wish your father were here to see this."

Bastien and Godric exchanged a look, but it was fleeting.

"Mom, did you invite your boyfriend?" Bastien asked.

"Boyfriend?" Godric asked.

"You didn't hear?" Bastien asked. "She's got some art collector boyfriend named Pierre."

"He's not my boyfriend," she said quickly. "But yes, he'll be joining us."

Bastien exchanged another look with Godric then winked.

Godric smirked back, like they wordlessly agreed to a plan to interrogate the fuck out of this guy.

The butler entered the room and announced the arrival of Pierre before he walked off.

His mother was in a purple dress with high heels that showed how lithe and agile she was. "Be on your best behavior, boys."

Pierre stepped into the room in slacks and a matching vest with a collared shirt, looking very refined, just like Bastien's mother. He gave her the warmest smile before he kissed each one of her cheeks.

"Pierre, thank you so much for coming." She walked with him up to Bastien and Godric, six-foot-something men who were intimidating to the most ruthless criminals. "It's my pleasure to introduce both of my sons." Her eyes watered when she looked at them, like there truly was no greater pleasure than the sight of the two of them. "Godric and Bastien."

Bastien shook his hand first. "Pleasure to meet you."

Godric shook his hand as well but said nothing.

"So," Bastien said. "What are your intentions with our mother?"

"Bastien." His mother swatted him on the arm. "You're ridiculous."

"Just a question," Bastien said. "He's a man, he can handle it. And if he can't, he can leave."

His mother had been beaming a moment ago, and now, she looked mortified. "Let's sit down and eat."

"It's okay," Pierre said, chuckling like he found this whole thing amusing. "They're good sons, looking after you." He gently patted her arm before he addressed Bastien. "It's been a long time since I lost my wife, and all I desired was companionship. But that companionship has blossomed into something more...probably because your mother is such an exceptional woman." He looked at her as he said all that, like he truly was enamored of her beauty and elegance.

Bastien smirked as he watched the two of them. "Good answer, Pierre." He made his hand into a fist and gently fist-bumped him.

Pierre chuckled before he reciprocated.

"Okay," his mother said. "Let's end this soap opera and have dinner."

We had a long dinner and chatted for hours.

Bastien and Pierre were still locked in an extensive conversation about art and politics while Delphine listened at the head of the table.

Godric had stepped into the sitting room and lit up a cigar by the fire, like his social meter had expired.

I joined him, taking the seat across from him.

He took a couple puffs to get the tip to burn and the smoke to rise in a cloud. Then he looked at me across from him before he reached inside his coat pocket and held out a cigar for me to enjoy.

"No thanks. I quit smoking."

He returned it to his pocket and smoked in silence, his attention on the fireplace, his aura calm and borderline indifferent. He was very unlike his brother, a complete enigma.

"I'm glad you and Bastien are talking again," I said, trying to take a stab at conversation.

His eyes shifted back to me, and he stared for a while.

"I hope you and I can have a relationship too."

He smoked his cigar and continued his stare. "I'm not pleasant company, if I'm being honest."

"Well, I already like you, so you don't have to try to be pleasant company." He'd already earned my love and loyalty when he'd shown up and shot those guys in the head. He'd spared me from a horror I wouldn't have recovered from. Bastien wouldn't have been able to go on either. Our relationship would be permanently altered.

He released the smoke from his mouth then a slight smile moved over his lips. "That makes it easy."

I looked at the fire for a while, trying to find something to say to him, but he was harder to pierce than Luca. Luca's front was just an act, but I could tell that Godric was exactly what he seemed. "I was wondering…if you would walk me down the aisle?"

His eyes immediately flicked to mine at the question.

"I don't have any family. It's just me."

He let the smoke rise from his cigar as he held it.

"And I know you'll be my brother, so..." I didn't want to force it. Didn't want to make him uncomfortable. Didn't want to burden him with a job he didn't want.

He was quiet for a long time, so long it seemed like he might ignore the inquiry altogether. "I can do that."

"Yeah?" I asked, unable to restrain my enthusiasm.

He nodded. "Sure."

21

BASTIEN

It was the night before the wedding.

Fleur wasn't going to be staying elsewhere for the night, not when I didn't believe in that traditional bullshit. I would fuck her before bed like usual. In the morning, she would leave and get ready in another part of the house, and then we would meet at the gardens to marry.

I spent my last night as a bachelor at my brother's house, smoking with him in the drawing room, the two of us reminiscing with some good memories but mostly bad ones.

He sat with the cigar burning between his fingertips, in the dim light from the chandelier that hung overhead. "It doesn't matter now, but where did you dump his body?"

I could tell that had been on his mind awhile. He just didn't want to ask.

"Wrapped it in plastic and threw it in the dumpster outside my building." I took a drag and let out the smoke like the cloud was packed with my sins.

"And no one noticed?"

"He'd only been dead for a couple hours by the time the garbage trucks came to empty it. And I wrapped him really well, so the smell was probably contained for at least a week afterward. By then, he would have already been in a furnace or a landfill." It was ruthless and barbaric, to treat the man who had sired me with cruelty. But at the time, I hadn't had many options. "It wasn't intentional, just the resources I had at the time." His grave in the cemetery was empty. The tombstone was a eulogy to a man who wasn't even there.

"Not once did I suspect you."

"I knew no one would." Because they underestimated me. Everyone did.

Godric looked away, but not in anger. "Do you ever think of telling her?"

My eyes focused on the cigar because the guilt suddenly gnawed at my flesh. "Sometimes."

He let the conversation drop when I didn't say more.

"What's next for you?"

"Business as usual," he said as he released the smoke. "But in accordance with the Fifth Republic. Luca has already stopped by to do his checks."

In six weeks, I'd been replaced, my legacy replaced by a new French Emperor, but I knew the transition wouldn't have been so smooth if Luca weren't so capable of the position. Everyone already knew him, already respected him. I'd turn into a friend…or someone they used to know.

"Is this really enough for you?" he asked.

"This?"

"Retirement. Domestication. Monogamy."

I wasn't surprised by his incredulity, because I'd had the same opinion not too long ago. I'd said I would never leave my job for anyone, especially a woman. Didn't think I'd meet anyone who would make settling down somehow exciting. "The thrills and adrenaline are still there, just in a new way. After the wedding, we're going to travel for a few months. I want to take her through Italy and Greece."

He nodded. "Nice honeymoon."

"Yeah."

"So, you're gonna do the kid thing too?"

"At some point."

He watched me like he expected me to say more, but he didn't want to push.

"I don't think I'm fit to be a parent, but I'll try my damnedest to do a good job."

"What makes you say that?"

"Well, I killed my own father and dumped his body in the garbage, so…"

"But that wasn't by choice," he said. "You've always been the good one, Bastien. You've always been the one to fight for those who can't fight for themselves. Stand your ground when it would be far easier just to cave. I see the way you love Fleur, so you're definitely capable of caring for another person."

It was the nicest thing he'd ever said to me.

"I think you'd be a good dad—if that's what you want."

I looked at the fireplace and kept a straight face, unsure how to accept his kindness. "Dad didn't want me…and I'm afraid I won't want them." I couldn't look at him as I said it. Hadn't even said that to Fleur.

He stared at me.

I couldn't see his stare, but I could feel it hot on my flesh.

"Dad was a fucking asshole. He was a psychopath who only cared about money and power and getting more money and power. He didn't give a shit about us as people, but free labor. He didn't care about Mom. He'd cheat on her all the time. I'm like him in more ways than I want to admit—but you are nothing like him."

I finally found the courage to look at him again.

"You'll be fine, Bastien."

The butler let me into the house then ushered me into the drawing room. Over the fireplace was an old family portrait, the four of us together, Godric and I almost teenagers at the time. I stared at it and felt the racing of my heart. It was a Maserati on the racetrack.

My mother entered the room behind me. "Bastien, is everything okay?"

I stared at the picture a moment longer before I manned up and faced her.

She must have seen my crestfallen expression because she stepped forward and grabbed my arms. "Honey, what is it?"

I gently guided her hands away, unable to accept my mother's love right now.

She grew more upset. "It's natural to get cold feet. I felt the exact same way before my wedding. But just take a couple breaths—"

"It's not that." Fleur was the only thing in my life I never had to doubt. But everyone else, including myself, was cast in the shadows of unease. The only doubt I possessed was wondering if I deserved her at all.

"Then what is it?"

I'd decided to keep this from her for years, said it was for her own good because she couldn't handle this secret. But it was just an excuse to hide the truth, just an excuse to pretend to be something I wasn't. I was always good to her, always took care of her, and I wondered if I'd done those things out of guilt rather than genuine desire. "Mom, there's something I need to tell you."

"Okay...I'm listening."

"Let's sit." I moved to the seating area and dropped onto one of the couches.

Even though it was late, she was still dressed and in full makeup, like she didn't allow herself to relax until she was about to put her head on the pillow.

Her hands were together in her lap, and she looked so scared that to an onlooker, they would assume I was there to kill her.

I suspected she wouldn't come to the wedding tomorrow. I suspected we might never speak again. But I had to tell her. Had to come clean and accept the consequences of my actions. "Dad stopped by my apartment before he died."

She stiffened when she heard what I said, her eyes big and round, like an owl in the dark. "He never told me that."

Because he didn't tell anybody.

"Did you two make up—"

"No. We got into a fight. He told me he hadn't wanted to have another kid, but you made him do it. Said I was a disappointment. Said he regretted having me." That was the easier part to say because I'd accepted that cold, hard truth already.

"That's not true, Bastien. He didn't mean that."

"It's okay, Mom. Your love has been more than enough. It's easily been the equivalent of two parents."

Her eyes watered like that either hurt her…or meant the world to her.

"He said he wished he'd never had me, and I said I wished he was dead, and it turned into a fight. He reached for his gun but—"

"Oh my god." Her hands immediately cupped her mouth, and she choked back her sob. "Oh my god…"

I ignored her cries and continued on. "But I got it first, and I shot him."

Her hands completely covered her face, and she sobbed, her chest heaving as she pictured the scene.

"I'm sorry."

She wailed in the silence, wailed like he'd been shot in this very room.

I didn't feel better, but at least I felt honorable. "I thought you deserved to know the truth." I left the couch and headed out of the room, listening to her cry behind me, knowing I was a monster. I'd taken her husband away. I'd broken up her family. I was responsible for every bad thing that had happened.

"Bastien." She stifled her sobs. "Wait."

I halted but didn't turn around, afraid of the look on her face, afraid of the slap coming my way.

"Bastien." Her footsteps grew louder behind me.

I took a breath before I faced her, saw the havoc the tears had wreaked on her makeup, saw a woman irreparably broken by my confession.

She took a breath and forced her tears to steady before she reached for my hands. She squeezed them.

And I didn't understand. Didn't understand anything at all.

"Bastien." Tears dripped down her face. "I know your father was a cruel man, but I didn't know just how cruel… You didn't deserve that, and I'm sorry that I didn't do better, that I didn't protect you and Godric, that I didn't leave…like Fleur left. You're so loved, Bastien. You and Godric are the single most important things to me, and I love you more than words could ever convey." She gripped my hands together in hers and squeezed them to her chest. "I'm sorry, baby. I'm so sorry."

"Mom…" I'd murdered my own father, but she treated me like the victim.

"It's okay, Bastien," she said. "You did the right thing. I can live without him, but I could never live without you."

22

FLEUR

I stood before the mirror and looked at myself in my gown, white with little straps over the shoulders and an opening in the front to show my cleavage. When I saw the price tag, I almost didn't get it because I would never spend that much on a dress. Might as well buy a car at that point.

But then I remembered Bastien would want me to have whatever I wanted, so I handed over his credit card.

Delphine came into the room behind me, and within the first glance, she glowed like I was really her daughter. She came up behind me and squeezed my shoulders. "My son is going to lose it." She smiled at me in the reflection. "Everyone is seated and ready for you, honey. Nervous?"

"No." I wasn't nervous at all. It was my second marriage, just months after my first divorce, but this felt different. "Not at all."

"Good. I was a nervous wreck when I got married. Should

have known what that meant." She gave me a sad smile and stepped away. "It's such a beautiful day. You got lucky."

"How's Bastien?"

"Happier than I've ever seen him. Smoking and drinking with his boys."

I smirked. "Of course he is." The only person more certain of this than me was him.

"He's a good man. And you're a good woman. I'm glad you found each other."

"Me too. Your son means a lot to me."

"I know he does. I appreciate your standing by him, even when things got tough."

The door opened, and Godric stepped inside, looking somehow like a younger version of his brother because he was less bulky. He was in a suit and tie, and he immediately gave me a restrained glance over. "Bastien said to hurry up, so let's go."

Of course he did. "Alright." I grabbed the bouquet of flowers and took his arm. He guided me through the palace, the very place where Bastien had taken me as a date to a social event and I'd tried to run because everything had moved too fast. He'd cornered me by the bathroom until he'd gotten what he wanted.

And now, he got what he wanted again—in the same place.

We moved down the hallway to the double doors that led to the gardens, rows of hundreds of people facing the flowered trellis behind Bastien and Luca at his side. When the doors opened, the music hit me from the four-piece string quartet.

Then everyone rose to look at me.

My stomach was in my throat, and Godric's arm suddenly felt like a life raft in the middle of the ocean. I used him for balance as I walked forward on the highest heels I could buy, wanting to look Bastien in the eye when I married him. I didn't grow nervous easily, but when five hundred people stared at me, I felt weak. My dress felt heavy, my train like a burden.

But then I looked up at him—and all those fears faded away.

Because he looked at me like I was the prize he'd earned, the trophy he would display on his mantel, the beautiful rose he'd gardened through all the seasons until it bloomed. With the handsome smile on his lips and deep affection in his eyes, it was as if no one else was there but us. It was the way he looked at me when he came home from work, the way his eyes softened before he kissed me on the hairline, the look of a man not deep in lust, but deep in love.

I smiled back and couldn't wait to get there.

We finally made it after what felt like an eternity, and instead of taking me by the hand, he circled me with his big arms and squeezed me hard, his chin resting on my head, and he held me there for a second before he kissed me on the forehead.

I melted.

He took my hand, and we faced each other before the priest, ready to declare our undying love for each other before God and the five hundred people gathered to bear witness to our union.

He continued to look at me the same way, the most handsome man I'd ever seen, eyes bluer than the goddamn sky. He'd shaved, so his jawline was smooth, and the shadow along his mouth was even more distinct.

The priest continued, and I mouthed, "You're so hot."

He smirked, and the twinkle that moved into his eyes was pure joy.

We didn't exchange rings because I already had mine, and he'd inked his days before to make sure it was healed for the big day. So we took each other, there under the Paris sky with the Eiffel Tower in view, and promised to love each other forever.

The reception at the Four Seasons was a big blowout, everyone drinking and partying, having the best time of their lives. I'd never seen Bastien dance, but he moved on the dance floor like it was yet another thing he was good at.

The party went until two in the morning, and most of the guests were still there when the party ended. The lights flicked on, and people began to grab their jackets and coats to prepare to depart.

Bastien wrapped his tux jacket around my shoulders. "I'll be right back, sweetheart." He said goodbye to a friend and his wife, and what should have been a brief departure turned into a long conversation.

I stepped into the hallway, keeping the jacket tight around my body to stay warm.

"Sad it's over?" Luca appeared, drunk in the eyes like he'd had a great time.

"Not as sad as you, I think," I teased. "I get to go home to Bastien and see him naked. The rest of you don't."

He chuckled. "I've already seen him naked, so you can't hold that over me."

"Why have you seen him naked?" I asked.

He shrugged. "Long story."

"It shouldn't be that long."

He rubbed the back of his head and gave a quiet chuckle. "Something I've been meaning to tell you. Bastien didn't want any speeches, so I didn't get to say it then, but...the two of us got a drink together months ago. This was before he asked you to move in, before things got super serious."

"Okay."

"He said he knew you were going to be his wife. Said he knew you were the one."

I'd never understood Bastien's love for me, but I would

never question it, not when it was the greatest thing that had ever happened to me.

"I told him he was crazy, that he barely knew you, but he told me he just fucking knew. And he wanted me to tell you that on your wedding day."

I felt my eyes soften so much they actually ached. "I know how lucky I am, Luca." I knew that any woman would resort to any deception to have what I had, the unwavering love and loyalty of a man like him.

"I think he's luckier, if I'm being honest with you." He came close and gave me a one-armed hug. "Congratulations."

"Thank you. See you later."

"See you later." He walked off and disappeared into the crowd of people.

Bastien returned, his arm moving around my waist before he pulled me in close for a quick kiss on the mouth. "Ready, sweetheart? It's raining, so I'll bring the car around."

"It's raining?"

"Yeah."

I loved the sunshine, loved the fact that I could wear this dress without being cold, but I loved the rain the way I loved my husband. "Can we walk?"

"You want to walk home in the rain?" he asked, slightly amused.

"Yes." I loved it when he smelled like the rain, when his hair was slightly damp, when the scent was heavy on his clothes. It reminded me of those nights together, in my bed or in his house, sitting outside in cafés or when we'd left the bar after my shift. It was special to me. "Then when we get home, we can warm up in front of the fire…"

He kissed me again then took me by the hand, a smile on his face and happiness in his eyes. "Let's do it, sweetheart."

EPILOGUE

BASTIEN

I spoke to Pierre in the sitting room.

"You know how she is," he said. "The most stubborn woman I've ever met."

"Oh, I know."

"I love her that way, but sometimes it works against me."

I nodded.

"I think it's time for both of us to go into assisted living. I found a really nice place in the Loire Valley, but she won't even consider it. Too proud to admit the stairs are too much. Too proud to admit she doesn't need all this space. She says she's too young."

"I think she doesn't fully understand what assisted living can be."

"I agree," he said. "I think it's better to make the move now than when it really is too hard. Do you think you could talk to her for me?"

I nodded. "I'll give it a try, Pierre."

"Dad?"

I looked over my shoulder to see him across the room, looking at an old family photo over the fireplace. I turned back to Pierre. "I'll have dinner with her this week. And if that doesn't work, Godric can give it a try."

"Thank you, Bastien."

I stood up and gave him a quick hug before I joined my son across the room, who continued to look at my old family portrait. The last time I'd really looked at it had been the night I'd told my mother what I'd done to my father. It kinda blurred into the background after that. We all smiled in the picture—but it was a fucking lie. "What is it, Bruce?" My son was fifteen and in secondary school. He'd received high marks ever since he started school, and all his teachers said he was bright. I wasn't sure if he got that from me or Fleur, or perhaps neither. Perhaps he just had a better environment than either of us ever did.

"Why don't we ever talk about him?"

"My father?" It was true. I never mentioned him, and neither did my mother. He'd just faded out of our lives. A couple years ago, my mother had asked me for more details about our childhood, like what he'd done to me and Godric when she wasn't around. I'd watched her revere his memory then hate his ghost.

"Yeah." Bruce looked at me, having my blue eyes but his mother's dark hair. He was a good-looking boy, and once he became a man, he would have his pick of the crop. He'd be smart enough to pursue anything he wanted. Handsome enough to charm his way into and out of any situation. Fleur had given me a son, but she'd also given me a daughter too, but she was home with her mother. "I call Pierre my grandpa, but I guess he's not."

"He is." He was a better grandfather than my father would have been if he'd lived. Our whole lives would be completely different. "You can have more than one."

"Whenever I asked Grandma about him, she changes. It's like she doesn't want to talk about him. How did he die? Did he get sick?"

I didn't want to lie to my son, but I didn't want to tell him his father was a murderer. "We don't talk about him because he wasn't a good man, Bruce. He did a lot of hurtful things to me, your grandmother, Uncle Godric. Family is everything, but it takes more than blood to make a family. That's why I say Pierre is your grandfather, because he loves you like his own. That's what counts."

Within the last year, Bruce had become more interested in family ties and previous generations after taking a genetics class in school. He became interested in genealogy. I was afraid one day he would figure out how we'd earned our family fortune. He would figure out my father was a criminal—and I had been a bigger one. "What did he do to you, Dad?"

I looked into his blue eyes, eyes identical to mine, and felt my heart skip a beat.

Because I loved him so much.

When he was born, our lives were upside down, even with a nanny and doula, and the adjustment was hard on me. I never complained, just supported Fleur in every way that I could. The attachment wasn't there at first. He was just a baby who went through twenty diapers a day.

But then…it changed.

I became a father, and I couldn't imagine my life any other way.

When my daughter was born, I was pumped. I was so freakin' excited. Excited to have a little girl and give Bruce a sibling.

It took time for me to be who I was, but it happened, and I could never look at my son and think, even for a fucking second, that he was unwanted. That he wasn't enough. That he was a disappointment.

"It doesn't matter." I put my hand on his shoulder, and I gave it a squeeze. "It's best to let things go and be happy. I learned that the hard way." I pulled him in and gave him a quick kiss on the side of the head, like he was still a boy. "Let's pick up some pizza and head home. You know how your mother gets when she's hungry."

He laughed. "Not as angry as you, Dad."

The Fifth Republic Series continues with Luca's story in *The Emperor*. Flip to the end of this book to read the first few chapters of his story and **preorder it now**.

If you're looking for something new to read while you wait for *The Emperor*, I've got another mafia romance with a golden retriever that falls first and hard for the woman he's forbidden to touch. Read ***It Kills Me*** now!

For those who are looking for a dark romance about a *very* morally grey alpha with black cat vibes where the MMC makes the FMC earn her freedom, read ***Buttons and Lace*** now.

And for my romantasy readers, I also write dark fantasy romance under Penelope Barsetti. My newest release is ***The Death King***, a necromancer intent on revenge...and will unalive anyone who touches his woman.

Fifth Republic Special Editions

I'm so excited to announce the Fifth Republic Special Editions! These stunning hardcovers are designed for diehard fans like you. These Special Editions also come with exclusive content -- additional epilogue chapters with Fleur and Bastien!

Preorder now!

Follow Pene...

On the G: **@penelopeskyauthor**

And TikTok: **@penelopeskyauthor**

Sign up for Penelope's newsletter to hear all her fun stories and stay up to date on new releases. There's also giveaways and access to limited edition hardbacks!

THE EMPEROR - CHAPTER 1

Aliénor

It was midnight when I finished my shift as a sommelier at Septime. The bottles were wiped down and returned to the case, and the wine glasses were dried by hand before being hung on the rack. It was a small restaurant with only a handful of tables, but the cramped atmosphere added to the charm.

I put on my long black coat and threw the rose-colored scarf around my neck before I stepped into the cold. The restaurant was on a narrow one-way street, and most of the other businesses were already closed. There were normally pedestrians on the sidewalks at all hours of the night, but it was quiet in the city in late winter. Spring was in the distance, close enough to see but not close enough to touch.

I headed down the street toward my apartment, my heels making a distinct tap against the cold stone of the sidewalk.

With my bag drawn close, I glanced at my phone to check the time before I stowed it in my pocket once again.

My chin lifted, and I noticed a man across the street, smoking a cigar, dressed in all black with a black beanie, looking at me like he knew who I was.

I quickly looked ahead and pretended I hadn't noticed his silent aggression.

I walked everywhere in Paris. Taxis and ride-hailing services were way too expensive for a bottom-feeder like me. I was a sommelier because I'd grown up privileged—but that was a long time ago.

I'd been poor so long I forgot what it was like to be rich.

Another set of footsteps accompanied mine, and I knew he was following me. I noticed the way the sound changed when he left the sidewalk and stepped onto the cobblestones. His legs were so much longer than mine, his stride would quickly catch up to me.

"Shit," I said under my breath.

I kept my head down, kept a low profile, did everything I could to be a nobody.

But he'd kept his word and sought me out—even years later. Hell-bent on revenge that shouldn't be my debt to pay, determined to add my head to one of the spikes outside his castle, desperate to fill his glass with the last drops of my family's blood.

I finally reached the end of the narrow street, the sidewalk opening to other shops under the lampposts, all closed early in the off-season. A couple cars passed on the street, but it was mostly empty.

There was only a single car, a blacked-out Range Rover with midnight-black rims and blacked-out tinted windows. A muscular man stepped away from one of the shops and headed toward the Range Rover. The side-view mirrors immediately popped open at his approach like it was his vehicle, and he hit the button on the key fob before he came into my sight.

I didn't have time to think.

Just before he opened the driver's door, I sprinted down the stone pathway next to the trees and the park bench, aware that my assailant was in pursuit even though I couldn't hear his boots in my hustle.

I threw open the passenger door and jumped inside. "Fucking drive!" I slammed the passenger door shut and hit the lock button—like that would stop a bullet from shattering the window. I turned to the driver and expected to have to yell or explain, but he hit the gas and took off down the empty road, his powerful engine making us accelerate with the speed of the wind.

I turned back to stare at the man who had pursued me and then heard shots fired, hitting the back window of the Range Rover. Two little cracks appeared in the glass, but it somehow didn't break. "Fuck." I faced forward again and glanced at the driver.

He was calm, almost indifferent.

The light at the intersection was red, but he turned left on Rue du Faubourg Saint-Antoine like it was just a normal day. He dropped his speed, like he believed the gunman would never be able to track us on foot.

Once the immediate danger had passed, I looked at the driver of my getaway car.

Dark hair and dark eyes, his muscular arms stretching the sleeves of his long-sleeved shirt, he was the definition of calm and collected. An Omega watch was on his wrist, the kind worth over one hundred thousand euros, and the only reason I knew that was because my father used to have one very similar. A shadow was along his jawline, like he had to shave every morning to keep a clean look, but the darkness was back by midnight.

One hand remained on the wheel while he relaxed in the seat, eyes on the road. "Where to?"

In shock, I stared for a solid three seconds. "That's it? No questions?"

"Your business is your business."

"You aren't going to demand that I pay for your back window?"

He had a relaxed grip on the wheel, the light from the center console basking his face in a glow. "It served its purpose."

"But at your expense."

He came to another red light, but this time, he obeyed the law and stopped. He turned to look at me for the first time, and I was stunned by what I saw.

The most gorgeous man I'd ever seen.

Ruthless eyes that were as unforgiving as the underworld. Hard and chiseled bones in his face. Cords up his tight neck. Masculinity so potent it was toxic to breathe. It was hard to gauge his height when he was seated, but I could tell he would tower over me greater than the Eiffel Tower over Paris. And he was thick like a slab of meat. Not just his arms but his shoulders and his chest...everything.

He continued his stare like he'd asked a question.

I was as immobilized by his gaze as if it were a loaded gun. One blink and my life would be over.

"Where to?" he repeated.

The light remained red for what felt like an eternity. The intersection was deserted, but he kept his foot on the brake anyway. The city was quiet until the sound of sirens came from somewhere in the far distance, an ambulance passing through the streets to a civilian in need.

His coffee-colored eyes continued to bore into mine.

I remained speechless.

He looked ahead once more. "You've got nowhere to go."

My apartment wasn't safe. Someone was probably already sitting in my living room with a loaded gun, just waiting for me to walk in so they could execute me. Or hidden behind the door so I'd walk in and they'd end my life with a silencer attached to the barrel.

"Too proud to ask but too desperate to pretend." His blinker hadn't been on and he was in the lane to go straight, but he suddenly turned to the right and ran the red once he had a destination. "You can stay with me for a couple days."

"Some man just tried to kill me. What if he follows me?"

"He won't."

"You don't know what I'm involved with. The men who want me dead are dangerous—"

He chuckled like I'd made some kind of joke.

"I'm serious."

"I know." His smile continued for a moment, the lights from the lampposts we passed reflecting in his eyes. "I'm not worried about it. And if I'm not worried about it, you shouldn't be either."

Who the fuck was this guy? "Who are you?"

"Luca Fournier."

"That didn't answer my question."

He continued to drive with one hand on the wheel, relaxed and casual, like his heart rate hadn't elevated once during this adventure. "My business is my business."

"What if you're dangerous—"

"I'm very fucking dangerous." He made another turn and entered the 6th arrondissement, one of the most luxurious parts of the city, where apartments were in the millions and entire buildings were owned by celebrities and politicians and aristocrats, the other ultrawealthy. "But not to people like you."

"People like me?"

"Women. Children. Innocents."

"How do you know I'm innocent?" I watched the buildings go by, remembering a childhood spent among the elite, extravagant parties with fancy canapés and expensive champagne.

"Just a hunch." He slowed the car when he approached iron gates that were thirty feet high, the crest of a garden in the center. They gently swung apart at his approach, and he waited until they were fully open before he entered the property.

A small driveway lined with cobblestone emerged into a roundabout with a fountain in the center. He came to a stop in front of double doors with two potted trees on either side, like this used to be the entrance to a hotel. Men flanked the door with rifles.

My spike of adrenaline was instantaneous.

Luca exited the car, and one of the guys got in. One of the guys with a rifle opened my door for me, like some kind of gentleman.

I stepped out and tried not to look like I'd just swallowed a bug.

Luca didn't wait for me as he approached the double doors that opened for him like he was a king.

I followed and entered a majestic entryway as high as the gate outside. Full of Parisian artwork and enormous statues, it looked like the lobby of a luxurious hotel before it became a personal asset to this enigmatic man.

A butler appeared in a tuxedo, hands behind his back. He said nothing, just emerged and waited for orders. He glanced at me, dark hair slicked back with gel, a thick mustache across the top of his mouth. He looked at me like he didn't know what to make of me but didn't dare ask.

Luca had just texted on his phone before he looked at his butler. "Prepare the guest room for—" He turned to look at me. "Who are you?"

"Aliénor."

He looked at his butler again. "Aliénor. She'll be staying for three days."

"Of course. Anything else, sir?"

"No." Luca headed to the stairs and began to walk up.

I felt out of place in this villa, but I felt even more awkward just standing there with no purpose, so I followed him up the stairs. It wasn't just one flight of stairs, but several, three to be exact. Luca made it to the top without being winded, but I felt the tightness in my chest, probably because I wore heels.

By the time I caught up to him, he was already heading into his bedroom. "Wait." I gripped the banister as I stood with my hand on my hip, trying to catch my breath.

He turned to look at me, eyebrows slightly raised like he couldn't believe I'd issued an order.

I caught my breath enough to approach him, the stitch still in my side.

His stare continued, growing in hostility.

"Why are you doing this?"

"What?" The coldness was in his voice, expressing his annoyance candidly.

"Letting me stay here."

"Because I wasn't given a choice."

"You do have a choice. You could have just thrown me out, and to be honest, you seem like the kind of guy who would." He'd saved me, but he didn't strike me as some altruistic gentleman who would open a door for a woman or pull out the chair for her. He was complicated. That much certain.

He stared at me with that hard gaze without needing to blink. "Would you like me to throw you out?"

"No—"

"Then don't annoy me." He turned to enter his bedroom.

"Wait—"

"Tell me what to do again in my goddamn house, and your ass is on the street." He said he was no danger to me, but when he looked at me again, his eyes were like bullets. Once he squeezed the trigger, my entire body would be pumped full of lead. "You have three days. Use them wisely."

THE EMPEROR - CHAPTER 2

Aliénor

The guest bedroom was an extravagant primary suite. Parisian in every way, from the furniture to the wallpaper and the artwork, it screamed luxury in the sexiest whisper. I had large windows that showed breathtaking views of the city below and the adjacent buildings. It smelled like a garden when there wasn't a plant or flower in sight.

I knew nothing about Luca, but I knew I was untouchable here.

Even if those assholes did follow me, they wouldn't cross the threshold.

And if they tried, Luca would smile.

The butler served me breakfast at the door like room service, entering with a rollaway cart that had a small vase of roses that looked like they'd just been cut from the garden. A drop of dew was even on one of the petals. When he removed the steel lids over the dishes, he revealed an elaborate meal of eggs smothered in Gruyère cheese tucked into a crepe along with a side of French toast and bacon and a bowl of strawberries and blueberries so pristine they looked as if they had been hand-painted by Michelangelo. There was a pot of coffee and a side of cream as well.

I'd been shot at last night, and now I felt like I was on vacation. "May I speak with Luca, please?" I didn't have his number, and while his bedroom was down the hall from mine, I wouldn't dare rekindle his anger.

The butler stared at me like he didn't understand what I said.

"He just expected not to see or talk to me at all?"

He returned the lids to the plates on the cart then left my bedroom without entertaining either of my questions.

"Well, that was rude." But no amount of coldness could chase away my appetite at the sight of this feast. It was the prettiest meal I'd ever set eyes on—even more beautiful than Christmas dinner.

I ate alone, savoring the gourmet food prepared by a chef and forgetting my troubles for a while. I'd have to abandon my apartment and all my belongings because it was unsafe to return there, and now I'd have to start my life over again. New name, new paperwork, new job...everything.

Leaving Paris would be the smart move, but I loved this city too damn much to flee it. I was too stubborn to abandon my first love, the only city in the world that actually loved me back. The worst things had happened here...but the best things had happened too.

The door opened without a knock, and Luca appeared in nothing but black shorts and running shoes. Completely shirtless and bare-chested with a sheen of sweat across his beautiful skin, he looked at me with that same piercing stare.

I stilled at the sight of him and forgot how to speak again.

He stared at me as if he'd asked me a question, and the longer I didn't answer him, the more irritated he became.

"I—I wasn't expecting you to just walk in here."

"In my own house? You called for me."

I tried not to snap back because beggars couldn't be choosers, but snapping back was pretty much my entire personality. "I meant right this second. Jesus, you help me but then jump down my throat."

His eyes remained vicious. "You have my attention, and you're wasting it."

"Can we talk?"

"What the fuck are we doing?" he snapped.

"I mean like civilized people. Stop yelling at me."

Oddly enough, his anger dimmed slightly.

"You can take a shower first." I tried not to stare at anything but his eyes. Tried not to inspect the hardness I'd noticed when he was clothed. He was covered in sweat like he'd just run for five miles, but I suspected he'd been lifting in a private gym. Bars and dumbbells…and probably some cars.

To my surprise, he entered and dropped down into the seat across from me. He had wireless headphones in his ears, but he took them out and tucked them into his pocket. He crossed his thick arms over his chest and stared.

It took all my strength to look at only his eyes.

Not the popping veins in his arms. The biceps that rivaled the size of my head. The shoulders that were large like mountains. The hard pecs that looked like slabs of concrete that held up the bridges over the Seine.

He stared, eyes bright with both intelligence and annoyance.

My god, this man was beautiful. But fuck, he was ornery like a stallion that refused to wear a saddle.

I was used to receiving attention and looks from men when I was out and about. At restaurants and bars. When I was at work. If I wanted to get laid, it wasn't a struggle to find someone to share a passionate night with. But Luca stared at me like he wasn't the least bit impressed. Like I was one of many. A name not worth remembering. Like the women he bedded were far superior to anything I had to offer.

I was definitely attracted to him, but he clearly wasn't attracted to me.

It stung…a little.

His impatience shattered the silence. "What do you want from me, Eleanor?"

"Aliénor. It's pronounced with an a—"

"Get on with it."

Asshole. "First, I want to thank you for helping me last night. I'd probably be dead if you hadn't been there."

"Not probably."

Did he talk to everyone like this? "Well...thank you." It shouldn't be so hard to show gratitude to my savior, but it was like pulling my own teeth out. Shoving bamboo under my damn fingernails.

He hadn't moved. Hadn't blinked. Just stared with silent hostility. "Is that it?"

"I said thank you, and that's your reaction?"

"I didn't save you to hear your gratitude. If you want to show your appreciation, there are better ways to do it."

"Like what?" I snapped. "Because as far as I can tell, you're made of stone."

He continued that intense, unblinking stare, still as the statue I accused him of being.

I waited for an answer because I couldn't read this man if the words were written on his forehead.

"Like what?" I repeated.

He tilted his head the other way, the only movement he'd made during this interaction. "A blow job would be nice."

My eyebrows rose at the request.

Okay...maybe he was attracted to me.

"So, that's why you saved me? To demand sex from me?"

"I've demanded nothing from you," he said calmly. "You sat me down so you could thank me, and I'm just suggesting a better way to show your appreciation than taking up my time like this. It's not an obligation, just like a tip at a restaurant is not obligatory but very much appreciated."

My eyes shifted away as I scoffed at his forwardness. "Wow."

He showed no disappointment at my dismissal, like he really didn't care whether I submitted or not. He didn't seem to care about anything. "If there's nothing else, I have a long day ahead of me."

"I want to know who you are."

"What does it matter?"

"Because I want to know who I'm dealing with."

"I told you I don't hurt your kind."

"Just ask for blow jobs."

He didn't grin, but I spotted a hint of it in the corners of his mouth. A shadow of a smile. "You've already gauged what you need to know. Whoever you're afraid of is afraid of me. You have three days, now two, to plan your next move. Don't waste that precious time interrogating me."

"It wasn't an interrogation."

He relaxed his arms at his sides and revealed his full chest, the top of his hard abs. The sweat that had covered him minutes ago had already mostly evaporated. "I can give you money if you need it. Identification, paperwork, whatever."

"And you offer that to me freely?"

"Yes."

He was almost unbearable to talk to, but then he did something uncharacteristically kind. "And you don't expect a tip?"

This time, he smirked—and it made him that much more handsome. "No. But it would be appreciated."

I didn't have a plan right now. The life I'd rebuilt had been demolished in a single moment. The sentimental belongings I still had were locked up in storage because I was too afraid to keep them at my apartment. I was glad I'd had the foresight to prepare for this moment. All my clothes and possessions were now gone. The only things I had were the clothes on my back and the purse that had been on my arm. "I don't want to accept more of your help after what you've already done for me, but I'm desperate."

His smile was just a memory, and his eyes showed a shadow of empathy. "Consider it done."

Luca delivered on his promise, and his butler delivered all the paperwork and cash to my bedroom. A passport, ID, even a driver's license, even though I'd never driven a day in my life. And there was a stack of cash, at least thirty thousand euro, way more than I needed.

But I also had nothing, so I took it.

I looked at apartments online and picked a different arrondissement this time. Two million people lived in this city, and with the influx of tourists all year-round, that easily added several hundred thousand people roaming the streets. Finding someone was like finding a needle in a haystack—if you didn't know where to look.

I picked the 18th arrondissement because it was the least safe. Lots of people around on the streets all hours of the night, people coming and going, not the ideal place for a single woman on her own. They would look for me again, and that was probably the least likely place they would search.

I found a furnished apartment this time because I knew I shouldn't get attached to any physical possessions. Maybe they would find me again in a week and I'd be off once more. A traveling tourist in my own fucking city.

When the third day came, and I had my affairs in order, I knew it was time to leave. Leave this private hotel with the beautiful flowers and the sexiest asshole who ever lived. Leave the gourmet food that was delivered straight to my door like I'd ordered room service while on a fancy vacation. Leave the protection of the iron gates and the armed men outside—and the man who feared no one.

I hadn't visited the rest of the house, just stuck to my bedroom during my occupancy. When I didn't call for Luca, he didn't come to me, so I didn't see him again. I left my bedroom and took the stairs down to the very bottom where the entrance had been.

The butler was there, as if he'd heard my footsteps from the floors above. "Are you leaving residence?"

"Um, yeah." Unfortunately. These three days had been a silence in my racing mind, a gentleness in my pained heart. It was nice to have peace, just for a moment, not to look over my shoulder or sleep with one eye open.

It'd been a long time since I'd felt that way.

"Could I speak to Luca before I go?"

Both front doors opened, and he stepped inside like he'd just gotten home. He was in a long-sleeved black shirt, dark jeans, and boots, similar to the way he'd been dressed the first night I saw him. He had an air of command to his presence but also potent, don't-give-a-fuck vibes. He turned his hard gaze on me, and I noticed when his eyes settled on my face, they weren't as annoyed as they'd been in our previous interactions.

His stare seemed to be his words because he didn't speak.

"I was just leaving."

He gave a slight nod.

The butler silently excused himself and stepped through the double doors of another part of the house, maybe the kitchen or the drawing room. I had no idea because I'd only visited a minuscule part of the grand home.

"Thank you for everything."

"Take care." He never asked about the night we met. Never asked why a gunman was trying to hunt me down. Either he didn't care or he respected my privacy. I wasn't sure which it was.

"I hate to ask for anything else, but...I don't know how else to get it."

His eyes looked tired, like he'd been out all night and the day before, but they still had the sharpness of a sushi knife. They narrowed slightly as his attention on my face deepened.

"Can I have a gun?" I'd bought one before, but I'd also been scammed before, and I needed something I could count on.

Without hesitation, he lifted up his shirt and reached for the back of his jeans, showing a glimpse of his hard stomach before he handed me the gun by the barrel.

"I don't have to take yours."

"I'm not sentimental."

I took the gun, the metal warm from being pressed against his skin.

"Know how to use it?"

"Yeah." I checked the safety before I placed it in my purse. "Thank you. For everything. Seriously..." Anyone I'd been close to was dead, and anyone else who had been in my life was off-limits. The second I visited them, they would become targets. I'd been on my own for years, lonely in existence, the city my only companion.

"Need a ride?"

"No, I'm fine." I wouldn't ask him for anything else.

He pulled out his phone. "What's your number?"

I hesitated before I said it out loud.

He typed it into his phone then hit the call button. A vibration was distinct in my purse as the call went through. Then he quickly hung up and shoved his phone into his back pocket. "Call if you get into a jam."

That was surprisingly nice. He was cold as ice, but he'd given me enough money to survive without employment for a year and given me his own gun. He'd given me a place to stay when I was a stranger. "I'm sorry I called you an asshole."

After a pause, a slow smirk grew over his lips. "Never apologize for being right. Always double down."

I felt an inexplicable attachment to him, a sadness at our parting. Or maybe I just didn't want to leave the safety he provided, the way his world reminded me of mine...before it was taken away.

I felt a surge of nerves when I looked at him, seeing a man I would have pursued across the bar on a late night. A night that would have ended in fireworks, followed by a morning masked in a dreary fog. I would never see him again, so I went for it.

I moved in and gave him an instant to react, a pause in case my advance wasn't reciprocated.

But it was definitely reciprocated because he smiled.

A full-on smile, a sunrise to his twilight, an antidote to his seriousness.

I closed the distance to plant a quick and simple kiss on his lips, just a touch of our mouths, affectionate rather than sexy.

But his hand quickly cupped the back of my neck, and he turned a simmer to a boil the second the pot was on the stove. I initiated the kiss, but he took over like a pirate that commandeered another's ship. He tilted my head back where he wanted it and felt my lips with his, searing my mouth with his mark, a kiss so hot that it sizzled with smoke. He felt my bottom lip between his before he turned his head and kissed me again, this time with tongue, like I was his long-term lover rather than some woman he barely knew. Like I was the love of his life, the wife he came home to, the woman he vowed to love forever.

I pulled away first, taken aback by the intensity and the way it affected me so deeply. I'd intended to kiss him, turn on my heel, and strut out of there, but I was frozen in place for a moment, locked in the dark eyes that reminded me of the fresh coffee I had every morning.

He smirked again slightly. "Thanks for the tip."

THE EMPEROR - CHAPTER 3

Luca

I entered Loup, the restaurant on the corner of Rue Du Louvre and Rue Coquilliere. There was a moose head over the entrance to the bathrooms, and the many tables and booths were vacant at this hour. The place was open until one in the morning, and I walked in fifteen minutes before closing because no doors in Paris ever closed. Not for me, at least.

Baptiste Escoffier was already seated at the table near the window, having an espresso as if his day had only just begun. He acknowledged my presence with a steely stare. The contact didn't break as he watched me pull out the chair across from him and take a seat.

The waiter walked straight to our table and asked what I wanted.

"I'll have the same," I said without looking at him.

He walked off. Music played overhead in the empty restaurant. A car passed by the window behind him.

Baptiste took a drink of his espresso. "What are you going to do, Luca?"

I gave a sigh because I was already exhausted by the topic we hadn't even discussed yet. "I don't fucking know."

"You need to figure it out—and quickly."

"Their beef was with Bastien, not me."

"Well, that inheritance has passed on to you. Oscar's death hasn't been forgotten. The violation of the truce hasn't been forgotten."

"They were going to violate it themselves."

"Can't be proven. You struck first."

"They quickly forget that all of this started because they took Bastien's wife." They'd violated the Fifth Republic when they'd taken an innocent woman and pulled her into the shadows of the underworld. But the bigger mistake was who the woman was.

"Adrien's wife, technically." He took another drink of his espresso.

Hard to believe she'd ever belonged to anyone but Bastien.

"The Aristocrats have drastically changed their organization. My sparrows tell me they're going to take the Louvre next."

I blinked several times as I stared. "The Louvre." It was ridiculous, so ridiculous I wasn't sure why I said it out loud.

He gave a slight shake of his head. "They believe some of those pieces belong to them. Relics and heirlooms from their family lines, taken from their ancestral homes and put in a museum for obnoxious foreigners to see."

"After all the shit that went down, they've gotten crazier?"

He gave a shrug. "Seems so. People believe they're behind the theft at the National Gallery in London. Only the French pieces were taken...a little obvious."

It was outside of Paris, so outside of my jurisdiction, outside of my concern. "Subtlety isn't their style." It wasn't mine either.

The waiter arrived and brought two plates of what Baptiste ordered. Onion soup with the beef tartare. The soup was so hot I could see the steam rising from the bowls. Baptiste dropped his linen across his lap and immediately scooped his spoon into the dark broth with melted cheese and took a bite.

He tapped his spoon against the hard pieces of cheese and forced them to drop into the broth before he took another bite. "How are things with you?"

I went for the tartare instead. "It's been a smooth transition." Bastien had given me no notice when he left. Put me on the spot then took off with Fleur. They'd traveled for a few months, visiting the Greek Islands then Sicily and

Tuscany. I'd rarely heard from them while they were away. I'd spent that time restoring order to the Fifth Republic and maintaining compliance with the gangs. Most of those who'd turned on Bastien had fled before they could be executed. New leaders came into power, and the entire ecosystem of crime had drastically changed over the last few months.

But it'd finally calmed down again. Probably because everyone knew I wasn't as easygoing as Bastien. I preferred to shoot first and then think about it later. I didn't hear testimony before I passed my judgment. I was the judge, the jury, and the executioner all in one. No such thing as second chances. Barely first chances.

Baptiste focused on his soup for a while, decades older than me in appearance but still hearty under the flesh. He'd always been smart, playing chess when his opponents played checkers. It was how he'd been around so long, evolving and adapting to the environment. "You've come a long way, Luca."

From rags to riches. From civilian to The Noose. The Emperor.

"Your father would be proud of you."

I watched another car pass by the window on the empty street.

"As proud as I am."

I sat in the booth alone and faced the windows and the main door at Holybelly. The street outside was one-way, and a motorcycle passed and then a town car. Then there was a black SUV. It came to a stop, its taillights turning red.

A moment later, Bastien emerged in a long-sleeved shirt and sweatpants, a permanent grin on his face as if a plastic surgeon had manipulated his facial muscles to stay that way. When he walked in, he spotted the waiter we saw on a regular basis, and they immediately greeted each other with a handshake and then talked football.

I drank my coffee and looked out the window again.

Bastien finally came to my booth and fist-bumped me. "Been a while."

"You look tan."

"It was surprisingly warm, especially in Sicily." He grabbed the menu and glanced at the specials. "Which really worked out because Fleur had this little bikini that barely covered the goods, so I got to stare at that all day." He smirked then flipped the menu over.

"You don't care about anyone else looking at her?"

"No," he said with a scoff. "You think some asshole is gonna go for it with me lurking around?"

Bryan came over. "The usual?"

"Yep," Bastien said. "Fucking starving."

"Me too." I set my menu on top of his.

Bryan walked away to put the order in.

I already had my coffee, so I took a drink of it.

Bastien sat with his arms on the table and stared at me. "You look like shit."

"I look tired. While you've been fucking all over the Mediterranean, I've been restoring order to our Republic. President Martin breathed down my throat every single day until order was maintained. And it's still not fully there."

Bastien gave a slight nod. "Fair enough. How are things?"

"Not your problem, Bastien."

"Doesn't mean we can't talk about it."

I gave a slight shake of my head. "How's Fleur?"

"She's good. Had a great time on our trip. A side to her I've never seen before."

"Probably because she saw a new side to you that she hasn't seen before."

"True." He nodded. "Didn't shoot anybody. Didn't threaten to shoot anybody."

"Must be nice." I'd been executing the traitors and chasing the cowards.

"If you don't want the job, Nico is next in line since Mael moved on."

"That's not the problem."

"Then what is the problem?" he asked. "Because there are waves of resentment crossing the table right now."

Bryan appeared then, bringing our hot plates of food at the most contentious moment. He laid everything out without saying a word or making eye contact then walked off.

Bastien was hungry but didn't touch his food.

"It's not resentment."

"Then what is it?"

I wasn't sure what the problem was. I didn't think about these sorts of things too often. But when I was put on the spot, I was forced to confront the emotions I suppressed. "It all happened so fast. Fleur appeared out of nowhere, and within just a couple of months, our lives were forever changed. I didn't expect you to leave so quickly and so suddenly. It's just not the same without you."

It was a testament to our friendship when he didn't make a joke or sidestep my words. He held my gaze and confronted it. "So, you miss me."

"I didn't say that."

"But you kinda did." A slow smirk moved over his lips.

I rolled my eyes. "Saying it's not the same is not the same thing as saying I miss you—"

"I miss you too, man." His fair skin was a little darker from lying by the pool on his vacation, but his blue eyes were still hard and brilliant at the same time. "I'm really happy with my life with Fleur. Wouldn't change it for anything. But now that the honeymoon is over and we're back to normal life, there's definitely a void there that she can't fill. A purpose that's missing, a lack of speed and adrenaline. If her safety wasn't so heavily braided into the job, I'd be back. No question."

That shouldn't make me feel better, but for some reason, it did.

"My life was easier without Fleur. But not better. One day, you'll understand what I mean."

I scoffed before I grabbed my fork and started to eat.

"I said the same thing, remember?" He started to eat too, pouring the syrup all over his sweet stack of pancakes. "Look at me now."

"We aren't the same, Bastien."

"But we aren't different either, Luca."

I paused and looked at him before I bit the piece of hash brown off the fork.

"So, what's going on?" Bastien asked.

"It's fine. You're done with this stuff."

"Doesn't mean we can't talk about it," he said again. "What else are we going to talk about?"

I shrugged. "I wouldn't mind hearing more about this little bikini Fleur has…"

He chuckled before he took a bite of his pancakes. "Can't even describe it."

Don't stop now. **Order The Emperor** so you can find out what happens between Luca and Aliénor.

Made in United States
Orlando, FL
14 April 2025

60474902R00204